SEED

SEED

Lisa
Heathfield

RP|TEENS
PHILADELPHIA • LONDON

First published in Great Britain by Egmont UK Ltd, 2015.
First printed in the United States by Running Press Book Publishers, 2015.

Printed in the United States

Books published by Running Press are available at special discounts for
bulk purchases in the United States by corporations, institutions, and other
organizations. For more information, please contact the Special Markets
Department at the Perseus Books Group, 2300 Chestnut Street, Suite 200,
Philadelphia, PA 19103, or call (800) 810-4145, ext. 5000, or e-mail
special.markets@perseusbooks.com.

ISBN 978-0-7624-5634-5

Library of Congress Control Number: 2014949872
E-book ISBN 978-0-7624-5636-9

9   8   7   6   5   4   3   2   1
Digit on the right indicates the number of this printing

Designed by Frances J. Soo Ping Chow
Edited by Alison Dougal
Typography: Baskerville, Harman, Maxwell Slab, and PiS NeoPrint

Published by Running Press Teens
An Imprint of Running Press Book Publishers
A Member of the Perseus Books Group
2300 Chestnut Street
Philadelphia, PA 19103–4371

Visit us on the web!
www.runningpress.com/rpkids

For my beautiful, brave Mama,
watching from the moon.

CHAPTER ONE

•••••••••●•••••••••

Here, crouched beside the toilet, I'm terrified I'm dying. My stomach must be bleeding, or my liver, or my kidneys. Something inside me has somehow got cut. Spots of blood smear my underwear. I wipe myself with toilet paper and there's more blood. Am I being punished for something I have said or done?

"Elizabeth!" I shout, running from the coffin-small room. "Elizabeth!"

I run from room to room. Kindred Smith is mending a bed in one. Rachel sweeps in another. The children play in the day room.

"*Elizabeth!*"

I wonder if the bleeding is worse. I look behind, but there are no drops of red following me along the wooden floorboards. I rattle the doors of the rooms that are locked. Elizabeth is not in the dining room, but in the kitchen she is coming through the back door, her rain-drenched dress clinging to her pregnant belly.

"What is it, Pearl?" she asks, putting down a bag of muddied potatoes. "Is someone hurt?"

I don't want to tell her. I don't want to tell her that I'm dying.

Will the shock damage the tiny baby in her tummy?

"Pearl?" She stands, looking at me, and I see the worry in her eyes.

"My stomach is bleeding," I whisper.

"Where? How?" Elizabeth steps back, looks at my top. "Did you cut yourself in the field?"

"Inside. It's bleeding inside me."

"What do you mean?" she asks. I've never seen someone turn so pale in the time it takes for me to take a breath.

"I'm sorry, Elizabeth," I say. And I can't stop the tears. Because I don't want to die. I want to meet her baby. I want more days swimming in the lake. I want more days dancing in the rain.

Then Elizabeth's face changes and she starts to smile. "Why do you think your stomach is bleeding?"

Why is she happy that I might soon die?

"Is there blood in your underwear?"

As I nod my head, she laughs and wraps her arms around me. I feel the bump of her baby under her skin. It presses against me. Against my stomach, which is bleeding inside.

Elizabeth steps back and I see that she's crying. So I'm right— I am dying.

She kisses her thumb, presses it to her belly, and then puts it onto my forehead, onto my chest and then onto my own stomach.

"Are you trying to heal me?" I whisper. And she smiles.

"You don't need healing. You're not dying, Pearl. You are fifteen years old and you're changing from a child to a woman."

Then she's hugging me again, and her words slowly sink in. So this is what I've been waiting for? A bleeding stomach?

I look at Elizabeth, but she doesn't seem like she's mocking me.

"Come on," she says, and she takes my hand.

In the bedroom, she changes my underwear, takes away my old ones, which are now heavily lined with a muddy red. I concentrate on the faded yellow wallpaper as she fills my new underwear with a thick, woven slab that makes me waddle like a duck.

"You'll get used to it." She smiles at me so warmly. "Now, not a word," she says and I follow her out onto the landing. I focus on her long blonde hair as we go down the stairs to the kitchen. In silence, she reaches for the lantern and matches on the shelf, and then we walk out the back door.

I'd forgotten it was raining and it hits down on us hard, soaking us within seconds. I hear nothing but its drumming on the ground as Elizabeth takes my hand again. She leads me through the herb garden with its high brick walls, where the smells have almost been washed away. She opens the rickety door at the other end and we're walking through the strawberry field. The plants are heavy with red fruit.

I feel the slab of linen rubbing my legs as I walk. I imagine the blood dripping onto it. Will I bleed forever now? Will I never be able to walk or run freely again?

I stumble after Elizabeth, confused about wanting to cry when I have waited so long to be a woman. In the distance, I see the figures in the vegetable patch, where I was less than an hour ago, when I was still a child. I see the shape of Heather, her long brown hair stuck with rain down her back. Then I remember. I'll be able to grow my hair. Finally, after all these years of waiting, I'll be able to let my blonde hair grow. I'll look like Elizabeth, with it flowing over my shoulders and down to my waist.

I'm filled with happiness. Suddenly the bleeding and the strange, uncomfortable way of walking are absolutely fine, because now I am a woman.

"Elizabeth," I say. But the water is falling too loudly for her to hear.

The sound changes as we head into the woods and the rain hits the leaves far above us.

"Where are we going?" I ask, but Elizabeth just smiles.

Finally, we get to the clearing where Papa S.'s Worship Chair sits in the middle. It has fresh ivy woven around its frame. Elizabeth walks toward it, and then she's going too close—she's walking into the forbidden circle. I look around, but no one is here to see. I look up into the branches, but no Kindreds are hidden there.

I hold my breath as she reaches for the chair. "No, Elizabeth," I whisper.

"It is bidden," she says quietly as she starts to lift the chair. I can see that it is heavy, but I can't help. Papa S. sees everything and Elizabeth is in the forbidden circle, touching his Worship Chair.

She drags it to the side and begins to kick at the thick leaves underneath. Then she's on her hands and knees, moving the leaves away until underneath I see a large metal hoop. She pulls it, and it opens a small wooden door flat on the ground.

"What are you doing?" I ask.

She is not smiling now. "I promise you will be okay," she says. She takes the matches from her apron, strikes one and lights the lantern.

And then I understand. I look down into the hole. There are steps that end in blackness. She wants me to go down.

"I want to go back to the house," I say. But I don't move. I don't run away.

"You must trust me, Pearl." Her wet hair still shines so blonde. She holds the lantern in one hand, the other hand resting on her pregnant belly.

And I know I love her, so I know I must trust her. I step forward, *into* the forbidden circle, and start to go cautiously down the steps. Elizabeth follows me and the light from the lantern shows us the way. At the bottom is a tiny room dug into the earth.

I look at Elizabeth. In the candlelight her cheeks look sunken, her eyes hollow. Is there fear hidden within her?

"I've seen it now," I say quietly. My voice sounds flat as it catches in the earth. "Can I go?"

"We have all done this, Pearl. Every woman at Seed. I promise you will be all right."

"What do you mean?"

"When you get your first Blessing, when you first start to bleed, you must stay with Nature so that she may give you the gift of a healthy womb," she says.

I don't understand. I just stare at her in the flickering light.

"You must stay deep in her womb, so your own womb may become fertile."

"What do you mean, fertile?"

"So that when it is your time, you will be able to have children."

"I don't want to be here, Elizabeth." My voice cracks as I start to cry. I look at the earth circling me and I'm suddenly filled with terror. Does she want me to stay here?

She puts the lamp down and wraps her arms around me, her face hidden in the shadows. "You know that you must not cry. Your life spirit will leave you and without it, you are nothing."

I can smell the sweetness of her vanilla scent. It masks the smell of the blood and the damp earth that is blocking the air.

"It won't be for long."

"So you'll shut the trapdoor?" The words fall from my mouth.

Elizabeth steps back and nods. She's trying to smile.

"But how will I breathe?"

Elizabeth picks up the lantern and shines it on the bottom of the curved earth walls. Tiny black pipes stick out all around. "I have been here, Pearl. It's all right."

"It's not," I say, and I start to cry again. "I don't want to stay." My voice is getting louder and Elizabeth looks up the steps toward the light above.

"Shh, now. Papa S. must not hear you cry. And Nature is hearing every word." Then she puts down the lantern once again and turns to go up the steps.

I can't move. Something holds me to the ground. I want to run after Elizabeth, pull her back, to escape, but I just watch as she goes up toward the air. The last thing I see is her blonde hair as she quickly lowers the trapdoor. It shuts with a muffled thud.

Faintly, I can hear Elizabeth scrabbling about with the leaves. Then I hear a dragging of something heavy. She must be pushing the wooden Worship Chair back over the top.

Every part of me wants to scream. Every nerve, every cell, wants to run up the steps and bang on that wooden door and scream until my lungs burn. But I don't. I know that Nature is watching me. And Papa S. will know.

So I stand and stare at the flickering earth walls, with their overwhelming dank smell. I stand and stare at the mud above me and around me and under me. I stand and listen to the sound of my own breathing.

Surely she will be back soon?

CHAPTER TWO

••••••••●••••••••

The candle is burning down so slowly. I don't want to move. The ground is cold through my trousers. I try to imagine that I'm dreaming, but I know I'm not.

Elizabeth does not come. The melting wax makes slippery shapes on the earth wall. The flame bulges and straightens, dancing in the silence.

I must have been here an hour, if not more. There's no one above me. No one is coming. When the candle burns down, I will disappear into the darkness.

"Elizabeth?" I call out softly. Of course she can't hear me. No one can hear me. There's no one there.

My stomach is starting to hurt with hunger, a rumbling pain. It's something I've barely felt before. At Seed, no one is hungry. There is always food, there is always drink.

"Thank you, Nature," I whisper. I kiss my palm, press it flat into the earth. It's bumpy against my skin. I imagine how deep the earth goes beneath me.

Kate and Jack will notice I'm gone. They will ask about me.

I close my eyes. It can't be long now.

But I'm finding it difficult to breathe. What if those pipes don't work? What if they're blocked and I slowly run out of air? My breath is sticking in my throat. It's got nowhere to go. Am I going to suffocate? Is this how I am going to die?

"Help me, Nature," I say. She must hear me, because there's a rustling of leaves above my head, a heavy scraping of the Worship Chair. And as the door is lifted, the sunlight floods in so sharply that I have to cover my eyes.

I am free. So I start to move toward the steps, just as Elizabeth comes down to get me. She is carrying something. When she reaches the bottom, she takes off the cloth covering it. It is a bowl of soup. A spoon and a chunk of bread sink into it.

"I must be quick," Elizabeth says, her voice hushed as she puts the bowl on the floor.

"But I'm coming with you," I reply.

"I'll be back in the morning. Just after sunrise." She tries to hug me, but I grab at her hands.

"No, Elizabeth, you can't leave me here." I'm crying, sudden and startling in the quiet circle of earth.

"Think of the rewards, Pearl. You will have a healthy womb. And when Papa S. says it is the right time, you will have children."

"No." I'm trying to stay calm. "No, I can't stay here."

"You must." She's trying to peel my hands away.

"I'll die if you leave me. I can't breathe in here, Elizabeth." I want her to look at me. I want her to understand, but she's looking back up the stairs. She's trying to get away.

"Pearl, you must let me go," she says quietly. Then she looks at me with those eyes of clover green. "Nature will protect you. There's no harm that can come to you here. You are privileged." Elizabeth finally frees her hands and kisses me on the head. "You are safe, Pearl, you are loved." Then she rushes up the steps. I reach for the material of her skirt, but she's gone.

The trapdoor has closed out the sunlight. There's just the silence and me. Somewhere, there are beetles burrowing, but I can't hear them. All I can hear is the sound of my short breathing and my heart thudding in the cramped air.

I kneel down and reach for the bowl of soup. The smell of it should make my mouth water, but as I bring the spoon to my lips, I feel sick. Still, I force it into my mouth, feel its warmth in my chest. It helps the ache in my stomach and so I gently scrape until every last drop has gone.

The smell of the ancient mud finds me once more. It creeps into my nose and slides down inside me.

I close my eyes and start to count. One, two, three. On and on. But the panic is rising again. *Breathe, Pearl, breathe. Trust in Elizabeth.* I focus on her smile, on the baby growing in her. Will I have a brother or a sister? I hope for a brother. If it's a girl, she will be forced into this hole. And I couldn't sit by, knowing that she is here.

I will think of the baby. Each little finger. Each little toe. Think about Papa S. and all that he gives us. Now I am a woman, maybe I can be his Companion. I imagine his hand in mine. I'm getting cold, but he will keep me warm.

I must sleep.

———※———

Somewhere there is music. And someone is singing, quietly. I open my eyes to blackness and silence. I am in the earth and the candle has burnt itself out. I move onto my knees as I sweep around with my hands. There's nothing but the rough, damp mud. Then my fingers hit the bottom of what must be the steps and I stumble up them. At the top I feel the closed trapdoor. If I'm desperate enough, I'll be able to open it. I push it with all my strength. I push it until I feel like my wrists will snap in two. But it doesn't move.

I bang it, feeble now. And I'm crying again as I curl myself onto the step. It's so dark that I can't even see my fingers. Darker than the silence in our sleeping room. Darker by far than the night. Nothing exists now, except the sound of my crying, getting soaked up by the earth. My life force dripping away.

Slowly I feel my way down the steps. I lie at the bottom. My bones ache from the cold and the hard floor.

"Please come, Elizabeth," I whisper. I kiss my palm and hold it above me, into the hollow blackness.

※————————————————

I'm woken by the sound of the trapdoor opening. There is light, muffled yet sharp enough to hurt my eyes.

"I'm here, Pearl."

It's Elizabeth. She lights a lamp and I can see again. "It's all right," she says. "It is over." And she smiles at me. "You can change into this."

She hands me a flowing green skirt. It's beautiful. I reach out to touch its material in the flickering candlelight. It feels so soft.

"It's silk," she says. "I made it for you when you were born."

I take off my trousers. As I put the skirt on, it feels like water on my bare legs. Elizabeth passes me a new slab of linen.

"Change this for the one in your underwear. We must leave the old one here for seven days."

"Will I have to come back to get it?" I ask, the panic rising like bile in my throat.

"You will not have to come back here," she says gently.

Elizabeth takes the old slab from me. It's heavy with my blood. When she has laid it face down in the earth, she turns to me. "You must never speak of this to anyone," she says.

She blows out the candle and starts to go back up the steps. I hurry after her.

When we're outside, she lowers the trapdoor, covers it with leaves, and pushes the heavy Worship Chair back into its place.

As we walk away in the early morning air, the birds are singing. The rain has stopped. My emerald-green skirt will tell everyone that now I am a woman.

CHAPTER THREE

••••••••●•••••••••

I watch Ruby's little fingers as she washes the mugs. In time, she too will become a woman. I know that it is years away, but I can't bear the thought of her being trapped in the earth. I try to push the memory away. Concentrate on the frothy water in the sink.

When Jack comes in, he notices my skirt immediately and stops. He looks at me. "A woman?" he asks, smiling.

Pride washes through me. "Yes," I say.

Jack hesitates. I wonder if he will bleed and then be able to grow his hair like the Kindreds. He's sixteen already, so surely it can't be long. "You won't change, though?" he asks.

"I might."

"You better not," he says. Then he reaches into the sink and Ruby smiles as he flicks water at me.

"Hey, watch my skirt," I say, laughing.

"I won't!"

So I splash him back and he runs from the room, straight into Kindred Smith.

"Careful," Kindred Smith says. But he's not angry. He never is. Of the two Kindred men, he's always been my favorite, even though favorites aren't allowed. With his beard the color of autumn, I can believe that he grew in the wood.

Jack reaches over and rustles my skirt. "Pearl's a woman," he says.

I see something flicker briefly in Kindred Smith's eyes, but then he smiles warmly. When he puts his arms around me, I feel a strange aching to stay as a child.

"I remember when you were born," he says as he shakes his head. "Your hair was so white it nearly blinded me. And that yell of yours came close to deafening everybody." When he laughs, the wrinkles around his eyes squeeze close together. He takes my hand between his. "You're no trouble at all now, though."

"Oh, yes she is," Jack interrupts. "You don't know the half of it, Kindred Smith."

I can feel my legs bare under my skirt as I laugh.

Ruby takes her hands from the sink and dries them on a cloth. She comes over to me and strokes the material of my skirt. "Are you really a woman now?"

"Yes," I say. "And one day, you will be too."

Her smile is wide. I try not to imagine her alone in the ground.

First meal is being laid out on the two wooden tables in the meadow. It's my favorite place to eat. And this is my favorite day, because Fridays are free days. Unless Papa S. says different, we can spend all day lying in the grass if we want, staring at the sky. As long as the tables are laid and the food eaten, the day is ours.

Through the window, I can see Bobby as he puts the forks in the right places. He pauses to hold one up to the sun. Although he's small for his five years, he seems wiser than most of us. He tells me that Nature speaks to him through sparks of light—I think he's listening carefully now.

"Can you take the bowls out, Pearl?" Elizabeth asks as she comes in from outside. "And Jack, there are glasses on the side. The table won't lay itself."

I grab the bowls and run out into the meadow. I hear Jack and Elizabeth laughing behind me as I reach the knee-high grass. I push through, careful not to make a path. I wish I wasn't carrying anything, so that I could reach my hand down and feel the strands on my fingertips.

When Bobby walks past, he kisses his palm and holds it toward me. It always makes me smile. He can't wait to grow up and be like the Kindred men.

"Did Nature tell you anything today?" I ask.

"It's a secret," he replies before he disappears into the house.

Jack catches up with me as I'm laying the bowls, one in each place. He's carrying towers of glasses in each hand.

"What did you worship this morning, then?" I ask him.

"I haven't been out yet. I had to help Kindred John with the drinking fountain. We fixed the leak."

I look at Jack. He's so proud that he's finally been asked to help the Kindreds with proper manual work. For years we've watched from where we've been playing, Jack fascinated by the hammering and clattering of mending and building. Slowly he's got older, and slowly he's been allowed to learn.

"About time you started to do some proper work around here," I say, laughing. He picks up a fruit cloth and swipes at me across the table.

We walk along the table together. For every bowl I put down, he puts a glass, until all eleven places are laid. I stop to watch an ant as it scuttles over a spoon. Press my finger in front of it, willing it to walk on my skin. But it turns back and disappears over the edge.

I look back at our home, at its many windows, the red bricks covered by ivy in places, the chimneys scattered on the roof. I know that there is nowhere else in the world that I would rather be.

Heather comes from the kitchen door. In each hand she has a vase filled with flowers from the meadow. She's woven some blue flowers into her hair, the petals ducking in and out of her curls. Soon, I will be able to do the same.

When she has placed the vases on the table, Heather comes to me. "Nature has made you a woman," she says warmly. She kisses her palm and holds it on my stomach. When she hugs me, her curls fall over my face.

"I'm so happy," I say as she pulls me back to look at her. I am sure that I see the memory of the circle of earth in her eyes. Maybe it is a good place.

"I am very proud of you," she says, and my smile is in every part of me.

Our arms empty, Jack and I head back toward the house. "What shall we do today?" he asks, running a hand over his cropped-short hair.

I don't answer him, because I have seen Kate standing by the kitchen door. I know she is looking at my skirt. I smile at her as she comes up to me.

"You made it, then," she says. Is she talking about the hole in the ground? We are forbidden to mention it. "Now we are the same again."

I feel her warmth as she hugs me. I imagine her stomach bleeding the way that mine is and how I never knew. But when she lets me go, there's something different in her eyes.

"I'll be able to grow my hair," I say with a smile. "We'll look like sisters again." I reach up to touch her hair. We are an identical color of blonde, but my hair is so straight and Kate's ripples slightly, like water.

Elizabeth stands by the cooker in the kitchen, stirring the wooden spoon through the enormous vat of porridge, humming quietly to herself. I watch the sun fall through the window onto her. It catches her red lips and almond-shaped eyes, and I know she's the most beautiful being in the world. As I always do, I make a silent wish that she is my true mother.

I know that it is wrong to wonder. I know that we are gifts from the earth and we belong to all of the Kindred women. But I want to truly belong to *her*.

I push the thought away. Today there is space for nothing but happiness.

"Right, girls. Carry this outside and I'll go and tell Papa S. that we're ready to eat."

Some of our family are already sitting at the table when we go out again. The porridge vat is heavy and pinches at my fingers, even through the cloth that I've wound around the handle. Kindred John gets up to help as we set it down with a muffled clunk on the end of the sturdy wooden table.

"Thank you, girls," he says, gently laying his hand on Kate's head. He is so tall, much taller than Kindred Smith, and his hand is so strong that he somehow makes Kate look young again. She winces slightly and moves quickly away. I don't know what's wrong, but she won't catch my eye.

We sit down just as Papa S. comes out of his door, and that

wonderful hush swoops over us. He makes his way slowly to the head of the table. Today it's Rachel at his side. Her eyes are smiling at him as she holds a flower to her lips, her other hand linked with his fingers. It seems like she has been his Companion for a long time.

Papa S. is barely taller than her, yet his goodness stretches into the air. He wears his long hair loose today, flowing like white sun over his shoulders. The feeling of love and awe I have for him swells within me. I gaze at the intensity of his eyes, the deep lines on his face that celebrate his years.

I touch the material of my skirt and smile, hoping that Papa S. knows. Hoping that he has seen. Maybe soon it will be me who holds a flower to my lips, and everyone will watch me and know that I am his Companion. The thought of walking with him spills sunshine onto my heart.

We all stand as he reaches his seat. As one, we kiss our palms and reach them out to the sky. Papa S. sweeps a hand over all of us and we sit.

"Begin your thanks," he says, his strong voice reaching out. So I lift my head and join the low murmuring around me. The air is warm. The long grass is silent around us. This is happiness.

I try to concentrate on my thanks, but my mind keeps drifting to Elizabeth's swollen belly. I imagine the child, curled like a nut, growing day by day. Waiting and growing and blinking into the inky, wet darkness. I will look at its face when it's born and see if it is like me. I'll look for signs to see if it is my true blood sister or brother. Yet I won't be able to treat it differently.

"Begin to eat," I hear Papa S. say softly, and so we all lower our heads and start to pass our bowls toward the vat of cooling porridge.

It's not my favorite food of the day. Elizabeth's magic has long gone by the time the bowls are put in front of us. There's always a rubbery skin on the top and the spoon has to pop through to reach the slightly sludgy porridge below.

"It's delicious, Elizabeth," Jack says and I know he means it. He has a warmth you can almost touch. I eat mine quickly, looking forward to the fresh bread and melting jam.

When we have finished eating, we clear the plates and bowls quickly. There haven't been so many warm days this summer, and as the Kindreds rest at the table, we want to make the most of our free time.

"Thank you, Pearl," Rachel says as she passes me her bowl. Papa S. smiles at me, and my arms tingle with pride. But he doesn't say anything and there's no flicker of recognition in his eyes. I wish I had the courage to ask him. *Have you seen? Have you seen that I am a woman?* But I gather their spoons and walk back to the house without saying a word.

Even though it's only mid-morning, the kitchen is becoming

uncomfortably warm. Jack has hooked the door open, and the windows looking over the meadow are as wide as they can go, but there's no breeze.

"Hurry up, you lazy bunch," Jack says, tickling Ruby and Bobby until their legs give way and they collapse on the stone floor.

"You're not exactly helping," Kate says, flicking bubbles from the bowl at Jack. He laughs as he wipes them from the suspenders attached to his trousers.

"That's enough," says a voice from the doorway. Heather doesn't normally sound annoyed. Earlier she had been so warm toward me, but now her eyes are dark and her mouth is tight. "Papa S. would like some more milk," she says to no one in particular.

"I'll get it," Ruby squeals, dropping her tea towel on the side and running toward the fridge.

"No, it's OK," Heather says, reaching for a glass from a cupboard above the sideboard. Ruby's face sinks into disappointment, but Heather doesn't even seem to notice. She takes the jug from Ruby's hand and pours milk into the glass. We all watch her as she puts the jug back, closes the fridge door and walks back toward the meadow.

"What's up with her?" I ask.

"She's jealous of Rachel, I reckon," Kate says. "I bet she was hoping Papa S. would choose a new Companion."

A new Companion. Will it be me?

"She can't be jealous," Ruby says, her little face shocked. "It's not allowed."

"You can't stop your feelings, though, can you?" says Kate. She looks at Jack, so quickly that if I'd blinked I wouldn't have seen it. But I know I didn't imagine it, because in that instant, Jack's cheeks flush red and he looks down at his feet.

A strange feeling suddenly creeps from my throat, down to my tummy. I don't know why it's there, and I don't know what it is, but then it's gone.

They do not know that I am here, locked away forever at the top of the house. That I watch them. That one of them is mine.

They do not know my memory of growing my baby in me. And when it was time, the thunder in my stomach, cracking me open. The stinging turning to burning and tearing and the final release of a head. I pushed the flesh and bones from me. My child.

I hadn't expected the slippery, snakelike cord that held my baby to me. My baby's screams as that cord was cut through.

"Are you hurting it?" I remember asking. I didn't know whether I had birthed a boy or a girl.

"The baby is fine." The Kindred had smiled as he pressed a cold flannel to my forehead. He wasn't doing it to help me. It was to keep me down.

"Can I hold my baby?" I asked. But then the cramps took over my body again.

My mother stood between my legs and she pulled that severed cord.

"What's happening?" I screamed.

The Kindred only smiled again. "Trust us," he said. "Trust us."

CHAPTER FOUR

•••••••••●•••••••••

He won't cry. Even though the drops of blood squeeze through the crack in his skin, I know he won't cry. So Bobby just screws up his face and keeps his eyes shut tight as I check his foot for any more thorns.

"They'll give us blackberries in the autumn," I say, gently touching the brambles with my fingertips. "So we can forgive them for this scratch."

Bobby's face stays scrunched as he watches me pick a bracken leaf. I press it onto his cut. He tries to move his ankle away, but I hold it tight, waiting for the leaf to work.

When it's done, I stand up and brush the dry mud from my skirt. "Come on, let's get back before it rains."

Bobby leans his head into me. "Thank you, Pearl," he says. And as we stand like this, I want to tell him: *I think you're my true brother.* Because I knew, those five years ago, as soon as Elizabeth and Rachel reappeared with their empty bellies and the Kindreds carrying two mewling babies. I knew the moment I saw Bobby that he was mine.

But I say nothing. Instead, I take his hand in mine and we pick our way carefully back through the forest, back toward Seed.

The rain comes soon, when we are busy helping Elizabeth in the kitchen. It's the first time it's rained again in the three days since I've been a woman. Kate walks in and she dips her finger into the soft cheese as I push it through the muslin cloth. I laugh as I try to snap it shut, but she pulls her hand away.

"Hey, dreamer," she says to me. "You'd gone to worship before I'd even opened my eyes."

"I went out early with Bobby."

"We found a robin," Bobby says. "It spoke to me."

"We managed ten rejoices before it flew away," I say.

"I ended up going out on my own," Kate says, that wicked smile tipping at her lips. "I chose mud."

I don't understand why she's saying such things these days. I want to ask her, but something is holding me back.

"There's beauty in everything," Elizabeth says, just as Ruby rushes in and the rain outside beats louder. We put down the cloth and go to the open door to watch it.

"I like the way it bounces on the ground," Ruby says.

"We'll have to go out in it later. We've carrots to pick," Elizabeth says. She stands next to us, one hand on Bobby's shoulder, the other pressing gently onto the glass.

I look at Elizabeth's fingers and put mine onto the glass next to hers. I'm sure our hands look the same. We both have slender fingers and small wrists.

She looks at me and smiles. "They're just hands," she says, and I wonder how she knows my mind.

"Come on, let's go out in it now," Kate says. "It'll be fun."

"Not you, Kate," a voice says from behind us.

Kindred John has walked into the room, his footsteps disguised by the heavy thumping of the rain. Ruby runs up and jumps into his arms. He throws her high into the air and catches her again. When she is back safely in his arms, she rolls the ends of his beard into her hands.

"You have lines in your hair," she says to him.

Kindred John laughs. "Nature is beginning to paint my beard gray," he says.

I am so used to the blackness of his hair, I cannot imagine it changing. I don't think I want it to.

Kindred John throws Ruby in the air again.

"She's too big for that," Elizabeth says.

"Five years old isn't too big for throwing in the air," Kindred John says, and Ruby laughs as he swings her up.

"You'll hurt your back," Elizabeth tells him, and he puts Ruby down.

"Heather needs some more flour," Kindred John says. "I need Kate to help with the wheel."

There's a strange look on Kate's face. "I'm helping Elizabeth," she says.

"I have asked you to come with me," Kindred John says.

Then he leaves the room and as she follows him, I'm shocked to see her pull a face behind his back.

I glance at Elizabeth, but I don't know if she's seen. If she did, I wonder what punishment Kate will get.

"Nana Willow needs her tincture," Elizabeth says to me. "Will you take it to her? She's not good today."

"Of course," I say, but there's a pebble of dread sitting in my stomach. I can't tell anyone, but Nana Willow frightens me. She has stayed in her room for so many years that her mind has become as withered as her skin.

Her bedroom is downstairs. Out of the kitchen, across the hall and down the tiled corridor. I can't help but glance at the door of the Forgiveness Room as I walk past. I have only walked through there once, and I never want to do it again. Another short corridor and I'm outside Nana Willow's room.

I don't knock. I know she can't hear. Slowly I push open the heavy wooden door and her smell rushes up to me. I try not to mind it. I tell myself it is as natural as the flowers in the field. But it smells of decay.

I force myself to step inside. I force myself to smile, even though from here I can see Nana Willow's eyes shut tight. Her chest sounds like a creaking bough as she sleeps.

My feet don't make a sound as I walk toward her. There's a small table next to her bed and I put the glass of fresh juice with tincture drops onto it.

"Nana Willow," I whisper. She doesn't stir. "Nana Willow." I lean toward her and her eyes snap open and are staring into mine.

"Sylvie, you came," she says, her voice like steam escaping through the crack in her mouth.

"It's me, Nana Willow. It's Pearl." But she doesn't see me. Her fingers reach out and stick onto mine. I want to run from here, but I know I can't.

"I knew you'd come back to me," she says. She tries to reach up. To stroke my face. I don't mean to, but I pull away.

"Nana Willow, I am Pearl." My hands are shaking slightly as I reach for the glass. "You must drink this." I should sit her up, but I'm scared of feeling her bones through her nightdress. Instead, I tip her head up slightly. She looks confused as I bring the glass to her lips, and I try to go slowly as she swallows, but some of the precious juice dribbles out from her mouth and drips down her wrinkled neck. And all the time, she looks at me with her cloudy eyes.

When the glass is empty, I reach for a brown cloth folded neatly on the table. I dab gently at the spilled juice on her skin. Nana Willow is staring at me when something changes in her. It's like she suddenly sees who I really am. A moan leaves her and now I'm wiping away her tears.

I wait until her crying stops.

"It's OK, Nana Willow." I dare to reach out and stroke her hair back from her face. *She is like a child,* I tell myself. *Just like a child.*

Her eyes are closed now, so I turn to go. As I dash to the door, I hear her move behind me.

I glance back and she's sitting up. I can see that she is about to call me over again.

I run from the room and don't even close the door behind me.

CHAPTER FIVE

·········•●●•·········

Elizabeth has explained that I might not get another Blessing for a while, but gradually my body will adapt and then I will have them every few weeks. It's a relief not to have the coarse slab in my underwear. Now I can swim again.

We see a glimpse of our lake through the trees. It's beautiful today. The sun makes the water glisten and as we get closer and push past the leaves, we can see it all. It's an almost perfect circle. The trees are stepped back slightly from the water, leaving the grass to run down to its edge. It's shallow at first, but out in the middle you could never touch the bottom. Today it's blue, shining off the sky. And as the heat tickles my shoulders, I know I want to jump in.

"Race you!" Jack shouts, pushing Kate and me aside, taking his shirt off as he runs. So we follow him, jolting the birds from the trees with our laughter.

"Get him!" Kate calls to me as I throw down my bag and pull my shirt over my head. She catches up with him as he struggles with his trousers, jumping on him until they both crash to the ground. My new skirt is easy to take off and I pass them both, my bare feet feeling the dry grass changing to damp.

In my underwear, I can feel the heat of the sun on my back as I run, splashing, into the lake. The freezing water whips at my ankles, stings my knees. I stop and gasp, just as Jack skims through the air and dives into the water. When he surfaces, he's a little way out.

"Come on, Pearl," he shouts. "It's easier if you're quick." He ducks his head under again, curls his body, and kicks until he disappears.

"Last one to the middle washes Kindred John's underwear," Kate says from beside me. Then she's gone, into the water.

So I go too. I breathe, tuck my head in and dive into the icy water. The shock hits my face, but it's so amazing down here— with the water above and around me, the world dissolves into a low humming. It's only me and the cold.

My head moves through the surface and so I breathe again, swimming until I reach Jack in the middle, where there's no way we can stand.

"It's so clear today," he says. His shoulders break through the top of the water and his hands mirror mine as we turn them in circles to keep afloat.

"It's good that it's sunny on our free day, isn't it?" Then I tip my body and lie flat on my back, my arms moving slowly. The sky above us is extraordinary, with not a cloud in sight.

I could lie like this and be happy forever.

There's a shouting that murmurs at me through the water. Reluctantly, I lift my head and see that Bobby is now in the lake, his skinny arms reaching above his head, his hands clutching Ruby's sandals.

"Give them back," Ruby shouts.

"I'll go and help her," Jack says, before he starts swimming toward Bobby. His feet kick water over Kate's face. She wipes her eyes, treading water all the time. We watch Jack's strong strokes breaking through the lake until he gets to the shallow edge.

"Enough," we hear him say, and he takes the sandals from Bobby's hands. Kate and I swim over lazily to join him.

"I'll throw her sandals in myself if she doesn't stop whining," Kate says as the water gets shallow enough for our feet to touch the bottom. It's sludgy between my toes. The mud oozes up like cold clay and I don't like the feel of it, although I know I should. I imagine the bones of a dead man, buried just underneath my feet. I move quickly, as I want to remember only the touch of the water.

We get out, and Kate and I lie side by side on the grass. Jack sits next to us, facing away, looking to the lake. Drops of water sparkle on his skin. I'm surprised how strong his shoulders look. Time is changing him as well, but sometimes I wish we could slow it all down. If I could, I might ask Nature to halt the ticking of her clock, just for a bit.

"Heather says I'm not allowed to go selling at the market for a while," Kate says, turning onto her elbow to look at me.

"Why?"

"Because she's been looking at the Outside boys," Jack says, glancing over his shoulder and smiling.

"Have you?" I ask. "It's dangerous, Kate."

"I haven't." She sits up, squeezes drops of water from her hair and flicks it toward Jack.

"Why else would they stop you going?" he asks.

Kate leans back onto both of her elbows with a sigh. She tips her head back and her hair touches the ground. She's been growing it for a year, since she officially became a woman. Jack looks away from her.

"Kindred John says I'm not allowed to speak to them. So I asked him how I'm meant to sell the Outsiders our homegrown beans if I can't talk to them. He wasn't having any of it and now he's stopped me going." She slumps down and swings an arm over her eyes. "Pig's breath," she says quietly into her skin.

Jack and I don't move. I've never heard Kate speak like that before, and about a Kindred. I don't even dare look at her. I'm suddenly terrified that Papa S. will come creeping out of a tree and strike us down. He's everywhere. He sees and hears everything. Will she be punished for this?

"Don't speak like that again, Kate," Jack says quietly, without turning around. She doesn't reply. She must know that, even for her, she's gone too far.

We share our lunch with the children. Chunks of bread with slabs of cheese. A mouthful each of potato salad, leftover from yesterday's supper. I bite my teeth through the skin of a small tomato and it pops and bleeds its seeds onto my tongue.

"Your shoulders are burning, Jack," Kate says. She goes to her bag as I wrap the leftover cheese in paper.

"I'll be OK," he says, touching his hot skin with his palms.

"Papa S. won't like it if the sun scolds you," she says. "It won't take me long." She kneels behind him, opens the bottle and pours some sunscreen onto her hands. I see Jack tense as she rubs the cream into his skin. He holds his head still, doesn't move.

And that strange feeling is back, somewhere in me. Nerves in my belly, a sickness in my throat.

Then Jack stands up quickly. "That'll be enough," he says and, without turning toward us, he runs and dives into the water and swims hard over to the other side.

When I look over at Kate, she's got a smile on her face. She's still kneeling, the bottle of sunscreen next to her, the imprint of Jack's body in the grass between her knees.

"Is he OK?" I ask.

She laughs slightly and looks at me and I'm sure she shakes her head. I want to ask why, but a thread of distance winds quietly between us.

"He's fine," she says, before she turns onto her belly in the grass.

I lie on my back, feeling the heat of the day on every part of my body. Behind my closed lids, I see the red of the sun. I can hear Ruby and Bobby splashing and laughing. Somewhere in it all must be the sound of Jack.

I don't think there's ever been a more beautiful day.

You were torn from me. Your little beating heart taken from me. The soft touch of your newborn flesh disappeared.

I tried. I promise I tried.

"I want to keep my baby!" I screamed at them.

"The baby belongs to Mother Nature. The baby belongs to all of us."

No. My baby belongs to me.

I screamed and bit and scratched at them, but they turned to stone.

And they hid me away. Cut me from you.

But I am your mother. I am your mother.

I reach up and touch the cold window.

"You are mine," I whisper through the glass.

CHAPTER SIX

•••••••••●•••••••••

It feels so different walking up to Dawn Rocks in a skirt rather than trousers. The sun hasn't yet risen and the air is cold around my legs. Jack is in front of me. His shoulders look broad and I can see the muscles in his arms, even through his shirt. He must sense me looking, as he turns around and smiles. He sees Ruby, still so sleepy, walking by my side, and he stops to pick her up. She buries her nose into his neck and he carries on walking.

It always amazes me how silent we are. How almost everyone from Seed can walk through the forest and up the craggy path to the hilltop rocks, yet there's hardly a murmur between us. Papa S. is at the front, leading the way through the lifting darkness. Looking back, I can just see Elizabeth and I can tell that she's uncomfortable. The baby in her belly must almost be full-size and it makes her steps heavy and slow. Her blonde hair is tied back from her face, but it still shines in the darkness. She leans on the staff that Kindred Smith made for Nana Willow.

The wind is resting and all around us the blackbirds are singing. Walking like this always makes it worth being woken from

43

my dreams.

Turning the corner in the path, there is the outline of Dawn Rocks in the hillside ahead of us. We will sit there to greet the sun. And as we get closer, I am sure that I can hear Mother Nature whispering to me, hiding just out of reach behind the solid gray.

When we reach the rocks, I sit next to Jack, who has Ruby on his lap. His warmth spreads into me and I barely shiver. I reach down until I feel his fingers in mine. Heather holds my other hand. She smiles at me, but she has lost something from behind her eyes. Each day it feels like the real her tiptoes away, replaced by someone edged in sadness. Is she really being taken by jealousy? It makes me uncomfortable, as no one is unhappy at Seed.

Slowly, the blackness around us changes and color seeps into everything. The cluster of trees below move from murky gray, to blue, to green. The fields shimmer purple, before the rising sun splashes them too. I hold my breath. This is my very favorite time and I want to slow it down, remember everything I see, everything I feel.

When the blue of the sky begins to push through, Papa S. stands up and lifts his palm toward the sun. We stay sitting, but we let go of each other's hands and reach our own palms upward. I can never be happier. I look at Jack. His head is tipped toward the sky and my eyes follow the line of his neck.

"Thank you, Mother Nature," says Papa S.

"Thank you, Mother Nature," we all repeat, our voices lifting to the sun.

Papa S. sits on the ground. We watch as he lays his hands flat on the grass. It's a hand I know so well, with white skin barely touched by the sun. When he looks at us, we know that it's time to begin.

"Nature," we chant. "We thank you for leading Papa S. to Seed. He saved us. He protects us. In return, we give you everything." The words flow out of me, and I speak with my family as one. "Because we need nothing more. We have Kindreds to guide us, we have food, we have love. We listen to you, Mother Nature, only you."

We kiss our palms, touch them onto the earth.

Suddenly Papa S. begins to shake. His arm is raised again, but this time it is as though someone invisible is yanking at him and his whole body jolts. His hair shudders against his back. Bobby looks toward me for comfort, but I'm frightened too.

Kindred John gets up.

"Stay back," Papa S. demands. His voice is deep and rumbles around the rock. I want to block my ears, hear only the comfort of his normal voice. But strange sounds are coming from him and words that make no sense, louder and louder until his head is thrown back, both arms outstretched above him.

When at last he sinks to the ground, his arms lie flat on the earth and he looks at us all with blazing blue eyes. Then he smiles.

"I have learned something new," he says quietly, his voice now his own. "I have learned that someone among us needs forgiveness. Someone here has let their pure soul become muddied."

Some of my family shift slightly where they're sitting. A sign of guilt? I am completely still, but my mind is flicking back in panic through my memory. *Is it me?* I think of being in that hole in the ground. Had he secretly been watching me? Did he know my fear? I try to stay calm as Papa S. looks at us all. I try to block out memories of the Forgiveness Room, but I can feel the beating wings in my lungs again.

I feel Heather's hand in mine. I glance at her and she shakes her head, as gently as a whisper, and I slow my breathing. Look at the horizon. Look at the beauty of the line of hills carved into the sky. I am sitting at Dawn Rocks. I am safe. The only sound is that of the birds and the air and the breathing of friends.

Papa S. stands up. He brushes the dry earth from his knees and wipes his palms clean. His smile is like honey and I know we have him back again.

"Dawn has been greeted," he says, his arms spread wide with love for us all.

He walks toward me. I see him notice my skirt and I blush with pride. He reaches out, but his hand goes to Heather. She looks up at him and suddenly she's happy. They hold hands and lead the way back down the path, through the forest and over the field to Seed.

⟫————⟨

"What was all that about?" Kate asks quietly.

We're kneeling side by side in the strawberry field. I look around and there's no one in the next few rows, but I don't answer her.

"Oi," she says, digging me in the side with her elbows. We laugh, but for some reason I'm nervous.

"Is it you?" I ask suddenly.

"What—am I the one with the muddy soul?"

"Shh," I say quickly.

"The strawberries don't have ears." She laughs again, popping one into her mouth and making herself go cross-eyed. "Besides, I love Papa S. I believe every word he says."

"Why are you being like this, Kate?" I whisper.

"Like what?"

"I don't know. Strange," I say.

Kate stops still and looks at me. "Maybe I'm not happy," she says. "Maybe I want more."

I don't understand what she's saying. No one is unhappy at Seed. There is no place on Earth as good as this.

"What do you mean?" I ask. But Kate doesn't answer me. She just keeps staring across the fields. "If they find out, they might punish you," I tell her, because maybe she doesn't know.

She turns to me, her smile defiant. "They'd better not find out, then." She picks another strawberry, throws it high into the air and catches it in her mouth.

I reach for one, pull it gently from its stem. It feels soft in my fingers. I want to eat it, but instead I add it to the pile in my little wicker basket.

CHAPTER SEVEN

························●●●●●●●●●············

"Come on," Kate says, once the last of evening meal has been cleared away. "Now you're a woman, you have to come with us."

I hesitate. I can't go into that hole again.

"It's good," she says, taking my hand. "It's in the Eagle Room."

Together we walk across the hallway and down the corridor. The door is open and the red of the Eagle Room spills out. The heavy curtains are already closed, even though it isn't yet dark outside. The deep red of the walls glow in the light. Elizabeth is standing by the table, lifting the cover from a sewing machine. Behind us, Rachel comes in and closes the door.

Instantly, the air changes. This somehow feels like a secret place, cut off from the rest of the house. Where we are all women. Excitement dances within me and I want to run and throw my arms around Elizabeth. But I stay standing quietly, waiting.

Kate goes toward the wooden trunk tucked in the corner. I have often looked at it and wondered what's inside. She lifts the lid.

"Careful, Kate," Rachel admonishes. But Kate doesn't seem to hear. She's pulling out some material decorated with large, green circles. She wraps it around her body and starts to dance.

"But that material is patterned," I say, looking at Elizabeth for an answer. "It's forbidden."

"We make these for the women on the Outside," Rachel says as she reaches into the trunk and takes out bundles of thread. "We write words that Papa S. has spoken, on pieces of paper that we sew into the hems. To help purify people from the poison around them."

"But we aren't allowed to do writing in the summer," I remind her. These warmer months are for working outside. It's only during the winter that we can read and write.

"Papa S. knows," Elizabeth reassures me. "It is his wish."

Kate has picked up a half-finished skirt, made from material that is covered with silver stars. She holds it, laughing, to her face, her eyes peeping through. I laugh with her.

So this is where Kate sometimes disappears to since she has become a woman. I can't believe that all this has been hidden from me. And now I'm here.

"Enough now, Kate," Elizabeth says, although her voice is kind. "Choose some material and start the panels of a skirt. Come here, Pearl, I'll teach you how to work the sewing machine."

For years I've watched the women sew our clothes. I have

never been allowed to help. Now I'm so happy that I want to run around the room like a child. Instead, I go to sit with Elizabeth. Her chair is pushed back slightly, but her pregnant belly still presses against the table. I nearly bend down and whisper to the baby inside. I want to tell it that I am here, that I am a woman.

"Watch," Elizabeth says. And I do. She threads the needle, picks up a piece of forbidden material, turns the handle, and begins to sew.

"Does Papa S. know?" I ask, above the gentle stabbing noise of the machine. "About the material?" Although the door is closed, I wonder if anyone can see us, can hear me speak.

"Of course." Elizabeth smiles. "They're not for us to wear. And our messages might save an unloved person."

Her fingers move gently on the cloth. It seems almost alive, the deep green covered with bamboo sticks and birds. I reach out to touch it.

"What's Papa S. got against patterns?" Kate asks quietly. Her legs are tucked under her on the sofa, her sandals on the floor.

Rachel scowls at her. "You know that it's not Papa S. It's Mother Nature who tells him."

Kate stares back. "So why does Mother Nature find nice material so offensive then?"

Elizabeth turns to her and there's a second of silence as the sewing machine stops. "All patterns are false, unless created by Nature."

She doesn't notice Kate making a face at her as she turns back to the sewing machine. I hope that the anger I feel is clear on my face. I can't bear that Kate is making fun of Elizabeth. Why is she being like this? But I won't let the magic disappear.

I watch the needle dig through the material, joining it together. Elizabeth has swept her hair over one shoulder, her eyes fixed on the work.

Suddenly she stops, sits back. "The baby is kicking." Her smile is wide as she takes my hand and places it over her stomach. Straight away, I feel it. A pushing against my palm. If it weren't for the skin in between, I would be holding a tiny foot, or a hand.

How will we hide that you are Elizabeth's? No one else is growing a child, yet I'll have to pretend I don't know. *Maybe, when you are old enough, we'll run together to the lake, and in the shadows of the trees, I will tell you. Then you'll never have the empty place I can't get rid of.*

The sewing machine spills its thread in a line. Elizabeth's fingers push the material along.

"Do you get upset?" I ask, before I can convince myself not to. "That it won't know you are its real mother?"

Elizabeth looks surprised. Because I have dared to ask? Surely the thought must have found its way to her before. Has she never thought it about me?

"I am only happy. I've been chosen by Nature to carry her child."

"Will you love it differently, though?" I persist. "Do you love your own children differently?"

"I do not have children, Pearl. I have birthed children, but they are not mine."

Her words are jagged in me. *Say it differently,* I want to beg her. *Tell me that I am the most special to you.*

But Elizabeth turns, puts her foot on the pedal, and the sewing machine starts again.

"Here," Rachel says. She has taken a pen and paper from the drawer and she puts it in front of me. The white of the paper is smooth under my fingers. A bolt of excitement stings my skin. "Write some of Papa S.'s words on here."

"Which ones?" He says so many wise things.

"Anything to save the unfortunate people on the Outside."

It doesn't take long to choose. I pick up the pen. It has been a long time since I have written and I watch carefully as the ink makes the words on the page.

Listen only to Mother Nature, I write. *She will save you.*

Rachel takes the paper from me, carefully folds it and tucks it into the hem of the skirt she has made. Swiftly, she pulls the thread behind it, locks it inside.

Will anyone find it? Who shall wear the skirt of silver stars?

Somewhere, on the Outside, a woman will feel the material against her legs. And hidden away, touching her ankles, my inky words will try to save her.

----◆◆◆◆◆◆◆----

So I watch. And I listen. But I hear very little through this thick, dirty glass that separates me from the outside world.

I see the children. They run across the fields, laughing. I watch them disappear into the trees.

And I wonder.

After all these years, I still wonder.

Each day I imagine that a different child is mine. One day it is the boy growing into a man. His gentle ways. One day it is the girl with hair like the sun. Today, the wild girl is my daughter.

Most days it is her.

CHAPTER EIGHT

••••••••●•••••••••

"I have some good news," Papa S. says.

He is standing at the head of our tables in the meadow. The grass around us is dry, as Mother Nature hasn't sent rain for over two weeks. The morning is cold against my back.

"We are to welcome three new members to Seed."

No one moves, but surely they feel the same shock as I do. There is only *us*. This is our family. We are complete, safe from the Outside. But now Papa S. wants someone else to come in.

"Don't be afraid." He smiles warmly at us. "I have asked Nature and she has agreed."

I look at Kindred John. His face is still, but his eyes don't seem happy. Elizabeth is smiling, but it doesn't look right.

Papa S. motions his hand toward Kindred Smith, who stands up. "Mother Nature guided me," Kindred Smith begins. He coughs slightly. "I have a good friend, Linda. I hadn't seen her for many years, but then Nature led me to her. Linda needs me. She needs us. Her heart belongs at Seed." He is beginning to speak quickly as he spreads his arms wide. "She will live here with her two children."

My mind is stuck. Strangers at Seed.

Elizabeth kisses her palm and faces it toward Kindred Smith. "We will welcome them," she says softly as she gets up.

Heather stands up next. "We will welcome them." Her voice is strong in the air.

We all rise. I kiss my palm and face it toward Kindred Smith. His smile is wide.

"We will welcome them," I say with my family. I try to mean it and ignore the doubt that is creeping around me. I look to Papa S., but his mouth is closed and I don't recognize the expression in his eyes.

We watch the car from the window, Kate, Ruby, and I. From here it looks so small, like a ladybug crawling closer. Slowly, it creeps up our long driveway. We never have visitors and Ruby has gone silent, standing on the chair beside me. Kate's hands go still in the sink as we hear the rumble of the car's engine. It comes to a stop outside the main door of our house.

A woman gets out. Her hair is pulled back from her face. Her trousers are blue, her top black, and she looks nervous. Even from here, I can see the bones through her skin. I have never seen any-one who looks so fragile, as though she could break. She bends to talk to someone in the back, just as the front door to Seed opens and Kindred Smith walks out. He is beaming, and the woman seems to relax slightly as he goes toward her. They kiss each other on the cheek.

"I'm so glad you decided to come." Kindred Smith's words are muffled through the glass.

"So am I." The woman smiles nervously and hesitates, before she opens the back door of her car. A little girl steps out, about the same age as Ruby and Bobby. She doesn't smile, but her eyes are wide as she looks around at the beauty of Seed.

"This is Sophie," the woman says, and Kindred Smith smiles and bends down and says something so quietly to the girl that I cannot hear.

"And this is Ellis," the woman says as a boy gets out of the car. A boy from the Outside. On the front of his T-shirt is a faded, wide-open mouth with a tongue sticking out. He must be Jack's age, but he has already grown his hair and his curls fall into his eyes. He puts his hands into his back pockets as he looks at our home. His eyes move slowly across the bricks, the ivy, the windows. Then he's looking at us. He makes me feel uneasy and I want to duck down under the sink, but I don't move. He smiles a lazy smile and seems to nod before he looks away.

"Well," Kate says. "Look at our new converts." She doesn't seem to notice that her hands are still dunked in the bubbly water.

"She looks nice," says Ruby. I think she means Sophie, who has silently taken the woman's hand as Kindred Smith talks quietly to them all, sweeping his arms across the fields beyond.

"I'll show you around," I hear him say and they all follow him toward the front door.

The boy still has his hands in his back pockets as he turns to glance at us again. I don't know why, but I wish I'd already looked away.

"Ellis," says Kate as she brushes a sponge around the inside of a mug.

"It's a nice name," says Ruby.

Kate looks at me, smiling. "It certainly is. And he looks like a nice boy, doesn't he?"

"Yes, he does," I say. "It'll be nice for Jack to have another boy our age."

"Oh, Pearl, please," Kate says. And I can't tell whether she's angry or laughing.

"Are they really coming to stay?" Ruby asks.

Just then, the kitchen door opens and Kindred Smith comes in. The new family are behind him.

"Ah, some more people for you to meet," Kindred Smith says. "Kate, Pearl, Ruby, this is Linda, Ellis, and Sophie. They are our new family members."

"I'm Kate. It's nice to meet you," Kate says, looking at Ellis.

"You too," he says. His voice is low and soft. Hearing it makes my skin tingle, like I've been out in the sun too long. He turns to look at me. "Hello," he says. It's strange, because I don't really know what to say. Maybe it's because his hair is already longer, it makes me awkward, unsure of who he is.

"So, are you Ruby, or Pearl?" He has a funny smile on his lips.

"Pearl," I manage. I suddenly wish I'd had just a few more months to let my hair grow as long as Kate's.

"Hi, Sophie," Ruby says. "Will you sleep in our room?" I know that Ruby is staring at Sophie's dress with butterflies all over it. I can't tell whether she's envious, or confused.

"Do you want to show her your room?" Kindred Smith asks.

"Will she not be sharing with me?" Linda looks unsure. From this close, I can see dry patches of skin on her face. They look sore.

"The women sleep in different rooms." Kindred Smith touches her arm, and it seems to melt her hesitation.

"It will be fun to share with other children, won't it?" Linda asks Sophie. The little girl doesn't say a word, doesn't even nod her head. She just looks at her mother with those wide eyes.

"I'll show you," says Ruby, and she reaches for Sophie's hand. Before the little girl has time to realize it, they're walking out of the room. Her mother's smile looks a bit forced, as though she's trying too hard to relax. *Mother.* Sophie knows her true mother. There's a rush of something in me, but I know it is dark, so I push it away.

"So, Ellis," says Kate. "Where do you think you'll sleep?" There's a crackle of unease in the air. Kindred Smith stares at Kate. If she notices the look he gives her, she doesn't show it. Her smile remains and Ellis looks right at her.

"I'll go where I'm told," he says, his own smile twinkling.

"Right, then I'd better tell you." Kindred Smith does a funny sort of laugh. "Pearl, you can show Linda where her room is." Then he turns to their mother. "When you've unpacked your car, Pearl can show you where to park it, around the back. Then you can give the key to me."

"Oh," she says.

Kindred Smith smiles at her. "We don't want the key to get lost. It's a big house."

"Of course," Linda says, but she twists her hair nervously in her fingers as she looks out the window toward her car, waiting in the driveway.

"And do you have telephones?" Kindred Smith asks. "Obviously we don't use them at Seed."

Linda looks flustered. "It's in here," she says as she reaches into the small brown bag hanging by her hip. She pulls out a black telephone. I've seen people from the Outside use them at the market, but it feels wrong to have one in our home. Nature has said that they block out her voice.

"Ellis?" Kindred Smith holds out his empty hand toward him.

"Are you serious?" the boy asks. He's looking at his mother.

"We've talked about this," she says quietly.

Kindred Smith laughs lightly. "I'll keep it safe."

I watch as Ellis takes his telephone from his pocket and reluctantly puts it into Kindred Smith's palm.

"We could show you around when you've seen your room," Kate says to Ellis.

"OK," he says.

I just stare at him. A stranger in our home. But he looks different from the boys I see at the market. And I don't want to turn away from him, like I do from them.

Kate is left in the kitchen as we go upstairs. Kindred Smith and Ellis continue up to the top of the house, where the boys and Kindreds sleep. I take Linda into the room next to ours. Heather is making up the spare bed in the corner.

"I saw you come up the driveway," she says as she goes up to hug Linda. "Welcome."

"Thank you." Linda's cheeks blush red. For a moment, I'm worried that she'll let herself cry.

"Shall I leave Linda here with you?" I ask Heather as she turns back to the bed. "Kate and I are going to show Ellis around."

"Ellis?"

"He's my son," Linda says.

Heather shakes the bedsheet and it cracks in the air.

"He's about Jack's age," I say.

Heather nods. "Well, you'd better go and help him settle in," she says as she tucks the sheet under the heavy mattress. "I'll stay with Linda." But her words are almost lost to me, as I'm already out of the bedroom and running down the stairs, two at a time.

I stand by the back door, waiting. I'm holding my sandals in my hand, feeling the bristles of the doormat on my bare feet. There's a bird, a wood pigeon, I think, making shapes in the sky. It lifts and swoops, a smudge of brown against the blue.

"You were quick." It's Ellis.

"Yes," I say. There's something about his eyes, as though he's seeing right into me. I touch the thin strap of my top. Does he notice that I'm wearing a skirt?

"Where are you going to show me first?" he asks.

I wonder if I should wait for Kate, but I'm not sure where she is. "Does Sophie want to come too?" I ask.

"I think she's with the other little girl."

"Ruby."

His eyelashes are a deep beetle-black, much darker than Jack's.

"Let's go, then?"

It's a question and the only reply I can give is to start walking. We go across the gravel of the driveway, the stones wincing my feet. I don't let it show, though. And anyway, the grass is only a few steps away.

"I'll show you the barn first," I finally say. "It's where you'll probably be working."

"Mom didn't say anything about working," Ellis says.

"Everyone works here." How can he expect otherwise? "It's good work. Jack loves it."

Ellis glances at me. "Who's Jack?"

"One of us." The grass is dry between my toes. "You'll meet him now, I should think."

I'm feeling a bit annoyed and I don't know why. Suddenly, I'm not so sure I want these new people here. I know I shouldn't feel like this, because Papa S. says we must welcome them. And I should willingly let them share in the beauty of Seed. But just this second, I don't feel like it. I want us all to be left alone.

So I don't say another word and then we're pushing through the big, rusting doors, into the banging and clattering of the work barn.

"Impressive," Ellis says as he looks around him, and I warm to him once more.

Instantly, I see Jack. He's looking at a green car's engine with Kindred John, pointing something out to him. The hood of the car is hooked open above their heads.

"Come on," I say to Ellis and he follows me, past the chaos and tables of oily springs and machine parts.

"Hi, Jack," I have to say as he hasn't even noticed us. His eyes are so focused on the ticking metal in front of him. He looks up and sees Ellis, and for a second he seems confused. "This is Ellis. The boy who's come to live here."

"Oh, hello." Jack reaches out to shake Ellis's hand, but must realize that his skin is dirty from the work and so he just shrugs lightly. "I'm glad you're here." If he is unsure about this boy from the Outside, he doesn't show it.

"And this is Kindred John," I say.

Kindred John wipes his hands on an old cloth slung over his shoulder. "Welcome," he says as he shakes hands with Ellis. "Do you want to join us?"

"I'm showing him around," I say too quickly.

"Yeah, I think I'll put off working as long as possible." Ellis laughs. But none of us do. We know that laziness disintegrates the soul.

Who are these people who Kindred Smith has brought into our home? And why do I not want to walk away? I can feel the air of Outside trickling off Ellis and yet I stay, standing by him.

"We won't be long," I say to Kindred John, but he's already turned back to the engine.

"See you later," Jack says, and something passes between them that tells me they will be friends.

It's quieter when we leave the barn. The whir and knocking of the machines is behind us as we start to walk through the meadow. I glance at Ellis's T-shirt, at his clothes from the Outside. They look so wrong. And they confuse me, because somehow I want to touch them. They make me have questions I cannot ask.

"It's nice here," Ellis says.

The long grass brushes against my legs and I'm so proud to show him our home. "It's the most beautiful place in the world," I say.

"Have you traveled?"

"No," I say. "I just know it is." He's unsettled me again and I don't know why.

"Well, I've lived in enough places," Ellis says. "And here is definitely one of the most beautiful." He smiles at me and then looks up at the huge arc of sky above us. "It's certainly better than where we've just come from."

"You're lucky. Papa S. rarely lets people from the Outside into Seed."

"Mom was desperate to come here after she bumped into that Smith guy, but he didn't think we'd be allowed. It took him a while to persuade your leader." Ellis laughs lightly. "I think because my mom and Smith knew each other when they were young, you know, it kind of convinced him."

The thought of Kindred Smith actually living on the Outside feels so wrong. I try to imagine him as a boy, but my mind won't let me.

"When she met him again, it was the first time I'd seen her happy in years." Ellis drifts his hand through the top of the long grass.

Kate is calling to us. We stop as she walks across the meadow. She doesn't run.

"You went without me," she says when she reaches us, but she's smiling.

"I didn't know where you'd gone," I say.

"Where are we going?" she asks.

"The lake?" I suggest.

"It'll be perfect today."

"Lead the way then," Ellis says. So we do.

We walk through the strawberry field, rather than around it, carefully stepping in a line over the rows of squat plants. The straw is scratchy on my feet and I tread carefully, not wanting rotten strawberries to squelch between my toes.

Kate stops and touches Ellis's elbow. "Here," she says, bending down and reaching under the soft leaves. She passes him a perfectly ripe strawberry. "Try this. I bet you've never tasted one like it."

Ellis puts it whole into his mouth and we watch as his jaw moves. He's smiling as he eats. He swallows and wipes the juice from his lips. "I think you might be right," he says.

We keep walking and take him through the vegetable garden. Elizabeth is picking some runner beans.

"Elizabeth," I say, rushing over to her. "This is Ellis. He's come to live with us." I'm speaking too quickly, dizzy in the sunny air.

She smiles at me, then kisses her palm and reaches out to touch Ellis's chest. "You are very welcome," she says.

"Thank you," Ellis replies. I wonder if he thinks she looks like me. Maybe I'll ask him later.

"We're going to show him the lake," Kate says, picking a green bean and crunching it raw into her mouth.

"Hey," Elizabeth laughs, gently slapping her hand away. "These are for evening meal. In fact, when you've shown Ellis the lake, you'd better come back and help me. The gooseberries need picking and sieving."

"It's Pearl's turn for that," Kate says. "I definitely did them the last time."

It's one of the tasks none of us like. The gooseberry thorns are sharp and long. Then there's the pushing them through the sieve to get rid of the skins. I try not to think badly of it, but it always seems a lot of work for very little to eat.

"I could help you, Pearl," Ellis says. I hadn't been expecting it and I feel my cheeks redden. "You'd have to teach me how to do it, though."

"You'll be needed in the work barn," Kate says.

"Talking here won't get anything done," Elizabeth interrupts. She rubs the base of her back.

"Come on," says Kate, and she pulls lightly on Ellis's arm. I think I should stay and help Elizabeth, but there's something about Ellis that makes me want to be close to him. Something I don't understand. So the three of us walk out from the vegetable garden, over the field and into the shade of the trees that hide our lake.

We walk without speaking. There's just the sound of dry leaves under our feet. When we get to the lake, I watch Ellis's eyes and I know that he's impressed. How could he not be? Surely there's nowhere on the Outside like this. The water is still as ice, patterned with striking sky blue and deepest greens. Patches of bugs hover and swoop and fly.

Ellis nods his head slowly as he looks around him. Kate and I are watching him as he bends down and picks a thick, flat piece of grass. He puts his thumbs hard on either side of it and brings it to his lips. A high, raspy call fills the air and shoots through the forest.

I stare at him. Did I just hear Mother Nature?

"How did you do that?" Kate asks. She seems uncertain of him, suddenly.

"You've never seen anyone blow grass before?" He's chuckling at us. And I realize now that it's a trick. Mother Nature wasn't working with him after all. And why would she? This strange boy with long hair has an edge that makes me mistrust him.

"No," I say strongly. I bet there's plenty at Seed he's never seen before. Things much more magical than making grass sing.

Ellis's expression changes slightly. "Have you lived here all your lives?" he asks. I don't think he's mocking us now. He seems curious. The change in him confuses me.

"Of course," I say.

"Yes," says Kate, more quietly.

"So you were born here?"

"Yes."

"So, whose mom is whose?"

It's only a few words, but they make my thoughts stumble. So it's Kate who speaks. "Papa S. says that Nature is our Mother."

"What, you grew out of the ground?" Ellis laughs, but when he looks at me, his expression changes. "Do you not know who your real mom is?"

A knot of anger is building in me. "We don't need to know," I say. But I know that's not true. Ever since I can remember, I've wanted to know. It's forbidden, but it pulls me, and almost every time I'm with Elizabeth, I long to really be hers.

"Teach me how you do that," Kate interrupts, pointing to the grass in Ellis's hand. He looks at me briefly. I think he's worried that he's upset me, so I hold my head high and smile at him.

"Here." Ellis bends down and picks two more pieces of grass. His hand touches mine as he passes one to me. "Put your thumbs like this. Hold them down hard. Leave a little gap, though." He reaches over and separates Kate's thumbs slightly. She doesn't say a word. "Then bring them up to your mouth and blow gently."

We do as he says. All I can hear is my breath, but straight away from Kate there is a high-pitched sound—faint, but definitely there.

"I did it," she says, laughing.

"Do it again," Ellis says, so she does. And this time it's louder, a confident call to the birds. She doesn't stop. Her head is tipped up to the treetops, her thumbs and lips making music.

"You try again, Pearl." Ellis isn't looking at Kate. He's watching me. "It's easy."

So I do. I press my thumbs hard onto the flat strip of grass, and watch as the skin around my nails turns blotchy white and red. I want to be able to do it. I want to show Ellis that I can make the grass sing too.

"Like this," he says, and I copy him as he puts his grass to his mouth. I blow gently against my skin, and the sound makes me jump. So sudden, so definite. A higher sound, it stretches up from my piece of grass and snakes off through the trees.

We stand like this, calling to Nature, trying to change the sounds we make. Our own, strange tune.

Eventually Kate throws her piece of grass down. She takes off her sandals, walks to the bank of the lake, and sits to dangle her feet in the cool water.

"Come and sit down, Ellis," she says. "I want to know about you." He seems a bit surprised, but he walks over to her and takes off his shoes and socks. I put my piece of grass in my pocket and follow them.

The water sends a bolt of cold through my feet.

"It's freezing!" Ellis says, dipping his toes in and out.

"You'll get used to it," Kate laughs.

"Wait until you swim in it," I say.

"I don't think I'll ever do that."

"You will." I smile at him. But he's staring at his feet in the water, keeping them down. It's strange that it feels so right that he's here.

"So, where do you come from?" Kate asks him. She pulls her hair back and drapes it over her shoulder, tips her head slightly to shield her eyes from the sun.

Ellis keeps looking at the water. "Near Southampton, most recently," he says.

"Where's that?" It's only a small question, but when he glances at me, his eyes have changed again.

"You don't know where Southampton is?" He's not laughing at me. It's something more than that.

"No," I reply, looking at Kate.

"How are we meant to know if we've never left here?" Her voice is strong as she glares at him.

"What do you mean, you've never left here?"

"What don't you understand?" She pulls her feet out from the water and starts to dry them with her hands.

"We go to the market," I say. I don't like the way he's looking at us, a sort of mixture of disbelief and pity. "We don't need anything else."

"How do you know what you need if you've never seen it?" He's taken his feet from the water too. He's trying to pull his socks back on, but they're sticking to his skin.

"If it's so great out there, how come you're here?" Kate's leaning toward him, making him look straight into her eyes.

"Fair point," he says and shrugs his shoulders. "I guess at least I don't have to go to school."

"What's school?" Kate asks.

Ellis has got that look again. "Have you seriously never been to school?" he asks.

Kate and I don't answer him. He knows what we'd reply.

"It's a place you have to go to learn things."

"Then school is here," I tell him. "We learn everything we need."

"I don't know whether to feel jealous or sorry for you," Ellis says. I can tell by his eyes that he's not being cruel.

"I know I'm happy for you that you've come to Seed," I say, summoning a smile for him.

We're silent again. We watch Ellis tying the laces on his shoes.

"So why are you here, then?" I finally ask.

"I told you. That Smith guy makes my mom happy."

"What do you mean?" Kate asks.

Ellis clears his throat. "She says it all makes sense, now she's met him again. That this is what will make her better."

"Better from what?"

"She's been in a bad way." He's looking at the ground, scratching the dry mud with his fingers. "Smith said he'd help her."

"He will," I tell him. "We will."

"What was wrong with her?" Kate asks.

I think that Ellis is uncomfortable, but Kate won't let it go. He picks up a piece of grass, rolls it tight between his fingers. "She's been really down, that's all."

"She'll be happy here." I want to touch Ellis's arm, to reassure him.

"But why was she in a bad way?" Kate won't leave him alone. "Is that what happens on the Outside?"

"It does to people who've got a dad like mine." Ellis seems to say it to himself.

"Your dad?"

Ellis stands up, brushing leaves from his jeans. "Aren't I meant to be in the work barn?"

I think Kate has finished her questions, because she gets up, sandals in her hands. As she makes her way out of the woods, we follow.

I watched the red car as it drove up the long, winding driveway. A woman got out, a girl, a young man. And I wanted to shout to them and break my window glass. Run! I wanted to scream. Run while you still can. But my dry mouth stayed clamped shut.

Flickers of memories reach me. They lick around my shadow and slip inside. My mother, my sister, and me, driving up that driveway. But before, before that. In a shop, where I had wanted the blue shoes with the rainbow strap. My weary mother and the stranger who came up.

"Are you all right?" he had asked her.

"I'm fine," she answered. But she wasn't, and somehow he knew.

"You look unhappy," he said, and touched her arm. He was younger than my mother. His face was warm and handsome, but already I didn't like him.

"I'm fine," she said again.

"Really?" He persisted. "I can help you." And that was all it took.

The next day, we were driving up this same driveway, with everything we owned in the back of our car.

The next day, everything changed.

CHAPTER NINE

••••••••●••••••••

"**H**ave you met him yet?" I ask Ellis. We're waiting at the table
for evening meal to begin.

"Who?"

"Papa S."

"No. What's he like?"

I look down the table. Kindred John has his chin pressed into
his hands as he watches us. There is a strange expression on his
face and it is not one of warmth. Linda is sitting next to Ellis, but
she is turned away from him, talking quietly with Kindred Smith.
All the time, she scratches at the red skin under her sleeve.

Ellis lowers his voice. "I mean, what's the setup here? He's
the leader, right?"

"Of course." *Please hurry up, Papa S.* I want the meal to start.

"So he tells you what to do?"

"No." I look at him. "Nature tells us what to do. She chose
Papa S. Through him, she tells us."

"Like what?"

"Like everything. She tells us when to pick the crops. And

when we need to choose something to worship in the morning. She knows what we should wear. Things like that." I touch the fabric of my skirt.

"How long has he been here?"

"Twenty-seven years. Nature built him our home and led him here." Pride begins to grow in me. "We are the lucky ones."

The door to our house opens and Papa S. comes out, with Rachel by his side. I watch Ellis. I want to see the moment that he first glimpses Papa S. I know he will love him instantly.

But his face is expressionless.

"She's his Companion," I whisper. I wait for him to have this moment in silence. But then something in his eyes changes.

"Have you ever been his Companion?"

"Not yet." I smile and I look down at my skirt. Soon, I hope. Now that I'm a woman, I hope it won't be long.

It's at the end of evening meal when Papa S. raises his hand, and we're all quiet. The sun is losing its heat, but it's not yet cold.

"It seems that there is much to be thankful for today," Papa S. says, gazing at us all, "for today, our family has welcomed new members."

I smile at Ellis, but he doesn't see me. He is watching Papa S. Already, he looks like one of us. I know he'll be happy here.

Papa S. turns his face toward the sky and holds his hands up high. "Show us a sign, Nature," he calls into the air around us.

"Show us that this is your doing."

I hold my breath. Many times Nature has heard Papa S. and answered him. I will her to do it now. To prove to Ellis the power that she has at Seed.

We wait. The sky is settled. The grass is still. No one calls from the trees. Nothing stirs.

But then, a flock of starlings appear. They glide toward us as one and swoop above our heads. I can almost hear their beating hearts nestled under their feathers, as they fly together just for us. Papa S. is joyous.

I glance at Ellis, knowing that he will he impressed. But his face doesn't show it. Instead he has an eyebrow raised and I see him glance at Kate. Is he doubting Mother Nature? Anger is whispering to me, but I won't let it in.

"Thank you, Nature," Papa S. says more quietly. "Thank you for guiding them to us. They bring love, they bring beauty."

Linda looks a bit awkward. I try not to feel uncomfortable that she is sitting at our table. This mother with her children. This woman from the Outside.

There is a long silence as we watch the starlings disappear. Ellis coughs. Finally, Papa S. lowers his arms. He smiles at Linda. "Come," he says warmly.

Linda hesitates, looks at Kindred Smith. He encourages her, pushing her gently toward Papa S. But Sophie holds tightly onto her mother's arm.

"You must come here too." Papa S. has his palm facing toward them. "And you." He is looking at Ellis.

Linda stands and lifts Sophie into her arms. She walks toward Papa S.

"Go on," I whisper to Ellis.

I don't think he wants to, but he gets up and walks to the head of the table. His mother smiles at him, but his face has no expression. It must be overwhelming, being so close to Papa S. for the first time.

Papa S. takes Linda's hand and places her palm on his chest. Does she know how lucky she is? Then he reaches out his palm toward Ellis, but the boy from Outside steps away from him. Papa S. must feel the shock from us all.

"Ellis." Linda's voice is quiet, but I can hear the anger in it. And it makes him step forward again.

"Now you are one with us." Papa S. looks at Ellis as his voice swoops down the table. "You have been saved. And now you must give yourself willingly to Seed. Shed yourselves of the bleak Outside. Do not think of it again. Do not let the poison eat your mind." Papa S. begins to shake. "Tell me that you want to be happy." He stares at Linda.

"I do," she says.

"And that you want a pure mind."

"I do." Her eyes are wide. She no longer carries the grayness from Outside. Finally she is alive.

"That you will give yourself completely to Seed."

"I will."

Papa S. radiates light as he turns to Ellis. "That you will give yourself completely to Seed," he repeats.

There is a sudden stillness. A silence that shouldn't be here.

Ellis puts his hands in his pockets. He shrugs and smiles. "I will too," he says.

For a while, Papa S. won't take his eyes from him. Then he tips his head to the sky. "It is done," he calls into the air.

We sit, unmoving. Linda glances at Kindred Smith and he motions for them to come back to the table. I beam at Ellis as he walks toward me. And I am filled with happiness, because now he is truly one of us. We have saved him. We have saved them all.

Rachel looks up at Papa S., her eyes wide. He reaches down to touch her long hair. His fingers hesitate at the red flower wound among the strands by her ear. He bends down and with his eyes closed, breathes in its scent. Then he takes Rachel's hand and leads her back to the house and we are free to talk again.

Elizabeth leans over and touches Linda's hand. "I am glad you came."

"So am I," Linda says. She picks lightly at the skin on her nails.

"Come on, then," Kate says, standing up and beginning to stack the plates. "I want to hear this piano playing."

"You play the piano?" Kindred Smith asks Linda.

"No. Ellis does," she says, looking at her son. She has such pride in her eyes that there could be no doubt she is his mother.

"I try to sometimes." Kindred Smith laughs. "But I wouldn't exactly call it music."

"It's not so bad," Jack says reassuringly.

"I'm sure Ellis can do better," Kindred Smith says as he gets up to take the heavy pan from Linda and carries it into the house.

Bobby stays near me as we gather the glasses. He glances over at Ruby and Sophie as they dance in and out of the tall grass. I kneel down next to him. "You're still her favorite friend," I tell him, but his face creases into a scowl and he stomps off toward the kitchen door.

I look up quickly. Papa S. is not watching from the windows, so hopefully Bobby won't be punished. But has he forgotten that if he lets jealousy in, it will burrow deep within him and eat through his veins?

"Shall I take some of those?" Ellis asks me. I've piled the glasses high and they tip as I stand up. I don't have a chance to reply before he's reaching over and taking the top half from me, all the time looking in my eyes. I hurry away from him before he can see my thoughts.

We gather in the day room, leaving the Kindreds to sit, talking, at the empty table in the meadow. Through the window, I can see Linda seated between Elizabeth and Kindred Smith. Already she seems different, as though the shell of her Outside self is falling away.

Ellis sits at the piano and we stand around him. All except Bobby, who won't move from beside the sofa. Part of me wants to sit with him too. Away from this stranger and the feelings that creep into me whenever I am near him.

"What shall I play?" Ellis asks.

"How should we know?" Kate laughs.

"OK, then." He moves slightly on the stool, looks down at the pedals and back at his hands.

Then he begins to play and it's nothing like Kindred Smith. I could never have imagined that any sound would make me feel this way. The music lifts into the room from Ellis, through his arms, his hands, and it fills me until there is nothing else. It feels like I'm underwater at the lake, yet floating through the sky. There are a thousand butterflies dancing on my skin. I want to close my eyes, but I don't want to look away, not when his fingers move so fast across the white and black of the piano.

Ellis stops suddenly. He turns and gestures at Bobby to come over. Bobby looks at him, but he doesn't move. It's unlike him to be so hesitant. Even when Jack walks over and kneels down next to him, he just shakes his head. So I go to him and take his hand. I have to help him get rid of these strange feelings before too much damage is done. And I want him to love this music as I do.

"It's OK," I say. "I wasn't sure at first either." Then I lead him to Ellis. Bobby looks small next to him on the piano stool.

"If you put your hand on top of mine," Ellis suggests, "then you can really feel the music."

Bobby doesn't smile, but he does what Ellis says. Slowly Ellis begins to play again. The music is instant.

Bobby's eyes are wide. Their hands play faster and faster, until Bobby begins to laugh. Ellis has healed him. There could never be a better sound than his laughter and this music.

Ellis is here. I never knew that life could get any better, but it has. Because of Ellis, it has.

CHAPTER TEN

•••••••••••••••••

On our next free day, the clouds gather in the sky, heavy and waiting.

"Show me somewhere new," Ellis says, leaning against the closed kitchen door. "I've been working too hard on those engines in the work barn." He's wearing proper clothes now, the same as Jack. Yet he still looks different. He has rolled his sleeves up to his elbows and it makes me want to look at the skin on his arms. "Come on, Pearl, take me somewhere I've never been before." His smile makes fingers tiptoe up the back of my neck.

"How about Dawn Rocks?" Kate says.

"Dawn Rocks?"

"We go there the first day of every month," I say, picking up a plate to dry. "To greet the dawn."

"What, like really early in the morning?"

"It's amazing then," I say. Ellis looks at me as if he knows better. Which he can't, because how can he? Kate carries on washing up with her back to us. "We don't have to go there," I say, turning my back to him too. Suddenly I don't want to take him there. I don't want to muddy our special rocks with his Outside ways.

"Go where?" asks Jack as he comes through the door with a pile of plates. Ellis moves out of the way for him.

"The rocks," Ellis says.

"Dawn Rocks," I correct him. He doesn't even know to say it right.

"Today?" Jack asks, and the water splashes up at Kate slightly as he drops the plates into the sink.

"Yeah," Ellis says.

"Sounds good. And if you actually started to help, new boy, we might get there quicker." Jack laughs.

So they go out the back door together, to gather more things to wash up from the tables. Kate and I watch them. Ellis, just a bit taller than Jack. They're deep in conversation and Jack tips his head back to laugh. Kate and I are in silence, though, and I don't know her thoughts. I'm not sure that I know mine.

When we've finished clearing and washing up, the day is ours. The children are building card stacks in the playroom, so it's just us.

We go through the meadow, where the Kindreds still sit at the tables, their shoulders hunched against the prospect of rain. I'm beginning to wish I'd brought a sweater. I thought it would be warmer than this.

"Let's go the shortcut," Kate says, so we head off to the right, along the edge of the cornfield. The plants are already shoulder height, the husks growing almost as we watch.

At the edge of the field, we walk along the bramble hedge until we find our little gateway to the other side.

"Race you," Kate suddenly says and she's running before I even think. So we chase her up to Dawn Rocks. Jack quickly catches her and puts his arms around her waist to pull her back. She's laughing, kicking her legs in the air as he lifts her off the ground.

I run past them, but Ellis is already ahead. He turns to me, starts to run backward up the hill.

"Is that them?" he shouts, pointing behind to the cluster of rocks which sit waiting for us.

Yes, that's them. I nod to him, and he turns away and runs again, up the last bit of the hill.

When I get there, he's gone. "Ellis?" I call. But there's no answer. My voice doesn't even echo. It just falls flat into the gray air. Jack runs up, ahead of Kate, her laugh breaking the quiet. She looks around.

"Where's Ellis?" she asks.

I shrug. "He was here and then he wasn't."

"He's hiding from us," Jack says. We don't often come here without the rest of the family. The rocks feel so still, so incredibly strong.

"Ellis!" Jack calls.

"I'm up here." We look up. He's standing right at the top. A place we're forbidden to go. A place of purity, touched only by the sun.

Even Kate looks shocked. "You're not allowed up there," she shouts to him.

But Ellis stretches his arms out wide and starts to turn around. What's he doing? Can he not hear her?

"Get down," Jack calls. He's looking around and I know he's checking for Kindreds, or Papa S.

"But it's great up here," Ellis shouts, still slowly spinning. "I can see for miles."

"You'll get us all into trouble," I say. Fear is creeping into me. "Please, Ellis." There must be something about the way I say it, because he stops and he starts to jump down, from rock to rock, until he's on the earth in front of us.

"Well, if you ask as nice as that." He laughs.

"It's not funny." I'm glaring at him, but he doesn't seem to care what he's done.

"Could you see the house from up there?" Jack asks.

"Yeah, I could see everything."

If he could see the house, then they could see him.

A buzzard swoops down on the wind. It perches on one of the lower rocks. Not even a bird dares go to the top.

Ellis moves toward me and it makes me look away. He's reaching out and his hand is under my chin. The feeling in me is instant. I let him gently move my face until his eyes look into mine.

"Sorry?" he says. I try to keep my eyes stern, but his hand is on my skin. This boy from the Outside is touching me. I struggle to think. But Jack and Kate are watching us and I know I must speak.

"Just don't do it again," I say.

"I'll try not to," he replies.

I glance at Jack. I need to feel that this is all right. That I haven't done anything wrong.

And then, without even talking, we all walk around to the back of the rocks. We climb up to the first stones, where we're allowed to sit, and we rest our backs against the hard surface, our legs all stretched out in a row. I'm next to Ellis and I can feel his leg against mine.

"So your mom's happier here, then?" Kate asks. She is staring at Ellis and he can't avoid her question.

"She's a different person."

"Different?" Jack asks.

"She just wasn't right. You know."

"No, we don't know," Kate says. "That's why we're asking."

A half smile happens on Ellis's lips, but it doesn't last. "Mom was all over the place. She couldn't even work anymore. I reckon she's been depressed for years."

"And Seed is healing her," I say, pleased.

"Yes." Ellis catches my eye. "I feel like I've got my mom back."

"What about your father?" Jack asks.

Ellis's face seems to shut down. "What about him?" He sounds so cold.

"Maybe he could come here too," Jack says. "We could help him."

"You wouldn't want him here."

"Why?" Kate asks.

"I don't want to talk about it anymore." Ellis looks out at the hills rising up behind Dawn Rocks.

"Papa S. is your father now," I reassure him. But his eyes stay turned away.

There's a low rumbling from the sky, just as it starts to rain. A few warning drops, but then, with no hesitation, the clouds pour their water on us. Kate jumps up, opens her mouth wide toward the sky. The rain beats on the rock, bouncing in all directions.

I jump down and Kate follows, and then the other two are with us. We all hold hands, lean out, and start to spin. I'm laughing and giddy and when we stop, we look at each other and our clothes are soaked through.

Kate takes off her top first. "Come on," she shouts above the pointing rain. She's laughing and she's reaching for the top of her skirt, pulling it down, peeling the wet material from her legs. Jack is staring, the rain dripping from his eyelashes, his top clinging to his chest. Ellis laughs, but he looks unsure.

"Come on, Pearl," I hear Kate say to me through the noise of the downpour. And so I reach for my buttons, undo my shirt all the way down, and take it from my shoulders and my arms.

"You too, Jack?" I smile at him. And Kate is laughing, pulling down his suspenders, tugging his shirt free. Jack pushes her hands away, but I'm sure he's shaking as he takes off his shirt, then his shoes, his trousers. He puts them on the wet rock. And they're dancing, Kate and Jack, half-naked in the rain, the water spilling on their skin as Ellis and I stand there.

I step out of my skirt. And I feel free. Ellis doesn't hesitate for long, and he takes his shirt off. His trousers stick, but he yanks at them. I look at Ellis's body. His skin is paler than Jack's and he's slimmer. The rain is falling on his bare stomach and I can't look away.

Kate and Jack take our hands and we're turning again in the rain. But we don't look at the sky this time. We watch each other, still laughing, the rain cold, but warm. Thunder cracks and Kate screams, but we keep on turning.

Ellis looks at me. I feel his eyes on my body, seeing my

underwear, seeing my skin, almost all of my skin. And a feeling rushes to my belly and fizzes down my legs. But then he turns away and I feel Jack's hand in mine.

Time rushes and stops and rushes and stops and gradually the rain slows down. The water now just taps me slightly. And then we're standing still, holding hands, soaked to our bones. Suddenly exposed. Suddenly aware. And I want to stay like this, but I want to cover myself too. Part of me wants it never to have happened, but I don't know why.

Jack is the first to put his clothes back on. He struggles to pull his trousers up, laughing as he tumbles to the wet grass. Kate smiles as she watches him with her hands on her hips. I reach for my shirt, pull it over my arms, fumble with the buttons.

"Getting dressed already?" Ellis asks me. That mocking smile is on his lips.

"I'm cold," I say. But I'm not. And I don't understand the feelings I have.

Kate is the last to put her clothes on. She's watched us struggle with the wet material, and now we watch her. She's slow, and doesn't look at us, as she bends over to pick up her skirt. She puts her legs in, pulls it up. I see the look on Jack's face and it makes me know that he is changing. Am I losing him?

And then we walk, in silence, away from Dawn Rocks, the last of the rain squeezed out of the sky.

He knows that I am here. The little boy. He watches me and he knows.

He speaks to me when no one sees. But I do not understand what he says. I do not know what he asks.

There are footsteps outside my room. I step down from the window and sit quietly on the chair. And I wait.

CHAPTER ELEVEN

•••••••••●•••••••••

apa S. has called me to him. I was hoping for good news,
hoping for the words that make me his Companion. But as
I stand in his study, he has barely spoken to me. He is sitting
in his chair behind his desk, with his back to me, his face toward
the window.

"Pearl," he says, his voice so quiet. "You have dissatisfied me
and Mother Nature." I want to ask why, but the word doesn't
come out. "You must ask for forgiveness."

I know, as soon as he says that word. I will be in that room
again.

He says nothing else, but beckons for me to follow him. Walking toward the room, I can hear the sounds of the children outside. And I'm walking, my bare feet on the wooden floor, toward
the door. I reach out for the perfectly round door handle. I hold
my hand there and I wait for my legs to run. But they don't,
because I trust Papa S., and I'm turning the handle. The door
breathes as it opens itself to me and I step inside.

I close the door and there's silence. It's like the world outside has disappeared and I'm the only one left. I walk into the small room and I want to run away, but I know that Papa S. loves me.

Then it begins.

At first it is so quiet that I can barely hear it. But it gets louder. The sound of a woman crying. She's asking someone to stop, but they don't, because her cries are getting louder. And she's begging them now, not to hurt her, don't hurt her, but they don't listen and she starts to scream. A sound from so deep within the core of her that I am shaking and even though I tell myself to breathe, she's still screaming and they're hurting her and it doesn't stop. My hands are over my ears, but it doesn't block out the noise. Nothing can block out the sound of her begging, the sound of her scream ripping through her body, her skin.

Then, that silence.

Nothing else.

It was her, the same woman who has haunted my dreams since I was in this room when I was a child. The woman who screams in the darkness of my nightmares, as she beats on my heart and blocks out my breath.

"Pearl," Papa S. says. He is not here, but I hear his voice. "Did you hear those screams?"

"Yes."

"These screams came from your bones. This time it was Nature calling to you, because you have displeased her."

What have I done that has made Nature cr
skin and scream within me? I have tried so har
right. To do all that I'm asked. But Nature is
knows my thoughts.

I remember what comes next. The walls slowly begin to close
in on me. Closer, closer. I stand with my feet on the ground, hold
my arms out to the side, as if that will protect me. Slowly, they're
walking toward me, inch by inch.

"You have done wrong, Pearl," Papa S. says. "You must ask
for forgiveness."

But I can't speak. My voice is caught between the woman's
screams and the walls that are coming closer.

"Pearl, admit that you have done wrong," his voice says from
beside me, above me, below me. "You are wicked. You must admit
it to cleanse your soul." But I don't know what I have done wrong.

The walls creep closer, touch my fingertips. But I don't know
what I have done.

I hear his voice, I feel the walls, and I cannot escape. I push
onto them, but they don't move back. They force my arms down.

And now it's me screaming, but I know no one can hear. No
one but Papa S., but he won't help me and I don't know why. I
have been bad, but I don't know how. I have been bad.

"I have done wrong!" I scream, the walls pushing on my back,
my front. "I have been bad!"

"What have you done?" His voice fills my skin. The walls stop.

"I don't know," I cry.

"It is Nature moving these walls," Papa S. shouts. "You must confess to Nature." And so the walls begin to crush me again. I cannot move my head.

"Try again," he says. "Because I love you, Pearl, and wickedness will fester in you if you don't release it in words."

"Ellis," I manage to say, my voice barely my own. I remember Ellis's body in the rain. The feeling when he touched me. "My bad thoughts are about Ellis."

The walls stop. They hold me there, just for a moment, before they begin to inch away, moving back to make the shape of the small room again.

My legs can't hold me and my lungs are still finding it hard to breathe. And lying on the floor, alone, I wonder at the words I said.

Ellis? Are my thoughts really bad? Round and round, I wonder. I think of him talking to me, looking at me. It's so different from Jack. Papa S. must have noticed and seen that somewhere deep within me, there were the roots of something he needed to drag out. Bad thoughts. He has helped me. He has wanted to cleanse me.

I leave the Forgiveness Room and walk back to Papa S.'s

study. He is here, waiting for me with his arms open and the warmth of the sunshine in his smile. I have pleased him and suddenly nothing else matters.

"Pearl," he says to me and I go to him and I am in the safety of his arms. His cloak smells of the lake. Gently, he strokes my hair. He kisses my head and then steps back to look at me. His eyes are like the brightest sky.

Finally, he kisses his palm and rests it on my heart. Through my dress, through my skin, I can hear the shuddering as my heart replies.

Papa S. kisses my forehead again, leads me to the door, and opens it for me. "You have been cleansed," he says. And I feel such relief that I won't have those feelings anymore. I shall look at Ellis as I do Jack. He is just a part of our family. One of us.

"Thank you," I reply, gazing at Papa S.

And he is still smiling as he closes the door behind me.

CHAPTER TWELVE

•••••••••●••••••••••

I know, as soon as I see Ellis at the bottom of the stairs, that it hasn't worked. In fact, everything is worse. Before, I hadn't known my thoughts about him. Yet now, I look at Ellis and my skin flushes warm.

"I'm meeting the others at the lake," Ellis says. "Want to come?" He's looking at me strangely. I feel the walls stepping closer. I can hear her screaming. "Is everything OK, Pearl?"

I nod.

"You sure?"

"I'm fine," I answer. But I don't think he believes me. Do I believe myself?

"I can wait, if you want to grab a towel," he says. His arms have become more tanned in the few weeks he's been here. His hair is a bit longer.

"OK," I say, although I don't mean to. I'd meant to say no and then I would have gone to my room quietly, on my own. But now I'm running up the stairs, two at a time, my bare feet slapping the wood. The echo of the screams are drifting away. I grab the first towel I see and run back and I'm standing next to Ellis again. I try not to sound breathless.

He laughs at me. "There was no rush. I wasn't going anywhere."

I laugh back and tuck my hair behind my ear. We start to walk, so close our arms keep brushing each other.

"Shortcut?" he asks. I don't need to reply. We head for the strawberry fields and begin to step carefully over the row of plants.

"Don't step on any leaves," Ellis says. "Papa S. might just take us up to the rocks and sacrifice us to the sun." He's laughing, but he's shot up that barrier between us again. I can't look at him.

"Just a joke, Pearl," he says, stopping and touching my arm. I carry on walking, so he holds me stronger until I stop. "Hey. It was just a joke."

"It wasn't funny," I say, finally looking at him. "It's important to us. He's important to us."

"And you're important to me," he says quietly. His words rest on me and then I let them sink inside.

Ellis bends down and I watch his fingers pick a ripe strawberry from its leaves. "Here," he says. And he holds it up to me.

I lean my head forward but he moves the strawberry away. I don't want to, but I smile. He puts the fruit nearer, so I grab his wrist and hold it steady until the strawberry is in my mouth. I feel his fingers on my lips and warmth shoots through me. The walls of the Forgiveness Room step closer, but I push them away. Ellis catches the juice with his thumb and as I eat, I watch him lick it off his skin.

He has that look in his eyes. I turn away from him and begin to walk quickly, stepping over the plants, toward the lake.

"You should try one," I say over my shoulder, as though being here with him is the most normal thing in the world. "They're delicious."

"I know they are," he says. Then he's at my side and we're walking together again.

I should say more. I should tell him that I think of him even when we're not together. But I keep my words inside me and hope my breath will bring him my secrets.

Kate and Jack are already in the lake. They're at the deeper end, leaning back against the edge and lazily kicking their legs to keep their bodies afloat. The sun is striking through the trees and sits on Kate's shoulders, yet it stops short of Jack. They're talking together, but we can't hear them from here. Ruby and Bobby sit by the bags and towels on the bank. Their little faces are a buzz of concentration as they pile small sticks on top of one another.

"It's a house for the ants," Bobby says, before we even have to ask. He doesn't look up as he balances a leaf for the front door.

"A mini Seed." Ellis grins and I know I'm staring at his lips.

And you're important to me.

My breath feels short, but I remember that Papa S. has cleansed me and I will not let him down.

I turn away from Ellis and stretch out the towel. "Your mother is very happy here," I say. My words seem to surprise him. I don't know what he was expecting.

"Yes, she is." He's too close as he sits down next to me. I should move away.

"And Sophie too."

"She loves it here. She thinks she's on vacation."

"And you?" I ask.

Ellis glances at me again, and as he shrugs his shoulders I can see what he must have looked like as a young boy. "Who cares what I think?" Then he's off and running toward the water, diving into its cold.

I look at his tanned back, his shoulders, the hair now wet on his face and I realize that I care. *I care, Ellis.*

I take off my dress. Underneath is the new swimsuit that Elizabeth has given me. Bright turquoise with tiny straps and two red buttons down the front. She told me how it used to be hers, when she was my age. It fits me perfectly, as I knew it would. I can feel that my body is changing every day, but in this swimsuit, do I look like a girl, or a woman? What does Ellis see?

I walk toward the water and hold my breath as it bites my

ankles. I don't know if he is looking at me, but I wade in gently just in case. As I swim to them, the cold burning my arms, I see that Ellis isn't watching. He's talking to Kate and she's laughing and dipping her long hair back into the water, where it swirls about her shoulders like it's alive. I refuse to feel envy. Ellis is not only mine to talk to. He is part of our family now.

Jack sees me, though, and he waves. He pokes me with his toes when I get to him.

"Where did you get to?" he asks. Such a little question, but it reminds me of the Forgiveness Room and the woman's screams. I take a deep breath and push myself down under the water. Its electric softness numbs my brain, until I run out of air and have to come back to the surface.

"You OK?" Jack asks.

"Completely," I lie, and I wonder whether I'll be punished for this too.

"Race you?"

"Maybe in a while."

"Suit yourself," he says as he pushes away from the bank and starts to swim. Instantly, I feel bad. Jack never speaks like that and I made him. But I don't follow him. I hold on to the bank, slowly making circles in the water with my free hand.

"Where were you, then?" Kate asks. In her bikini, she looks much more like a woman than I do.

"With Papa S." I won't tell her more. Maybe they'll think that Papa S. has made me his Companion. Kate raises her eyebrow at me.

"Alone?" she asks.

"Yes." I smile and look away. I know that I have Ellis's attention now.

"You're on the way up, Pearl," Kate says, but her words aren't filled with happiness, or even envy. It's more like pity.

"You'll be his Companion one day," I say to her.

"What if I don't want to be?" she says. What is she talking about? I look around quickly toward the trees. Anyone nearby could have heard. I don't answer her. I watch as her defiance suddenly slips into sadness. "Because maybe I don't," she says, so quietly that it must be to herself.

"Can I be his Companion?" Ellis asks, his face serious. But then he grins and rolls backward through the water. Kate laughs and tries to grab his ankles.

I wonder what it feels like to touch Ellis's skin. I could reach down now and touch his shoulders, his back.

My thoughts make me swim away.

CHAPTER THIRTEEN

•••••••••●•••••••••

"You should take Ellis with you," Kindred Smith says.

"To the bees?" Ellis asks.

"You'll need to learn," Kindred Smith tells him. He bangs the hammer down hard on the chair leg and it slots into place.

"Come on," I say. "Ruby's coming too." I put my hand on his elbow and start to pull him with me. "You've been here over three weeks and haven't even seen the bees." When Ellis stares at me, I wish I could take back my words. Have I been counting the days I've known him?

"I'll tell Kindred John where you are. He won't mind," Kindred Smith says. So Ellis has no more reason to hesitate.

It's a strikingly hot day. Everything seems dry and thirsty. Ruby runs ahead of us as we go around the back of the house. We walk through the East field, which is resting this year, and the ground feels knobbly under our feet.

"Who is Cedar?" Ellis asks. "I heard Bobby talking to Sophie about him."

I hesitate. "He used to live here."

"Where did he go?" Ellis asks.

I turn to him. He's looking at me as he walks. "I don't know. One morning they were just gone." I had almost forgotten about Cedar, and the memory licking at me makes me feel uncomfortable.

"They?"

"Sarah and Cedar," I say reluctantly.

"What made them go?"

I look down at my feet. Dust is creeping into my sandals. "Papa S. says she was poisoned by the whispers."

"What whispers?"

"They come from Outside. There was a storm that night and the whispers were carried on the clouds, clothed in thunder. They made Sarah and Cedar run away."

Ruby has stopped. I walk quickly toward her, thankful that I don't have to say any more. She's holding something in her hand. When we reach her, she shows us the smooth, round stone with its swirls of poppy red.

"Look," she says to me. "The sun has painted it."

"You should borrow it," I say warmly, and she puts it in her pocket.

We reach the bee shed in the corner of the field. When I open the door, the smell of old honey rushes out. I love coming in here. As a child, it was always the job I begged to do. Elizabeth taught me everything.

We walk to the hooks where the hats hang like fish skins. I reach up and pass one to Ellis.

"Just this?" he asks. "What about the rest of the suit?"

"This is all we use," I say.

"And gloves too?"

"No." I laugh at his expression. "The bees won't hurt you."

"They sting."

"Hardly ever," I say as I pick up the basket with the pine needles and matches. I pass Ellis the wooden box and Ruby reaches for his other hand as we walk from the shed across the field, to where the hives sit waiting for us. I can't wait to show him. The world of the bees is magical and I want to be the one to share it with Ellis for the first time.

As we get closer, we put our hats on so the veils cover our faces.

Ellis laughs beneath his veil. "I feel like a spaceman."

"What's a spaceman?" I ask.

"A man who goes to space."

I don't know what he means, so I just keep walking.

"You know?" he asks.

"No," I say.

Ellis shakes his head. I can see his eyes looking at me through the net over his face. "Have they never told you about people going to space? Walking on the moon?"

I stop and look at him. The anger he has placed in me makes my head so hot. He is ruining it. Ruining everything. "I'm not stupid, you know," I say.

"I know you're not," Ellis says.

"So why test me? Tell me stupid things to see if I believe them?"

"I don't," he says.

"Someone walking on the moon?" I raise my eyebrows at him. I hope he can see.

"Yes. They did. They do. And they have helmets like these." Ellis reaches up and touches the white surrounding his face. "But harder and with oxygen pumping into them."

"Then you're the stupid one, Ellis," I say. "Is that what you learned at the school? I wonder what other things you believed." I laugh, the air warming my lips even more. Ellis just shakes his head and carries on walking.

I forget about his words as soon as we get to the hive. I light the pine needles and hold them, smoking, into it. Then Ruby pulls Ellis toward us.

"Watch," I say to him as I reach for the first wooden frame. I pull it up and it's heavy with bees. Their noise immediately fills the air. Thick, solid buzzing pushing right inside me. I look at Ellis, but it's difficult to see his eyes. Have they got into him, the way they have in me?

I hold the frame and watch their black and orange streaks.

Today they sound annoyed; they didn't want to be disturbed. But I want Ellis to see them properly. I move the frame toward him, but he steps back quickly. Ruby shakes her head and laughs at him, and then carefully places her bare hand on top of the bees.

"See," I tell him. "They don't sting."

"How does she do that?" he asks, his voice muffled.

"You can do it too," I say.

"It's all right, thanks," Ellis says. "I'm fine right here."

Gently, I knock the frame against the hive until the bees fall off. Some fly around Ellis, and he stands still as a rock.

"You can do it next time," I suggest.

"There won't be a next time," Ellis mumbles.

When we've gathered enough frames, we walk back to the bee shed. Ellis keeps his hat on until he's safely inside. His hair is sticky with sweat.

"Can I go and play with Sophie?" Ruby asks.

"Of course," I tell her and she runs from the shed, the door closing behind her, shutting the heat in.

I scrape the top layer of honeycomb from the frames and slot them into the machine to spin them.

"You won't be frightened of this too?" I turn to Ellis.

"I don't like bees," he says. "It's no big deal." He watches me as I turn the handle faster and faster and the honey begins to drip into the glass jar below.

"That's pretty cool, though," he says.

Slowly, the jar fills. The flow of honey stems to a drip, so I reach for a lid on the shelf behind me and screw it on tight. When I hold the jar up to the window, the sunlight catches on it. I know that Ellis is impressed and I beam at him.

"Can I try some?" he asks.

"Of course not," I reply. "You haven't got the drops, have you?"

"What drops?"

"For the honey," I say. Ellis is looking at me, as though he doesn't know what to say. Maybe he's never had honey before. Maybe he doesn't know.

"You can't eat the honey like this," I explain. "If you do, the eggs will hatch inside you and bees will fill your stomach." Ellis looks shocked. So he didn't know. "They crawl up your breathing pipes. They sting you on the way up, and they sting inside your mouth before they swarm out."

"That's not true," Ellis says. His face is blank. He's just staring at me.

"The people on the Outside have the drops," I carry on. "They put it in the honey and it kills the eggs. But we can't use them because we know that they're poisonous."

"The drops?"

"Yes."

"It's a lie, Pearl," Ellis says. His eyes suddenly look angry. "There's no such thing as the drops. It's rubbish."

"You just don't know about them," I say. "Have you never tasted honey?"

"Of course I have." He laughs, but it's a nasty sound. And I don't want it here. I have never felt anything but happiness in the bee shed. "Many times. Without any stupid drops." Ellis reaches over and takes the jar from me. "Watch."

Roughly, he unscrews the lid. Before I can stop him, he dips his finger into the honey and puts it, dripping, into his mouth. My stomach clenches.

"See?" Ellis says. "It's delicious. And not an egg in sight. Here." He puts his finger into the jar again. The honey is thick on his skin and he lifts it toward my lips. "Try it."

I step away from him, my back against the wood of the shed wall. "Stop it," I say, looking out of the window. I don't think there's anyone watching us.

Suddenly, Ellis hunches over. He's clutching his stomach and moaning. I want to go to him, but I dare not. A strange noise comes from his mouth.

"Ellis?" I whisper. He should have believed me. And now it's happening so quickly, the eggs are already hatching. The horror of it crashes into me. Ellis is going to die.

I reach for him, but he's standing up and laughing, his eyes sparkling. He must see terror on my face and he stops.

"I was only joking, Pearl," he says gently. "I'm fine. There are no eggs. I won't have bees crawling inside me."

My hand is shaking as I snatch the jar from him. "It won't be that quick," I tell him. "But soon you'll have bees in your mouth."

Ellis passes me the lid. I turn away from him as I put it back onto the jar. And I ignore the drops of honey clinging to the glass.

I wake, sweating, from my nightmare. The same one. The one that mingles the days with the darkness of night.

They are there, the men with the burning rods that they press into my skin. My skin hisses and melts and blinds me with pain. And I scream, but they won't stop. The smell of my burning flesh claws at my nose, begging me to make them stop. I scream.

Then blackness. Always at the top of the pain, on the spike that takes my brain away, the blackness happens.

And then I wake, my sheet soaked with sweat. Just me and my breathing and the hard beating in my chest, alone in this room. But when I look down at my arms, the skin there is shriveled, like wax.

And I know.

I know.

........●........

CHAPTER FOURTEEN

"Shall we sleep in the dip tonight?" I ask Kate. "We haven't been for ages." The sky is clear and I know the night will be beautiful.

"What's the dip?" Ellis asks. "Put that card down, Soph," he adds, pointing to one in her hand. She picks it carefully from the ones she holds and puts it on the pile.

"It's the best place in the world for seeing the stars." I haven't really spoken to Ellis since we were in the bee shed, but now I can't help being excited to show him somewhere new.

"Will we really sleep there?" Sophie asks as Ellis picks a card from the pile.

"If you'd like to," Kate answers.

"Sounds good," Ellis says. "There we go, full house." He takes the cards from Sophie and lays them in a fan shape on the floor. Jack leans over to look.

"Will you play the piano again?" Kate asks. She stretches out her legs and nudges the cards with her bare toes.

"Yes," Sophie answers for Ellis, and she jumps from his lap

and is pulling him up.

Jack and I go over to the piano to listen. Kate stays on the floor, lying back and closing her eyes. Before Ellis even begins, the feeling is in my belly again. Every time he plays, it's there. And as soon as his fingers move on the notes, the room comes alive. The air dances. The music breathes on me, licks my skin and fills my mind until everything else disappears.

It's just Ellis and his music.

The door opens and Kindred John walks in. Without a word he closes the piano lid, so Ellis has to pull his hands away. Instantly, the magic is gone.

"Papa S. needs quiet," Kindred John says.

For a second, Ellis just sits. It's as though he's still with the music somewhere. Then he stands up. "Sorry," Ellis says. "No problem."

Kindred John looks over at Kate, where she lies on the floor, her eyes still closed. "Get up, Kate," he says.

She doesn't move. Has she heard him? There is a slight smile on her lips. *Kate?*

Kindred John stands, looking at her. An anger spreads from him. He seems unsure what to do. Then he looks sharply at Ellis before he walks out of the room. Kate opens her eyes, stretches her arms above her head.

"I loved that, Ellis," she says. She turns onto her side, rests her head in her palm. "How did you learn to do it?"

Ellis shrugs his shoulders. "Practice," he says.

"Let's go to the dip," Bobby shouts, and he's pulling blankets from the sofa.

"Will we need more blankets?" Jack asks.

"I reckon so, if we're staying all night."

"Really, all night?" Sophie asks, and I laugh.

"You'll love it," I tell her. "I promise."

We are ready by the kitchen door when Elizabeth comes in.

"Come in if you get cold," she fusses.

"Sure you don't want to come?" Kate asks her.

Elizabeth sweeps a hand over her stomach. "I need the comfort of a bed," she laughs.

Linda stops Ellis by the arm. "Will you be OK?"

"Of course," he says.

"Look after Sophie," she tells him.

Ellis grins. "Mom, we're only in the field."

"Don't worry, she'll have a good time," I reassure her. Sophie is standing with Ruby and Bobby and already they are looking sleepy, their eyes wide as they try to keep awake.

The moon is glowing, the sky almost black. The blankets I am carrying are awkward to hold, but they keep my arms warm. Jack and Kate are in front and we all follow them toward the forest, curving around the edge of the trees until we get to the West field. We walk carefully; it's difficult to see where the dip starts.

It is here. In this light it looks like a dark hole. Sophie hesitates, looks at Ellis.

"Is this it?" he asks as Bobby and Ruby hurry down it.

"Trust me," I say. "It feels like a black blanket when you're down there." I reach my hand out to Sophie and she takes it. Together we step down the sides of the dip, closer to the darkness. I can see the shapes of the others already sitting down and we curl up with them. There isn't much space for Ellis.

"Here," Kate says and she moves closer to Jack. Ellis sits next to her and she reaches the blanket over him. I must push the flicker of jealousy away.

Kate lies back, and we copy her. Sophie gasps. "Are they the stars?" she whispers. Above us, the dark sky is sprinkled with the brightest white.

"I wasn't expecting that," Ellis says.

I hear Kate move. Maybe she's looking at him. "Don't they have stars on the Outside?" she asks.

Ellis laughs. "Of course they do. I've just never seen them like this. In the city, the sky is mostly just a bit of gray at night."

"They are the brightest at Seed," I say.

"That must be it," Ellis says.

"Do you know how they make the stars?" I ask Sophie.

"No," she says.

"They are holes made from Nature's tears. And every time someone does something bad on the Outside, another hole burns through the sky."

"Don't be filling her head with nonsense," Ellis says.

"What do you mean?" I ask.

"You don't really think that's what stars are?" Ellis asks.

"What else are they?" Jack asks.

"Ellis thinks that on the Outside there are men who walk on the moon," I say.

Jack laughs so loudly that I feel guilty. "How do they get up there, then?" he asks.

"A rocket," Sophie says.

"Is that possible?" Kate asks quietly. Does she believe him?

"Yes," Ellis says.

"Have you been there?" Kate asks him.

Ellis laughs. "No."

"I'm going one day," Sophie says.

"Me too," says Bobby.

We let the silence in. It creeps down the side of the dip and sits on our mouths. It holds my arms so I don't even move. And it brings doubt with it. Could Ellis be right? Is there someone looking from the moon now? Can they see a black hole in the middle of a field, with seven silent figures looking up? Surely it can't be possible. The thought spins my mind into a million different directions.

A cry comes from the forest.

"What's that?" Sophie asks. She sits upright, grabs Ellis's arms.

"It's just a fox," I say. The scream echoes from the trees.

"No, it's a baby," Sophie says. She sounds scared, as though she might cry.

"That's just the noise foxes make," Jack says. "They won't hurt you."

The cry again.

"Are you sure?" Ellis asks.

"Of course," Kate says.

"I don't want to stay here," Sophie says. "I want to go back to the house." She looks at Ellis. The moonlight shows the fear in her eyes.

I stroke her hair. "It's OK, Sophie. It will stop soon."

"No," she says and she starts to cry. Ruby sits up, but Bobby stays lying still, his eyes open wide.

"How about you just try to sleep?" Ellis says gently. But Sophie just starts crying more.

Bobby screams. He's pointing to the top of the dip.

"What is it?" Kate asks, sitting up.

"There's someone there," Bobby says and he tries to burrow his head into me. I look up. There is nothing but darkness.

"Right," says Ellis. "I'm taking Sophie back to the house. Anyone else coming?"

Ruby and Bobby don't answer. They just stand up, holding each other's hands.

Ellis turns and his shape bends down toward me. He whispers in my ear. "That honey thing is rubbish."

Then they are all scrambling up the steep slope. At the top, Ellis looks back.

"Night," Kate calls up.

"Are you really staying?" Ellis asks.

"Of course," Kate answers.

"Then I'll see you in the morning. If you haven't been eaten by wolves," Ellis says. Sophie starts crying again, so he takes her hand and they disappear.

There is an emptiness now that he has gone.

"What did he say to you?" Kate asks.

"Nothing," I say.

I lie to her because something has happened that I don't understand. There are no bees in Ellis's mouth, no sign of them in his stomach. Yet he ate the honey without the drops and there should be eggs inside him. Shouldn't there?

The silence again. Just Kate, Jack, me, and the stars.

Kate finally breaks the quiet. "Do you think he was serious about the man flying to the moon?"

"I think someone's lying. Either him, or those who told him," Jack says.

"He goes to a place where you learn things," Kate speaks quickly, as though she wants to know.

"They taught him rubbish, Kate," I say.

"Sometimes I can't work him out," Jack says.

"I know exactly how he works," Kate says.

"How?" I ask. I need her to help me make sense of everything, make everything straightforward again.

"I'm going to sleep now," Kate says. I want to keep talking. There is so much I want to say. But Kate is quiet and I think that she has closed her eyes. I keep mine open, hoping the sky will wipe clear my thoughts.

Slowly, Kate's breathing changes. Jack turns on his side and I think he's asleep too. The night sky stays almost touching me.

There is a sound. I look up the sides of the dip. Something, someone, is walking across the field. Cold grass is crunched underfoot. Closer still and then it stops. I know someone is here.

"Ellis?" I whisper. No one replies.

Someone is watching. Can I hear their breath? I pull the blanket tight to my neck. I want to cover my face, but I'm frightened that if I do, they will come down.

"Is that you, Ellis?" I whisper again. "Jack? Kate?"

They're sleeping, while someone is looking at us. *It is just the night,* I tell myself. Maybe Nature herself has crept here to keep us safe.

Something moves. The footsteps are going away. They are gone. I want to run up the sides of the dip to see, but fear stops me.

Gradually, I let the stars back in. Now that is all I see, all I hear. My eyes ache, but I won't sleep yet. Not yet.

He brings the bowl in. And the glass with the juice. Always the glass with the juice. Sometimes he will hold it to my lips, so that I have to drink. Other times I want to drink, because afterward it makes me sleep and then I am free.

In the dark, I can fly out of the window, float down to the meadow and run and run and run and not stop. The air is in me, the fresh, clear air. It swoops around my mind and wipes away the pain. That throbbing pain of loss and loneliness and sickness and bleakness. I will run to the trees, to the lake I remember there. To the rocks.

In the darkness I am free.

He can't hurt me.

No one can touch me.

And so I eat and so I drink and so I live. In this room, this tiny room, this suffocating prison. Watch my child through the glass. Hear my heart beating out my days in the silence.

Maybe one day I will not drink. Maybe one day I will not eat. And the next, and the next? Maybe one day I will make myself truly free.

CHAPTER FIFTEEN

••••••••••●•••••••••

"Don't you ever think it's odd that you're all so fussed about Mother Nature, but then you're working on cars that pump pollution into the sky?" Ellis asks Jack.

I'm with them in the barn, sitting on seats we've made out of straw. The children are here, jumping from the bales, ducking in and out of the tunnel they've created. Outside it's getting dark, but Kate is still with Kindred John, helping him in his room.

"We make good engines, though," Jack replies.

"Good engines?"

"Yeah, to kind of balance out those on the Outside." Jack pulls his shirt on over his head.

"How does that work then?" Ellis asks. He has a piece of straw in his hands and he's slowly splitting it in two.

"The oil that we rub into the engine, it's that."

"What?"

"That cleans the air. Kindred John discovered it a few years ago. So the cars we make for the people Outside actually help stop the pollution."

"They told you this?" Ellis asks. He throws down the piece of straw and looks at Jack.

"Yeah. It's amazing, isn't it?"

"It gets rid of pollution from other cars," I say.

"So, the engines we work on at Seed are filled with some magic oil?"

"I suppose you could put it like that," Jack says proudly.

"And I suppose you believe in the tooth fairy too?" Ellis asks.

"What's that?" asks Jack. Ellis just shakes his head, but I wish that he would walk away.

Then Kate is here. She comes running in, her wild look in her eyes. There's no space for her, so she climbs up and sits on Jack's lap.

"Finished with Kindred John?" he asks.

"Yes," she says, pulling her cardigan across her body.

"Why did he need you?" Ellis asks.

"Just stuff," she says. Then she scrambles up and runs for the hay tunnel. She crawls through and grabs a squealing Bobby by the ankles.

"Stay in my prison!" she cackles. "You cannot escape." So Bobby sits in the tunnel, giggling, as she runs over the bales. "You'll all be mine!"

Sophie tries to dodge past her, but Kate holds her by the waist and throws her in the air. "To my lair," she shrieks as she bundles

Sophie into the tunnel. Kate pulls a straw bale to block one of the ends.

Jack jumps up, grabs a spade leaning against the wall, and goes to join her. "I'll guard them," he says in a gruff voice, spreading his legs wide, holding the spade high.

I watch Ruby start to scale the big wall, made from heavy bales stacked high next to the tunnel. She's not allowed up there, it's too dangerous.

"Ruby," I call out, but I don't think she hears me. She rushes up, gleefully trying to find hand and foot holes.

And then the tower falls. It's as though it happens in slow motion, as I watch the bales piled high up on each other begin to lean too far. Ruby is screaming as she's falling backward, still clutching onto the straw, and it all just crashes down, piles and piles of bales smashing the tunnel below.

"Sophie!" Ellis yells, and he's running and pulling at the bales. I'm with him and I can't see Sophie, or Ruby, or Bobby, or Kate, or Jack.

I run to the door.

"Kindred Smith!" I scream into the darkening air.

I'm back beside Ellis and he's throwing the bales behind. Together we grab them away. They're so heavy, as if they're made from bricks. The dust clogs my throat and we're both coughing, but we still can't see the tunnel, still can't see or hear anyone.

"Hurry," I hear Ellis wheeze. Jack's hand appears and we push the straw from him and he's coughing and retching. He doesn't seem to notice the blood coming from a deep gash on his chest where the spade has sliced into the skin. His white shirt is soaked red. He stumbles to the side, just as Kindred Smith runs in.

Ellis finds Ruby and pulls her free. She's shaking and Kindred John is by my side and he takes her from me.

We're pulling at the straw, the thick air dragging at my throat. I'm screaming in my head, screaming for the children. Screaming for Kate to be safe.

We find the tunnel and there, huddled inside, are Sophie and Bobby. They're clinging to each other, their faces alive with fear.

"She's not breathing," I hear Kindred Smith say, but I don't understand because Ellis has pulled Sophie out and she is breathing because she's crying and he's holding her.

I look up and it is Kate lying motionless. Her hair is tangled with straw, her body bent at an angle, her face white as a star. Everyone is standing, just staring at her.

"Do something," I hear Ellis shout, but no one moves. I don't know what to do.

"Kate?" I say, but she's lying there and everyone just stands, looking down at her.

Suddenly Ellis pushes Sophie into Kindred Smith's arms

and he's kneeling next to Kate. He's feeling her neck, feeling her wrists.

"Come on, Kate," he says. He bends his face to her lips. No one moves, no one helps him. "She's got a pulse," he says, but he looks bewildered. Then Jack is by his side, his hand covering his own skin where the blood is pushing through.

"Can we help her?" he asks. The Kindreds look at him. Still they don't move.

But I do. I run to Kate, try to lift her in my arms and shake her. "Kate!" I scream into her quiet face.

Ellis starts to push both his hands hard into her chest. "Rub her arms, keep her warm," he says.

So I take her arm in both my hands and I rub it as though it is a stick, and I am lighting a fire. The Kindreds' eyes watch us as I work on that spark to bring it to a flame, and Ellis pushes on Kate's heart, and Jack whispers into her ear, telling her to wake up.

Then Ellis leans in and it looks like he is going to kiss her, on her lips, but she moans and turns her head and she's opened her eyes, looking straight into mine. I watch her fire burn again as I rub her arms and I'm crying and laughing and hugging her into me. Ellis pushes me gently away and he picks her up into his strong, safe arms.

"We need to get her to a doctor," he says.

But Kindred John is blocking the way. "She is fine now. Take her into the house," he says.

"But she needs to see a doctor," Ellis says.

"No, she stays at Seed." Kindred John reaches out to take Kate, but Ellis won't let him.

"Fine," Ellis says and then he barges past Kindred John, out of the barn. I follow him toward the light of the house.

CHAPTER SIXTEEN

...........●●●●●●...........

"They would have let Kate die." Ellis's voice is hushed, but I can hear his anger in the almost-dark. Kate is lying in her bed, sleeping. The moon through the window provides the only touch of light. "They just stood by and watched."

"They thought it was her time," I say. But the words feel wrong. I watch the blanket rise and fall with Kate's restful breaths. And I know I couldn't have let her go.

"Bollocks," Ellis says. I don't want to ask what he means, but his harshness smacks into me. I don't move. His legs are touching mine, his arms, his shoulders. We have never sat together on my bed like this, but he's like a block of stone.

"Nature didn't want her yet. She let her stay," I say quietly.

Ellis turns so quickly that I think he wants to hit me. "For fuck's sake, Pearl," he says as he gets up. He lashes out at the books on the table by the door, and they smash to the ground as he goes from the room.

I stare after him, at the door that has slammed behind him. Listen to his feet as he pounds down the corridor to the stairs.

To where?

I look over at Kate and my thoughts whir and crash and try to escape, but there's nowhere for them to go, just round and round and round.

Would I really have left her because it was Nature's way? Could we really all have stood by while her breath dripped out of her and vanished like the wind?

Would I have done that? Would I?

The door opens and Elizabeth comes in. She has a steaming bowl and a flannel, but when she sees Kate sleeping, she puts them on the floor next to her bed. She leans over, her belly bulging in the moonlight, and she kisses Kate quietly on the forehead. She smoothes her hair back gently, without waking her.

"Kindred John didn't help her," I whisper. "Or Kindred Smith." But it's like I haven't said a word.

The door opens again. It's Heather.

"Jack is asking for you," she says to me. "He's in a lot of pain."

I get up from my bed quickly. In all of this, my thoughts have not been with Jack. I should have been with him, not sitting next to Ellis. I step over the books left scattered on the floor and follow Heather from the room.

Jack is sitting in the Eagle Room. He has material clenched in his mouth, his teeth biting down hard, trapping the roar in his throat. His eyes look like a wild horse's. It fills me with fear because he looks nothing like my Jack. But I go to him and take his hand, which is locked into a fist of iron.

Linda is here. She is sewing his skin. The cotton pulls through him as though through material, but it's soaked in blood.

"He'd be better in a hospital," she says quietly.

"It is best for him here," Kindred Smith replies. "He is in good hands."

"I'm not a doctor," Linda says abruptly. Kindred Smith smiles calmly and rests his hand on her shoulder. Maybe she doesn't realize what doctors really do.

Rachel rushes in with a glass of brown liquid. She stands by Jack's side, takes the material from his mouth, and holds the glass to his lips.

"Have some more of this," she says. "It will help." Jack drinks, coughing and grinding his teeth. Rachel puts the material into his mouth and he bites down hard.

"Trust us," Kindred Smith says to Linda. "He wouldn't want to go to the hospital, would you, Jack?" Jack shakes his head violently. Linda looks confused and she's making me have doubt. I know deep down that they are bad places, but a part of me would try anything to help take Jack's pain away.

I hold his clenched fist and make him look into my eyes. I talk to him of the hills and the lake and the sunshine at dawn, as Linda drags the needle through his skin again and again.

The pain reaches into Jack and the material in his mouth drops to the floor as he jerks his head forward to push into my shoulder. I hold him there. Put my hand to the softness of his cropped hair. I am sure he is weeping but doesn't want to show it.

Linda cuts the end of the cotton. She reaches for a cloth soaking in water and wipes gently at Jack's jagged wound. Then she takes a bandage from Heather and begins to wrap it tightly around his chest. She splits the end of the bandage and ties it in a knot.

"I'll have to change it every day at first. There's always the chance of infection," she says, but she seems less angry now, less scared.

"I'm proud of you," Kindred Smith says, and Linda smiles.

"I think I surprised myself," she says. She looks so different from when she arrived here. It's as though Seed has burned away the gray clouds that were settled on her.

Heather goes over and puts her arms around her. "Thank goodness for you, Linda," she says. Then they're picking up the pieces of Jack's sweater.

I can feel that he has stopped shaking. He moves his head back from my shoulder and I lean down, put my hands on his knees.

"Are you OK?" I ask. He nods. But the pain still shudders in his eyes.

Have we done wrong, Jack? By not getting you help?

I watch as Kindred Smith helps him out of the room. Jack, with his quiet ways and love growing out of him like wings.

"Thank you, Nature," I whisper. "Thank you for not taking them." But my words hang lifeless in the air and I don't think anyone has heard them.

CHAPTER SEVENTEEN

........•••••••........

I am bleeding again. My Blessing has returned. But this time I will tell no one. I can't risk being sent into that hole again. Forgive me, Mother Nature, but I can't. So I find one of the linen slabs that Elizabeth has left for me in my drawer, and when it's soaked through I shall wash it in the bathroom and leave it around the back of the barn to dry in the sun. She has left me five slabs in all. Surely the first will dry before I have to use the last?

I sit next to Jack at morning meal. He's obviously in pain. Elizabeth has put cloves into his food, but they don't seem to have helped much.

"I won't be able to swim in the lake for a while," he says. "And I'm not allowed to work on the engines for a few days." There is a bit of porridge on his bottom lip, so I reach over and wipe it off. I smile at him, but he doesn't smile back. If anything, he just looks a bit angry. It's not like Jack.

"Does it really hurt?" I ask quietly.

"Yes," he says.

"You'll still be able to watch the work on the engines. You can learn that way," Elizabeth says, smiling gently at him. "It won't be long before you are healed."

"And you can go to the lake and wade up to your waist," I say. But Jack doesn't answer. He just spoons the porridge from the bowl into his mouth. "Kate says she'll get up after breakfast," I tell him. "But she won't be working today either."

"Where's Ellis?" Jack asks.

"He took her some porridge. He's probably eating with her." I look up toward the window, certain that he's watching us, but there's no one there. "You could sit with him while he works on the engines."

"I think I'll spend the day with Kate."

"Don't let her do too much," Elizabeth says.

"I'll make sure she rests," Jack assures her. He drinks the juice from his glass, not stopping for breath until every last drop has gone. I watch the bump in his throat move in and out. Every day he is changing. Moving away from me? I can't tell. I just know that I think my heart will break if he goes too far.

Ellis and Kate are lying on her bed together. Her eyes are closed, but she is laughing lightly. For some reason I don't think the Kindreds would be happy to see this. Ellis sits up as soon as he sees me.

"Feeling better?" I ask, going over to them.

Kate opens her eyes and smiles. "A bit," she answers. Her skin still looks pale, though, and her eyes don't seem as bright. "But don't tell anyone. So long as I've nearly died, then I won't have to do any work."

"It's not funny, Kate," I say. "You scared me."

"Not them, though," Ellis mumbles.

"What do you mean?" Kate ask, turning to him.

"Nothing," is all he says.

Kate reaches out her arms to me and I pull her up. "You're still with us." I smile and happiness is everywhere.

"It'll take more than a few straw bales to get rid of me." She laughs.

Ellis stands up, and I look at his arms as he reaches for the two empty bowls. "I'll take these down," he says.

"Thank you, servant." Kate smiles at him before he goes out. That feeling is there again and I hate myself for it. It burrows deep within me, twisting what is good. Kate is alive and I shouldn't have any jealous thoughts.

"Jack wants to spend the day with you," I say. "But he's not happy about not being able to work."

Kate raises her eyebrows. "That boy," she says.

"What?" I ask.

"They've well and truly got him."

"Who? What do you mean?"

Kate looks at me. I don't know what I'm meant to know. I don't know what's in her mind.

"Nothing," she says as she gets up slowly. "Will you find Jack and tell him I'd love to?" She reaches her arms above her head. Her hair is so long and though mine is growing, I envy her even that.

Sophie and Ruby are standing on chairs, helping me wash up, when Kate comes into the kitchen. She's wearing trousers. They don't seem to notice, but when Jack comes in I can tell he realizes straight away. He puts down the stack of bowls and looks at her legs and then at her face.

Sophie and Ruby don't stop their chatter and washing, and they don't notice the new feeling that has crept in here and is circling our heads.

"Do you want to sit down?" Jack asks.

"I'm OK," she replies, but she doesn't sound sure.

"Do you need a drink?" Jack gets her a glass of water before she has time to reply.

"How's your cut?" Kate asks him. "Does it hurt?"

"It's getting better already."

"Don't heal too quick," she says. "I've got lovely lazy days planned for us."

"They'll want you back in the fields soon."

"Not if I can help it."

"I won't be much fun. I can't do much."

"I'm sure we'll find something to entertain us." Kate smiles at him and pulls her long hair over her shoulder. Jack suddenly seems awkward and he moves her glass into the sink.

"Like cards!" she laughs as she pulls herself up to sit on the side, crossing one bare ankle over the other. "Or I could get us together a picnic and we could go up to the orchard, or the dip?"

"That's not fair," I say, reaching for Sophie's sponge to scrape at a bowl she's struggling to get clean.

Kate licks her fingers and presses them onto the crumbs on the breadboard. "You could always nearly die and come join us," she says.

"Did you really nearly die?" Ruby asks. Sophie takes her wet hands from the sink and stares at Kate.

"Maybe," Kate says lightly. She hadn't seen Sophie and Bobby in that airless tunnel, the terror sitting starkly on their faces.

"Everyone's fine now though," I say brightly, lifting Sophie from the chair and into my arms. She doesn't stay there long. Even after all this time, she doesn't really like to be held by anyone apart from Ellis or Linda. Her mother. "And we're going to have a lovely day picking food for the market."

"Can I come to the market?" Sophie asks.

"When you're a bit older," I say. I wonder if she misses the Outside. Did she have friends who wonder where she's gone? I'm so lucky to have been born here, to know only this. I kiss my palm, hold it up to the window to face the sky. But nobody else joins me.

Out in the vegetable patch it's too hot to put on a cardigan, so I'm just wearing Kate's yellow dress. It feels like I'm wearing sunshine, but there's a heavy stone sitting within me. I don't know where it is, or why it's there, and I try to wish it away but it stays, humming quietly to itself.

I pick the beans with their rough skin, snap them from the plant they grow from. With the soil and the sun and the wind and the rain, they have grown for us. Nature has provided.

My thoughts drift to Ellis, working right now in the barn. I try to crowd my mind with the blue sky and the biting sun so that I do not think about how it felt to sit so close to him on Kate's bed. But he's there and he's taking so many of my thoughts. More than anyone else. I hope that Papa S. can't see into my mind.

I try to concentrate on my task, and by mid-morning I have three baskets full. I can take a bunch of beans to Kate and Jack for their picnic. They can crunch the peas raw from their pods. I hook the baskets over my arms and walk back to the kitchen.

Ellis is bending over the kitchen sink. He's taken his shirt off and he is rinsing his hair under the running water. He doesn't know I'm here. I watch the muscles click in his back, and the need to touch his skin is so strong that I have to hold my breath.

He squeezes his hair out and straightens up, and I am still watching him, the baskets of beans on my arms.

He smiles. "Do you want to help?" Water drips slowly from his curls onto his bare shoulder. I watch as they slide down his stomach and disappear into the top of his trousers. When I look back to his face, he is gazing at me.

"I'm taking beans to Jack and Kate," I say. I walk to the table, lift up the two baskets and place them on the side. I must not look back at him.

"Can I come?" Ellis asks.

"I don't know where they are."

"Where are you going to try?"

I have to turn to him and he's smiling, leaning back to squeeze the ends of his hair once more into the sink.

"The orchard? Maybe the dip?"

"I'll come with you, then."

"I'm going to join them for their picnic. I need to take food."

"I'll help get food, then."

"Fine," I say. I don't know why my words come out so roughly. I'll be walking in the fields in the yellow dress, with Ellis to talk to and food to eat. Where is the bad in that? "That'll be good," I add as I turn my back on him once more and take a bunch of beans from the basket. I look out of the window quickly. There's no one to see us.

Ellis cuts two wedges of bread from the loaf freshly made this morning. I take a small pot of chutney from the cupboard, as Ellis puts a chunk of cheese and a handful of tiny tomatoes into the bag he's taken from the hook.

"Milk, or juice?" I ask, standing next to him by the fridge.

"Both," he says.

As I put the bottles in the bag, he looks at me. "That dress suits you," he says, but then instantly he's walking to the door, grabbing the T-shirt from the chair with his spare hand. I'm left to follow him, wondering at the words and the smoothness of his back and the feelings he's planted in me like seeds. I must not let them grow.

"Where to first?" Ellis asks. I don't look back at the house, although I'm sure someone is watching us. I'm scared that it's Papa S. I wish I was so small that he could not see me. If we walk quickly, I will only be a dot in the distance, a moving sunflower.

"The orchard?"

"Sounds good."

We walk in silence for a while. I've put my sandals on and it's strange not to feel the dusty grass beneath my feet.

"Do you miss your home?" I ask, without thinking.

"Isn't this my home?" Ellis does that mocking smile again.

"Of course. I mean your old one, though."

"My past life?" He turns his head away from me.

"Yes," I say. But he doesn't answer and we keep on walking. "Do you like it better here?"

"Mom does. And Sophie likes it too."

"But do you prefer it?"

"I don't know." He moves the bag onto his other shoulder. "But if I hadn't come here I wouldn't have met you." His words stumble into me and I don't know what to say. Silence speaks for me instead.

"Do you like it here?" Ellis eventually says.

"Of course."

"But do you really like it? Like Papa S. and all that."

"I love Papa S.," I say. I feel that sharpness settling in me again.

"That's OK, then," is all he says as we head toward the edge of the orchard.

Kate and Jack are sitting by one of the farthest trees. They don't see us at first. Jack is lying in the grass and Kate sits, looking over him. As we get closer, we see her lift her hand. She starts to run her finger from the top of Jack's head, down over his forehead, his nose, his mouth. She doesn't stop at his neck, his chest. All the time, Jack is looking at her.

When Kate notices us, she pulls her hand back quickly, as if she's touched something hot. The spell that danced around them has been broken.

"We've brought you beans," I say, pointing to the bag on Ellis's back. Jack sits up awkwardly. I don't think Kate wants us here. Suddenly I wish we hadn't come.

"So, what have you been up to?" Ellis asks, laughter dancing in his eyes.

"Just talking," Jack says, but his cheeks color slightly. Ellis sits down beside Kate.

We are here, but nothing is right.

Ellis tips out our bag of food. The bread lands in the grass and we'll have to pick the strands from it.

"We've already eaten middle meal," Jack says.

"We've brought you fresh beans, though," I say. It feels like Jack wants to get up and go, but I don't want him to leave. I want him with his happiness back.

Ellis passes some bread to me. "How's your wound?" he asks Jack.

"Getting better." Jack smiles and my little knot of worry begins to unravel.

"How come they didn't take you to the hospital for the stitches?" Ellis asks, eating chutney straight from the spoon.

"They didn't need to," Jack replies. He reaches for the bottle of milk that we've brought. "Linda made it better."

"Not properly."

"She did it perfectly. Nature will do the rest," Jack says. He opens the bottle and the white liquid disappears as he drinks.

"You could have had proper pain relief. You wouldn't have felt a thing."

"Why would he want that?" Kate asks. She stops shelling the beans in her lap. "To feel pain is to feel alive. It is a gift." She's looking hard at Ellis.

"That's mad. The doctors would have given him an injection in the arm. Numbed the pain."

"Now I think *that's* mad," Jack says, shaking his head. "An injection of what? Doctors are just the devil in disguise. Messing with Nature like they do."

But I had wanted it. I had wanted someone to take his pain away.

"Are you serious?" Ellis asks, his eyes wide.

"We know it's true," Kate says, putting a bean into her mouth and crunching on it, hard.

"Jack's fine, so that proves we're right," I say. I wish my bad thoughts had never happened.

"Then you're all mad," Ellis says. He takes a bean from where it nestles in its pod, pulls it out, and throws it high toward the tree next to us. It hits an apple hanging there.

"Bull's-eye," he says. When he smiles at us, I think about

his ability to make me so angry one minute and almost love him the next. Does that make Ellis bad, or good? I don't think I want to know.

CHAPTER EIGHTEEN

·············●·············

Kate has been asked to take Nana Willow her tincture. Heather does it most days, but as Kate says she still can't work, she's been given the task. I'm glad I don't have to. Recently, Nana Willow has slipped into my dreams and sometimes, even when I'm sure I'm awake, I hear her rattling breath creeping around my bed.

Elizabeth and I are cutting up tomatoes in the kitchen. She pops a piece in her mouth and smiles at me. Today she has knotted her hair high up on her head. The skin on her neck has burned slightly from the sun.

"How long now, do you think?" I ask her.

"A month? Maybe less, maybe more." She rubs her stomach gently. "You just come out when you're ready."

"Is the baby heavy?" I ask, scraping tomato seeds from my finger.

"No, it's fine," she says.

"Does it hurt at all?"

"It's too beautiful a thing to make me feel hurt." Elizabeth scoops up the tomatoes and puts them in a bowl.

I want to ask her what it felt like when she carried me. If she carried me.

"You'll know it one day," she says, standing up to take the bowl to the side. But instead of happiness, I just remember the worms in that circle of dirt.

Kate comes in, not looking ill at all. It's been less than a week since her accident, yet Nature has healed her almost completely.

"Mm," she says, taking a chunk of tomato before Elizabeth can swat her hand away.

"How is Nana Willow?" Elizabeth asks.

"Barely awake," Kate says, sitting down next to me. She picks the knife up, puts its tip into the wood and gently twists it around.

"Did she call you Sylvie?" I ask.

"Why would she call me that?" Kate laughs. Elizabeth stops moving.

"Because she thought I was someone called Sylvie," I say.

"Stop doing that with the knife, Kate," Elizabeth says. So Kate does, but Elizabeth still looks unsettled.

"Who's Sylvie?" I ask her. I'm looking right at her, so I don't miss the hesitation that crosses her face. "Do you know who she is?"

Elizabeth turns from us and starts to wash her hands in the sink.

"What are you talking about?" Kate asks.

I watch Elizabeth as she rubs her fingers through the water. She takes her hands out and dries them gently with the cloth hanging on the tap. She breathes in heavily. "Sylvie was Nana Willow's daughter," Elizabeth says finally.

I don't understand, and by the look on Kate's face, I don't think she does either.

"Where is she? How come we've never heard of her?" Kate asks.

"She died," Elizabeth says quietly. She's looking toward the kitchen door, but it's still closed.

"When?"

"A long time ago."

"How?" I ask.

Elizabeth looks like she doesn't want to answer, but she does. "She died giving birth," she answers. How? How is that possible? Elizabeth must see the panic growing in me. "It is very unusual. I will be fine," she says.

I know she wants to reassure me, but the thought is there now, and I feel sick with dread. I never knew you could die having a baby. "What went wrong?" I ask.

"Nothing went wrong. It was just Sylvie's time and Nature wanted to take her," Elizabeth says. I look at her pregnant belly and I imagine the child curled safely underneath.

"Did the baby die?" Kate asks.

"No," Elizabeth replies.

"So where did it go?"

"It stayed at Seed."

"What do you mean?" I ask. Nothing she is saying makes sense. Nana Willow had a daughter called Sylvie. And Sylvie had a baby. I try to piece it all together in my mind.

"So it could be one of us?" Kate asks. She is totally still.

And I begin to understand Kate's words. That there was another mother. That her baby was one of us.

Kate is staring at Elizabeth. "Was Sylvie my mother?" she asks.

"We are all your mother. And Nature is your greatest mother," Elizabeth says.

"But I want to know if she was my real mother," Kate says, her voice rising.

Then the door opens and Kindred John is standing here. How long has he been behind the door?

"Kate," he says. "I need you to help me in my room."

Kate doesn't move. If anything, she sinks lower into her chair. "I'm sorry," she says. "I am not well enough." She doesn't smile.

Something like anger is in his eyes. "I'm sure you are," he says.

"No, I'm afraid I'm not."

"Kate still needs to rest," Elizabeth says.

"Well, then," Kindred John says. "I shall just have to ask Pearl." But he's still looking at Kate, with a strange smile on his mouth.

"Pearl is helping me to prepare evening meal," Elizabeth says as she begins to drag a bag of earthy potatoes toward the table. I take the edge of the bag from her and heave it across the floor. "And if we don't start peeling these soon, no one will be eating anything." Her voice is lighthearted, but there's a slither of something sharp in her words.

"I'm sure Pearl can help me tomorrow then," he says. "Can't you, Pearl?"

I smile. "Of course."

"Unless you're better by then?" Kindred John looks at Kate.

Her confidence seems to have melted away. "I'm sure I'll be better by then," she says.

"Good," Kindred John says, and he goes and touches her lightly on the head before he walks out to the garden.

"I'll help him if you're not up to it," I offer Kate. But she doesn't say anything. She doesn't look at me as she gets up roughly from the table, storms toward the door, and slams it hard behind her.

The thoughts of Sylvie being her mother chase after her.

It's when I'm taking the plates to the table for evening meal, the day still warm enough to eat outside, that Ellis comes up to me.

"I've persuaded Kindred Smith to let me do the market with him tomorrow. He says you're coming too." Ellis takes some of the plates from me. "You and me together in the outside world." He laughs. "Maybe I'll steal you away and we can run off together."

"You'll never get me away from Seed," I say.

"You wait till you've seen the temptations of the Outside."

"I've been to the market many times," I say. "There's nothing tempting about the Outside." I put the last of the plates down in their places and turn to go and get the pans of food.

"You haven't been with me before, though." He catches up with me. "You never know, I might just tempt you." He says it so close to me that his lips almost touch my ear. A current shoots through my body, but I won't let it show.

"Hurry up, Pearl," Elizabeth calls as she comes out of the kitchen door.

Ellis runs to take the heavy pan from her. I watch him and I know he's right. Because there's a part of me, just a tiny spark hidden away, somewhere deep within me, that would be tempted.

CHAPTER NINETEEN

••••••••••●•••••••••

Everyone else is sleeping. There's no wind, no noise, just the sound of our shoes in the gravel as we walk to the van, and the songs of the birds. It's getting light, but the chill is still in the air, nipping at our faces. Ellis steps up first, and the seat squeaks slightly as I sit next to him.

Kindred Smith walks around the front of the van. He gets in, closes the door, and seals us off from Seed. I've never liked the van—its gasoline smell, the noise of its engine, the metal surrounding me. Carrying me away from Seed and all that I love, to the Outside and all that I fear.

"Excited?" Ellis looks at me and raises an eyebrow.

"No," I reply. Because I'm not. I've done this too many times to know that the Outside is full of poisonous things, which take days to wash away.

"I'll look after you," he says, reaching over to tuck a strand of my hair underneath my headscarf. Kindred Smith must notice. Even as he starts the engine, his hands fixed on the steering wheel, he must know. I move away from Ellis, but I can't go far. He looks at me silently. So I stare at Kindred Smith long enough for Ellis to know that he must not touch me.

I always have the same feeling when we drive from Seed to market. It's as though a thin blue thread attaches me to my home. It winds through the lanes, past the hills and houses, a thread that will never break and will always keep me safe. If I am lost, I can always follow it back again, to Papa S. And attached to it, he will always be able to find me.

Kindred Smith and Ellis talk about engines and water and oak trees until the van finally reaches the town, and we get to the street where we set up our market stall. As soon as we open the van doors, the smell of Outside rushes in. A dusty metal that sticks in my throat and clings to my clothes.

The only people around are the other market sellers. They all look so tired and worried and they move so quickly, always rushing. Kindred Smith speaks to them, but I only nod hello. It is safer that way.

I wish I had bought some gloves. The sun hasn't warmed up yet, and the boxes scratch at my bare skin as I lug them from the van to the tables that Ellis is setting up. Our food looks remarkable, though. Even the peppers have grown bigger than ever this year, and the colors are striking—the marrows against the tomatoes, next to the cucumbers and small baskets of red currants. Kindred Smith catches me as I pop a raspberry into my mouth, but he only smiles. It tastes of the morning and if I close my eyes, I'm no longer surrounded by buildings and noise and man-made fumes. I'm back in the fields of Seed for just a few seconds, until I swallow the sweetness and it is gone.

Ellis lifts a bag of potatoes onto his shoulder. It must be heavy, I can tell it in the concentration of his forehead. I try not to stare at his arms. Instead, I busy myself with finding the prices to put in all the boxes.

"Right," Kindred Smith says. "Ellis seems perfectly capable. I won't be gone long." He kisses me on my head before he picks up a large cardboard box and walks off, disappearing around the corner of a red-bricked building.

"Where's he going then?" Ellis asks.

"He likes to go and spread our knowledge about purity, about Nature," I say. I don't want Ellis asking any more questions, because I think the box holds our skirts with the messages sewn into the hems.

Ellis goes to get another bag of potatoes and lowers it with a thud on the floor. "You're very quiet," he says to me as he unthreads the top of the bag and rolls it down. A potato escapes and I stop it with my foot before it rolls away. Ellis bends to pick it up. "Don't you speak much on the Outside?" He wipes the mud from his thumb onto his jeans.

"I'm not here to speak. I'm here to sell our food. To let others share in the beauty of Seed."

"Right," he says. Then he goes to the van to get the last of our boxes.

The selling starts quickly. It's Ellis's first time, so he fumbles with the weighing scales, makes mistakes adding up. But it is good to have him by my side. I watch him as he picks up the fruit and puts it in the paper bags. I listen to him talk to the people, so easily, and I know I am proud of him too. He is ours now. He is part of us.

"What's your secret to making these grow like this, then?" It is a man speaking to me. Why does he need to ask such a question? Why can't he just pass me the bag like most of the other people? There is always someone who makes me feel even more uncomfortable than the rest. He looks about the same age as Kindred John, but he doesn't have a beard. I try not to stare at his smooth chin with the spot sticking out like a button on the end. I smile at him, but I can tell it's not enough. "Cat got your tongue?" he asks. I don't know what he means, so I look to Ellis for help.

"You should answer the man," Ellis says to me. "You know more about growing the food than me."

I stare at him. He must know that I don't want to. When I look back to the man, he is looking at me and I can't tell whether he's angry, or being friendly. "We just grow them," I say finally.

"With what, though?"

"With thanks," I reply.

The man looks like he will laugh, but he doesn't. "Oh, right. It's like that, is it?" He reaches over and picks up a sweet potato. His fingernails are ragged. "What do you recommend then—these, or your normal potatoes?" he asks me.

"You should have both," I say. I stand tall and look him in the eye.

"A natural salesperson." He laughs. Then he looks at Ellis. "She's good," he says.

Ellis smiles at me. "She is," he says.

"I'll have a bag of each, then."

When the man has gone, I turn away from Ellis. He touches me gently on the arm. He knows I'll look at him, and I do. His head is tilted, all serious and smiley at once.

"Sorry?" he says. I don't answer. "I thought it would be good for you."

"You have no idea what's good for me," I say.

"I think I do," he says and he grins in his way. I feel something flutter deep within me. I want to stop the feeling, but at the same time, I don't.

"It won't hurt you know, to talk to them," Ellis says.

He's wrong, though. I know what I've been taught.

"I grew up on the Outside and no harm's come to me."

"I wouldn't be so sure," I say, loud enough for him to hear. He laughs, but I don't know if I'm joking.

I'm glad of the distraction of a new customer. Someone young, not much older than us. He passes me a full bag of mushrooms and I put them on the scales.

"Where's Kate?" he asks. I look up quickly. How does he know her name when he's from the Outside? Has Kate been talking to him? I glance at Ellis and he's looking at the boy as though he wants to say something.

"One pound fifty, please," I say, passing the boy the bag.

He reaches into his jacket, pulls out some change, and counts it out. *Who are you?* His fingers touch my palm as he passes me the money and I pull quickly away.

"Is she back at your home?" the boy asks.

Does he know where we live? He doesn't move away. He won't go until I speak to him.

"Yes," I reply. Then I busy myself with putting the remaining carrots into rows.

He is still here. "How is she?"

My face is not friendly, and I hope that if I answer him he will go away. "She's fine," I say.

He smiles, relieved, as he pushes back his blond hair from his forehead. "Will she be here next week?" the boy asks gently. And suddenly I realize why Kate spoke to him. Why she told him her name. Because there is something about him that feels safe.

"No," I reply.

The boy looks disappointed and for some reason I want to bring his smile back. "Will you tell her Simon was asking for her?" he asks.

"Yes," I say quickly and I turn my back on him. Deep down, I know that trusting him is wrong. Simon must have walked away, because when I turn around, he's gone.

Ellis picks up a greengage that has fallen on the floor. He puts it in my hand.

"Don't you ever wish you were free?" he asks me.

It's such a strange question that I laugh. "I am free," I remind him.

"But really free. To walk out of Seed. To live on the Outside."

"Why would I want to do that?"

Does he not see what I see out here? How can there be any comparison to our home?

"Are you happy, though?" he asks.

"Of course," I answer. How could I not be? I have everything. "Are you not?" I ask Ellis. "Happy?"

He looks at me. "Maybe," he says.

Kindred Smith is back. I didn't see him cross the road, but now he is standing by the van, watching us. How long has he been here? I don't know if he saw Simon, if he heard Ellis. But there is a look in his eyes that tells me that he is not pleased with me. I have done something wrong.

This little piggy went to market, this little piggy stayed at home. This little piggy went squeal, squeal, squeal. And this little piggy had none.

I have none.

None.

Nothing.

CHAPTER TWENTY

•••••••••●•••••••••

lizabeth is ill. Her breathing is staggered and her face is flushed red with sweat.

"You must sit down," I say to her. "I can do the porridge." But she shakes her head and continues to stir that big wooden spoon through the oats and our cows' milk. Her stomach is so swelled with the baby that it pushes against the cooker.

Linda gently takes the spoon from Elizabeth. "I'll tell Papa S. He'll make you rest," she says. I can see the roots of their friendship as I watch them. Elizabeth tries to smile but I can tell she's in pain. It's difficult seeing her like this and I wish I could make her feel better.

"I'm fine. It's just uncomfortable, that's all," she says. But she's wrong. She needs to rest.

We eat morning meal inside, with the rain spattering on the windows. I'm thinking about how the days are changing when Elizabeth's face turns white. Her eyes are shut tight and her fingers grip her spoon.

Linda whispers something to her, but Elizabeth shakes her

head. A silence spreads up the table and it reaches Papa S., but he carries on eating, spooning his food into his mouth. Has he not noticed Elizabeth? The pain she is struggling with? I want to tell him, but I've never spoken to Papa S. in such a way. I look to Jack. He has stopped eating and I know he wants to do something. But it's Linda who stands up.

"I'm taking Elizabeth upstairs. She is unwell," she says. We can all see that there is food in both their bowls. They cannot leave it.

Papa S. puts down his spoon. He is staring at Linda, as though he's about to speak. But his lips stay shut tight. It's the coldness in his eyes that stop me moving. Linda doesn't seem to notice as she helps Elizabeth to her feet.

Kate rushes to her other side. She puts Elizabeth's arm over her shoulder and helps her from the room. They don't close the door and we can hear them, moving slowly and awkwardly across the hall and up the stairs.

There are three bowls on the table, the porridge still warm.

I dare not look at Papa S. But I don't understand his anger. They did not want to leave their food, but Elizabeth is ill.

I don't like the way that her face turned white. I want to run from the room to be with her, but Papa S.'s displeasure has tiptoed down the table and holds me back.

We eat the rest of morning meal in silence. Papa S. finishes his food and drinks the last drops of his water. When he stands up, I know his anger has not left him. It's caught in the lines on his face.

"The wasteful shall be punished," he says, his voice cracking into the air. I wait for him to say more. To say that he's made a mistake and it's all right for them to leave their food. Because Elizabeth is ill and we must all help her to feel better. But instead, he storms from the room. Heather, his Companion once again, follows behind him. There is no longer happiness on her face, only fragments of fear.

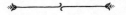

"Hold the flannel to her forehead," Linda tells me. "When it gets warm, rinse it again in the cold water."

Elizabeth's eyes are closed, but I know she's not sleeping. Within a minute, the heat from her skin has already soaked through the flannel and is warming my palm. But I must stay calm. I must not show that I'm afraid.

I take the flannel, float it in the ice-cold water in the bowl at my feet, then squeeze it through before putting it on Elizabeth's forehead again. She moves slightly, which I think is a good sign. Linda takes a small packet from her pocket. Inside, there is a strip of silver with little white circles. She pushes one of the circles and it pops out onto her hand.

"What's that?" I ask her.

"I have to bring her temperature down." She puts the white circle in a small glass of water and it starts to fizz and shrink and disappear. I grab the glass before Linda has time to pick it up.

"You can't do this," I whisper. The smell from the glass slips onto my tongue.

"It's fine, Pearl. It will help Elizabeth."

"No, it won't. This isn't from the earth. You will destroy her."

"No, Pearl. I've had these many times. So have Ellis and Sophie. They're good for you. They help get rid of pain."

"Pain is good for you," I say. "Elizabeth needs her pain."

"Right now, Elizabeth needs to get her temperature down. She is too hot. And if we can't cool her down, then she and her baby will be in danger."

"The flannel will cool her. You told me it would." But I can feel Elizabeth's illness seeping through the cloth.

"It's not enough, Pearl." Linda is reaching for the glass, but I won't give it to her.

"It's not what Elizabeth wants," I say.

"Do you want her to die?" Linda says. "Or her baby?"

Her words stop me. Does she really mean Elizabeth could die? Is it her time? Sylvie died having her baby. Sylvie died giving birth to one of us.

Linda's voice is calm. "If she drinks this, we can help her."

I look toward the door. It's closed, but is there someone listening on the other side? It's a risk I will take. I pass Linda the glass with the misty liquid. She nods at me and we lift Elizabeth's head.

"Drink this," Linda whispers in her ear. I am torn between pushing it away and letting her drink it. But I watch Elizabeth's lips open, the drink disappearing from the glass and into her body. I don't know what I have allowed to happen, but I know it is too late to change it.

＊───✝───＊

Kate has disappeared. She helped clear away morning meal, but then she wasn't working in the fields and I can't find her in the house. I thought maybe she was helping Kindred John, but Jack says he hasn't left the barn.

She wasn't back for middle meal, or evening meal. Rachel doesn't know where she is. Jack and I have looked in the barn, the forest, the bee shed. Maybe she's with Papa S.? But Heather is still his Companion.

"What's he done with her?" Ellis asks. We're gathering in the chickens for the night.

"What do you mean?" I try to laugh, but I know that I'm worried.

"Papa S. said she would be punished and now she's disappeared."

"He meant punished by Nature."

"She left a few spoonfuls of porridge, so she could help Elizabeth," he shouts, slamming down the empty metal bowl. "She didn't deserve a punishment."

"It's not like that. Papa S. hasn't done anything wrong. He is nothing but good to us."

But he didn't help Elizabeth. She was too ill to eat and although he loves her, he called on Nature to punish her.

"She's disappeared, Pearl." Ellis is right up close to me.

"She could be anywhere, helping one of the Kindreds, anything."

Yet I know I've looked everywhere. Jack has looked everywhere.

"Ask them where she is, then."

"No."

"Why not?" he asks.

"Because I know she's fine."

"What if she's not?" Ellis shuts the mesh fence harshly. Pulls over the lock.

"You have to trust them, Ellis." I know I'm trying to convince myself, but Ellis won't take my words. They fall from him as he turns from me and stamps back to the house.

I wake in the night so violently that all I can hear is my heart smashing in my chest. I sit up, confused, unsure where I've been in my dream.

Then I remember Kate. I slip from my bed and feel across the black air until I find her bed. It is empty.

The dark of the room makes me realize. I know where she must be. There must be other stages of being a woman, and she is back in the hole. I know she will be frightened and I know what I must do. And I must do it before I wake properly and think.

I find my sweater in the darkness. The noise I make seems loud, but no one wakes up. The children breathe in their sleep.

I walk out of our room and down the silence of the corridor. I falter on the top step of the stairs, as it creaks into the night. But no one comes. My feet carry me down, across the hall, into the kitchen. I unlock the door quietly and step outside. The cold hits my bare legs, wakes me up more. But I won't turn back.

It's so dark, so silent. The grass from the meadow brushes against me as I wade through it with my arms outstretched.

I'm coming, Kate. I won't leave you there. I hit the table with my palm, feel my way around it. *Just keep going straight.* Through the grass, until I reach the hedge. It is here, crackly against my hand. *Find the place to walk through, Pearl. Keep your hands brushing on the hedge, until it falls into a gap of air.*

There. I walk through. The grass is shorter here, the field in harvest.

Don't think that you are alone. The night is a blanket to protect you. The hidden animals are your friends. Don't look back at the shadow of the house.

Is someone watching me? *Keep walking. Don't wake up.*

The air changes; I'm near the trees. I can sense their height. I am here, walking among them, feeling the jagged bark of their trunks. They show me the way until I know I'm in the clearing.

I walk slowly forward.

"Kate?" I whisper. But I know she won't be able to hear me, as she is locked in the earth.

I can feel Papa S.'s Worship Chair. As I touch it, I wake up more and suddenly I'm alone, in the dark of the woods. I want to run, but I can't.

"Forgive me," I say as I pull the chair, hear it scraping through the earth. *Quickly, Pearl.* I kneel and push the wet leaves away until I feel the loop of metal. Pull it up, pull it up.

The trapdoor opens.

"Kate?" I whisper. But she doesn't reply. "Kate?" I say again. I don't want to go down. I can't go down. But what if she's hurt? What if she doesn't answer because she can't?

I put my foot on the top step. And the next. And the next. I am going down into that circle of earth.

"Kate?" I'm at the bottom and I kneel on the ground, feel

everywhere with my hands.

She's not here. Kate is not here. I feel up the walls, in every crack of the earth and I have to get out because I can't breathe and Kate isn't with me and I'm alone in the dark. I feel up the steps, so quickly until I'm out in the air. I lower the trapdoor and push the leaves over. Have I covered it all?

I pull the chair, the Worship Chair that must not be touched. Will he know? Will he be able to feel that my hands have been here?

I run back through the trees, my hands feeling the way. Through the rough ground of the harvest field. I can't find the hole in the hedge. Something grabs at my hand, cuts my skin, and then I'm free, in the meadow.

I run toward the dark house, where every light is off. But someone is watching me. I know someone is watching me.

I push open the kitchen door and lock it quietly behind me. I'm standing by the sink, trying to calm my breath, when there is a noise and the light turns on. It's Kindred John and Kate. They look shocked to see me. Flecks of red flame on Kindred John's cheeks.

"Pearl, what are you doing here?" he asks.

I look at Kate. She's been crying. "I'm getting a glass of water," I lie. "Where have you been?" I ask her, before I can stop myself.

"Kate, too, is getting a glass of water," Kindred John says. He walks to the cupboard as she stands in the doorway. There are marks on her arms. I look at them, but I don't ask how she got them. Kindred John reaches for a glass, then goes to the sink. The tap wheezes as he turns it on.

He goes to Kate, lifts the glass to her lips. She tries to take it from him but he holds her hand away.

"I will help you," he says, his voice kind. He has saved her. Wherever she has been, he has saved her. Hasn't he?

When she has finished the water, he kisses her on the forehead.

"Go with Pearl. You need to sleep," he says. His voice soothes away the last fragments of my fear.

I take Kate's hand, but she won't look at me as I lead her up to our room, up to the safety of our beds.

•••••••••••••••••••◆◆◆◆◆◆••••••••••••••••••

Ring-a-ring of roses, a pocket full of posies. A-tishoo! A-tishoo! We all fall down.

CHAPTER TWENTY-ONE

........●.........

"Where had she been, though?"

Ellis and I are balanced in an apple tree, hidden from the house.

"She was fine."

"But where was she?"

When I had asked Kate the same question, she had snapped at me. Told me not to ask again. She dressed quickly this morning, hid her arms from me, and now I don't know whether I imagined the bruises. But I did not imagine that she disappeared for a whole day, and that Kindred John must have known where she had been.

"Mom had to go into a room," Ellis says. "She won't tell me more." I pretend I don't notice him rip the leaf from its branch and screw it up in his palm. "She said it was the right thing and she didn't mind. But I don't believe her."

"Papa S. has forgiven her," I assure him. But did she really need forgiveness? Ellis throws the leaf down to the ground below us.

The apple that I choose to pick is half-red, half-green. I pass it to Ellis. "Elizabeth says your music takes her pain away," I tell him.

He holds my gaze as he bites into the apple. "Is she any better?"

"Not yet," I say. "Soon though." Because she will be fine. Nature won't take her away from us.

The hills in the distance are silent. I breathe in Seed's air and try to let it calm me.

"How can anyone want to live on the Outside, when you can have this?" I say.

"There's beauty on the Outside too, Pearl," Ellis says, tracing the musty bark with his finger.

"There's murder and dishonesty and laziness and liars." I look right at him, because I know he can't deny it. He's been there. I know he's seen it all.

"It's not all like that. Only bits of it."

"You know they poison the water, don't you?" I ask. I don't want to scare him, but if he doesn't know then I must warn him. "Papa S. has been to meetings with people in the government. They put viruses into the water, to make people sick."

"Why would they do that?" Ellis laughs, but he's not happy.

"They're bad people, Ellis, the ones who run the country. They think they can take Nature into their own hands."

"Right," Ellis says. "And I suppose you believe in the bogey-man?"

"Who's he?" Why is he being like this? I'm only trying to help him.

"It doesn't matter," he says. "But what does matter is that you shouldn't believe everything you're told."

"What about the floods?" I say.

"What floods?" Ellis asks.

"The floods that are taking over miles of land. They're Nature's revenge."

"For what?"

"For everything. Nature will destroy everything, apart from Seed," I say.

Ellis is smiling at me. Is he happy that he will be safe, or is he mocking me? "And Papa S. told you all of this?"

"He knows it all."

"Bit of luck I'm here, then," Ellis says.

"Yes," I say and I smile at him. He isn't laughing at me now. He understands.

"Will you kiss me, Pearl?" he asks.

The question stops my breath.

"No," I say. But I know it's not really what I want to say. I look over to the house, behind the trees in the orchard.

"Ever?" Ellis asks. He's looking at me so intently that I feel I might fall.

"No," I say. But inside, my stomach shoots through with a

feeling so strong that I don't move, in case I never have it again.

"You will," he says. Then he grabs a branch and swings himself down, landing on the grass below.

As he walks away, he looks back at me, just once.

And me? I sit in the apple tree, his words and my thoughts taking me to a red place I know I shouldn't go. But I do go there. Step by step, with my eyes closed and with burning feet, I go there.

CHAPTER TWENTY-TWO

·······•●•··········

I'm in the greenhouse, hidden in the corner. I'm sure Jack won't
find me here. I smell the cooped-up air, with its memory of
tomato leaves. It's mostly cucumbers in here now, and I crouch
among the plants. I can no longer hear Jack counting in the distance. We've scattered far and it will take him ages to find us.

My legs begin to ache, so I sit down and stretch them out.
The ground is dirty but it's dry enough to brush from my skirt.

I peer through the glass, but I can see no one. I could sleep in
here. Close my eyes and sleep until evening meal. The warm, stale
air mingles with my thoughts, but it doesn't help make sense of
them. About how I feel when Ellis is close. But how I hate his
Outside mind and the questions he has brought. The spittles of
anger growing in Papa S. Kate in the kitchen with Kindred John.

A fly is buzzing around my head. It's caught in here, beating
its wings to try to get to the outside. Slowly, I stand up and I quietly open the door, but the fly doesn't seem to see the way out.
Gently, I rest my hand next to it on the glass. The fly calms, hesitates, and then walks onto my palm. Inch by inch, I move to the

glass door, lift my hand and set it free.

"Got you," Jack says behind me. He has his arms around my waist and swings me in a circle.

"That's not fair," I laugh.

"It's very fair," he says, releasing me. "Now you have to help me look."

He takes my hand and we run to the blackberry hedge that circles the field. We duck down low and I have to pull my skirt up to my knees so that we can creep along unseen. When I begin to laugh, Jack holds a finger to my lips and silences me.

"If we do half the woods each, we'll find people in there," he whispers.

And so we separate as we reach the edge of the trees, walking slowly and quietly away from each other, hunting the others down.

I find no one. Not by the lake, not near the worship circle. But there is a noise by an ash tree. Silently I creep up to it, bend down low, and reach my arm around the trunk. I feel something and as I move around to see, there's a pain on my hand. Now something on my face, on my arm. They are bees, huddled around a wild hive. I blink and they swarm at me.

Suddenly they're in my hair, down my back, on my lips. They're in my clothes, stinging and stinging my skin. Stinging my eyelids and my bare legs.

I'm running and screaming as I try to brush them off me, but they stick to me. It feels like hundreds of them. Somewhere there is Jack and he's pushing them away, but there are too many of them under my clothes, stinging me. So I pull at my shirt, rip it over my head.

Rachel runs from the house and pulls me into the kitchen. There are bees tangled in my hair. Jack pulls them off, shakes them from his thumb.

"Run her a bath," Rachel orders him.

We're at the sink and she is holding my arms under cold water. The bees have hurt me. She runs a wet cloth on my face, over my eyes.

Kate and Ellis run in.

"Get me some nettles," Rachel tells them. "Bring them to the bathroom. Quickly."

She's taking me upstairs. My body is shaking. Kindred Smith comes to us, but Rachel moves him away.

Steam is rising from the bath. Jack leaves the room. Rachel takes off my skirt and underwear, as I hold my arms wide.

"Step into the water," I hear her say. It's hot. There are the stings. I sit down, feel the water. I can't stop shaking. The bees that I love have done this to me.

Kate is here and she pushes nettles into the bath. They float, little clumps of green, as she holds my hand and Rachel presses the flannel gently to my neck.

The sharpness of the stings turns to tiny little thuds that cover my body. Tiny little aches pinching into my blood.

"Shh," Kate says as she gently strokes my hair back from my face.

I hear the door open and her hand stops. I open my eyes. Papa S. is standing here. I am naked in the bath and he's looking at me. My hands go to cover my bare flesh.

Kate reaches for a towel, but Papa S. stops her. "Leave us," he says.

Kate doesn't move. "I need to stay with Pearl," she says. "She is in shock."

"Kate," Rachel says. She takes Kate's hand from mine and pulls her up. Papa S. kisses his palm and puts it on Rachel's forehead. Her smile is bright.

"I'll wait outside," Kate says as Rachel leads her from the room.

Papa S. steps forward until he's standing by the bath, looking down at me. I do not move my arms. I want him to say something, for his words to make it better.

"The bees stung you for a reason," he eventually says. "They were trying to stab away the rotten core that is growing within you."

Rotten core? The bees think that I am rotten inside? I feel

tears creeping to the edge of my eyes, my throat burning. I want to ask him what I have done, but no words come out. Perhaps I already know.

"Mother Nature told me that they would do it," Papa S. continues. "She has been watching you. They have been watching you."

My skin begins to shiver in the hot water.

"It is a warning. Next time it will be worse." Papa S. turns. I think that he is going, but then he moves back to me, kneels by the side of the bath. "We all love you, Pearl," he says. He kisses his palm and stretches it toward me. He pushes it through the water until it rests on my naked stomach. His skin on my skin. He holds it there and I do not move.

He holds it there and he makes me look into his eyes.

"We love you, Pearl," he repeats. Then he stands up, his fingers dripping wet. I don't watch as he walks away. But I hear the click of the door as he closes it behind him.

CHAPTER TWENTY-THREE

..........●..........

I'm working slower than usual as I dig the potatoes from the ground. The bee stings on my palm rub against the handle of the spade, and those under my clothes still feel sore. They remind me. Next time it will be worse.

I'm trying to hide my thoughts in the shapes of the trees when I see him walking up the driveway. He's on his own, slowly making his way toward the house.

Even from here, I recognize him. I know it's Simon, the boy who spoke to me last week at the market. The boy who asked after Kate. She hasn't noticed him and I watch as he comes slowly closer. I look around. There are no Kindreds to see him. But he shouldn't be here. I have to get him away.

I am meant to be digging up potatoes, but now I put down my spade and go to Kate, close enough so no one else will hear.

"Kate?" I whisper. She looks up at me. Her hair is tied back from her face, which is streaked with mud from her working hands. "When I was at the market, someone asked for you."

"Who?"

"Simon," I say, and her face shows me she knows.

"Why didn't you tell me before?" she asks.

"I don't know. I forgot." Did I?

She shields her eyes from the sun. "What did he say?"

"He asked for you, Kate. And I think he is here now." I look quickly toward the driveway and Kate looks too.

So much passes through her face in these seconds. She is happy. She is terrified.

She looks around us. Is Papa S. watching from somewhere in the house?

"Has anyone else seen him?" she asks.

"I don't know," I say. He's still far away. And everyone is busy working. "You must make him go, Kate."

But she's not listening to me. "I have to speak to him," Kate says. "If anyone asks, don't tell them where I've gone." She drops her spade and runs down the driveway, toward the walking figure. Her hand goes to pull the ribbon and her hair falls free. I want to shout to her to come back, but I don't and she doesn't.

She reaches him. Then they go quickly to the side and disappear behind the trees.

The wind whispers to me as I dig the spade into the earth. But it doesn't bring me their conversation. How can she be taking so long? I pull at a potato, the dirt snagging under my nails. There is a small thud as I put it into my basket, and the scrape again as

I dig down.

When I look up, Papa S. is standing on the front porch. He sees me, kisses his palm and faces it toward me. I should feel happy that he is here, but my stomach seems to fill with the earth at my feet. He's looking toward the trees, the trees where Kate and Simon are.

I look away and rub the skin of a potato clean. Papa S. is walking. He is heading down the driveway.

I can't warn her. There's nothing I can do. What if he doesn't know and I run to her and call out? He gets closer, his hair catching in the wind.

Move, Kate. Move.

Hide, Simon.

In the moment that I look up, Kate is there. She has come out from the trees alone. She goes to Papa S. and laughs, pointing to the sky. Papa S. has his back to me but he is motionless, while Kate is animated, reaching to him.

Papa S. must say something, because suddenly everything changes. Kate's movements stop, and her confidence slides away.

Then Papa S. steps forward and takes her hand. Out there, on the driveway, Papa S. takes Kate by the hand. She has never been his Companion before. Is now her time?

I try not to be jealous. I try to be happy for her. But how can I have got it so wrong, when Kate gets it so right? They are facing me now as they walk toward the house, so I get my spade and chip it into the earth, searching for the flesh of another potato.

I can sense them walk close by, but I won't look up. My spade scrapes and I will not look up, not until I know that they have gone.

And when I do, I see the shape of Simon. He's keeping close to the trees and he's running. Running away from us, away from Kate. I watch his back, fresh from the Outside, until he turns a corner in the driveway and he is gone.

⸻

Evening meal is inside. The nights are creeping earlier and it's too cold outside to eat. We are all ready and we are waiting. It's noisy, with laughter and the children and the talking. Ruby and Bobby balance spoons on their noses. Ellis is sitting next to me, but he's not smiling.

"Where's Kate?" he asks.

"With Papa S.," I say, because she is. I feel proud for her and my eyes challenge the doubt in his.

"Why?" he asks, just as the door opens and Papa S. is standing there with Kate. Their hands are linked and in her other hand, Kate holds a flower up to her lips. She looks beautiful and I want to rush up to her, because for years she has waited for this moment. For as long as I can remember, we have wished to be his Companion. And now is her time.

They walk slowly to their place, side by side. Papa S. is wearing a cloak of the deepest green and I can hear the sound of Kate's skirt rustling as she moves. When they reach their places, we all stand up, the scraping of the chairs on the floor breaking the silence. Papa S. kisses his palm and raises it skyward. We copy him, but I don't take my eyes from Kate. I want her to look at me so we can smile together and know that she has made it. But she doesn't look my way and when she sits down and takes the flower from her lips, her face shocks me. There's a defiance brighter than I've ever seen in her before.

"Begin your thanks," Papa S. says. We tip our faces and I close my eyes and I try to thank Nature, but all I can see in my mind is Kate, on what should be the happiest day of her life.

"Begin to eat," Papa S. says. The noise of the clatter of knives on plates and the talking and laughing starts again.

"When did that happen?" Ellis asks under his breath. He reaches over me and cuts his knife directly into the butter. The bread is still warm and the butter melts as he spreads it.

"Today," I answer him quietly. "I saw him take her hand in the driveway."

"It shouldn't be allowed," Ellis says. He bites into his piece of bread, rips some off with his teeth.

What does he mean? This is what Kate wants. But when I

look at her sitting there, picking at her bread, why do I feel doubt?

"He should choose the older women," Ellis says. So that's it. He wants his mother to be Papa S.'s Companion.

"He'll choose Linda soon," I say, but he just crushes the bread in his hand as he stares at me.

"I don't want him anywhere near my mother."

I'm so shocked I look away. My hand is shaking slightly as I reach for my glass to swallow down some water. Has anyone else heard? Next to him, Jack is laughing with Heather and the voices around the table are loud and joyous. But not Ellis. And I think Papa S. has noticed and Kindred Smith too, as I catch them looking at him.

"How's the engine work going?" I ask. Anything to wipe away his last words.

"How can you stand it, Pearl?" he asks. I don't answer. The butter from our cows tastes thick on my soft bread. "Because I don't know if I can much longer," he says. He looks away from me, jabs at the crumbs on his plate with his thumb. His anger is in his eyes, in his hands, in his whole body and there's no way he can hide it.

"Do you want to go for a walk after evening meal?" I ask him. In the air outside, Nature will heal him and wash away these strange feelings that are taking hold. He looks at me, more calmly now.

"Yes," is all he says, and it's time for us to clear the empty breadboards to make space for the stew that Heather and I have prepared.

The moon is already strong in the sky by the time we've finished clearing up, although it's not too dark. Jack is taking food to Elizabeth. I worry that she's still not eating enough. The fever seems to have settled into her bones. But Linda barely leaves her side and although she's not getting better, I don't think that she is getting any worse.

Ellis and I have put our coats on, and I can wear socks and my shoes now that my feet ache less from the stings. We walk together through the meadow, through the hole in the hedge and across the fields.

"You didn't tell me how the engines are going," I ask. I know he's proud of what he's been learning.

"It's fine," he says. His hand brushes mine as we walk.

"Just fine?" I look at him and smile. "Jack says you've picked it up way quicker than he ever has." But Ellis just shrugs.

We're quiet again as we reach the orchard. Up close, you can see the trees are heavy with their fruit. The children spend their days collecting fallen apples, filling basket upon basket that now sit out in the hall.

We walk to the farthest tree in the orchard and Ellis starts to climb. So I follow him. It's a strong tree and holds our feet and hands. The branches form a seat for us, but we have to sit close.

"Do you really want to leave?" I ask. I hadn't wanted to. I had wanted to just show Ellis the beauty around us. To remind him how amazing Seed is, and to make him love it all over again. But I've said the words now, and I can't take them back.

"Yes," he says, looking down at his hands. "More and more, I want to leave."

I hold my breath in the almost-darkness. Hearing him say the words. Knowing that he'd want to leave all this behind. And I don't understand it.

"But Mom won't go. She says she's got a reason for living now." He laughs bitterly. "And I'd never leave Sophie here."

"But how can you want to leave?"

He lifts his face and looks away, across the black fields toward the lights of our home. "There's evil here," he says.

His words stop my heart.

"Then I think you should go," I say. I feel my words bubbling up and I can't stop them. "Because you have absolutely no right to come here, and after all that we've given you . . ." I don't want to cry. I'm climbing down the tree, because I've got to get away from him. My hair catches on a branch, but I yank it free and almost fall the whole last bit as I jump on the grass and start to run.

"Pearl," Ellis calls after me. I won't stop. "Pearl!"

I run through the orchard, the trees protecting me. I hear Ellis running closer and he's quick, too quick for me. He has my arm and he's pulling me.

"No," I yell at him. I've never heard myself like this. Neither has the air, neither has the sky.

"Pearl, stop," Ellis says, his voice calm, but his grip on my arm is tight.

I stop and I turn and I'm hurting inside, just looking at him. But I pull my arm free. "You're the evil one," I shout. "This is what growing up on the Outside does. You should go back there. Leave us alone," I say and I start to walk away.

Ellis is just a few steps behind me. I won't say any more. I can't say any more. "Pearl," he says and hearing his voice makes me want to cry, because he is my friend, he is part of our family and he wants to go and I want him to go, but if he does it will shatter my heart. "I'm sorry," he says and he catches up with me and gently puts his hand on my arm.

"Don't you realize that it's the Outside that has made you this way?" I say. "Give yourself properly to us, Ellis, and you'll be happy."

Ellis takes a breath in. He runs both his hands through his hair, but his curls fall close to his eyes again. "Can't you see, Pearl?"

"See what?" I ask, staring at him, willing him to look into my eyes, willing him to have my happiness. Because I would give it all to him.

He looks up at me. Then he reaches out for my hand and I let him take it. "Nothing," he says quietly. "Nothing." He looks down. Gently he moves his thumb over my thumb. I feel his skin on my own.

"Are you really going to leave us?" I ask. I don't want to hear his answer.

"No," he replies. He looks into my eyes. "I won't leave you here, Pearl. And I can't leave my mom and Sophie."

"They wouldn't want to go. They're happy at Seed. And you're happy here too, you've just forgotten, that's all," I say. Ellis reaches out and touches my hair. A shiver runs through me and I close my eyes.

A twig cracks somewhere in the darkness. My eyes open and Ellis and I look. He drops my hand and I can hear the sound of someone walking away. Running.

Someone was here. We both know it.

"Who was it?" I whisper.

"I don't know," Ellis replies. "But we haven't done anything wrong, Pearl."

Haven't we? His voice sounds scared.

"I want to go back to the house," I say.

The night feels different now. The air is cold on my face. Back at Seed, everything will feel better. In the warmth of our family, everything will make sense.

I try not to remember the figure in the darkness, because when I do, a strange fear begins to creep into me. And Seed isn't a place for fear.

<hr />

Last night, I watched them come back through the fields. Two figures in the black shadows, side by side. She could not hide, not with her hair catching in the moonlight.

And today I keep this blonde girl as my child. Through my glass, I watch as she picks the lettuce. She works slowly, carefully. Sometimes, she takes a leaf from the edge and eats it. Sometimes she stretches her arms up toward the sky.

The door of my prison opens and he is here. I don't have time to step back, to pretend that I haven't been watching.

"Have you been looking out the window?" he asks, so close to me. I shake my head and he knows that it is not the truth.

He strikes my face so hard that I fall. The floor hits me. I put my arms over my head, but this time there is no more.

"I am sorry," he whispers in my ear. "But you know you have done wrong."

Wrong?

He is spooning the stew into my mouth as if I am a baby. My baby. My baby. I swallow. The soup is almost cold, but it is all that I have. And in it, there is the blackness.

Yet sleep is not long enough. It's not far enough away.

Soon. Soon I will be strong enough to go.

CHAPTER TWENTY-FOUR

·········•●•·········

Nana Willow's eyes are open wide when I walk into her room. She's sitting up and she watches me as I step toward her. I concentrate on the small tray that I'm holding, try to stop the glass clinking onto the bowl. I have never fed Nana Willow, it is always Heather or Elizabeth. The sweet smell of the soup crawls up my nose, but I don't want to breathe through my mouth.

She is still watching me. Carefully, I put the tray down on the small table next to her bed. I have to look up at her. The skin on her neck twists as her face is turned toward me. I try to smile, but she doesn't smile back. Her lips are now as pale as her skin, with lines of red where they have cracked.

"I have brought your food, Nana Willow," I say. She doesn't answer. She just looks at me with her old eyes that know a thousand things. Does she think I'm Sylvie? Do I dare to ask?

There's a chair next to the table, so I pull it around. When I sit on it, my knees are touching her bed.

"Are you comfortable?" I ask her. There are pillows behind

her back and her blanket is pulled almost to her chin. She nods her head.

I reach for the bowl. It's too full and I'm shaking and I'm worried that I shall spill it. But I dip the spoon in, blow gently on the soup, and slowly bring it to Nana Willow's lips. She opens her mouth like a child, her ancient tongue poking out slightly as I tip the soup so she can drink. And all the time, she watches me.

Again, I put the spoon in. Again Nana Willow drinks. And again. There's just the sound of the spoon scraping, Nana Willow's catlike breathing, and the sound of the soup as she swallows it.

She hasn't even eaten half the bowl when she turns her head away. Her lips are shut and she won't accept the spoon.

"Is that enough?" I ask her. She nods. The spoon sinks into the soup as I put the bowl back on the tray.

There are tears on Nana Willow's cheeks.

"Nana Willow?" I ask quietly. But now she won't look at me. "Are you hurting?" I ask her. She shakes her head.

Suddenly her fingers are around my wrist. She's squeezing my skin.

"She didn't die," she says, her voice rasping. "When Sylvie had her baby, she didn't die." But then her eyes turn in panic toward the window, where the curtains are pulled back from the skin of the glass and the black night looks in. She lets go of my wrist and pulls her blanket up to her neck.

"But Elizabeth said she died," I say. Nana Willow shakes her head violently. "Then where is she? Where did Sylvie go?"

Nana Willow doesn't move. Something has scared her. I get up and walk to the window and my hand reaches for the curtains. There's someone there. Out there, looking in, watching us. A man. Is it Papa S.? I yank the curtains shut, but hold on to the thick material, trying to steady my breathing.

My arms are shaking as I turn back to Nana Willow. Her eyes are closed. As I step closer, I can see that tears have dried in streaks on her cheeks.

CHAPTER TWENTY-FIVE

•••••••••●•●•••••••••

W e follow Papa S. and Kate through the meadow. Only a few of us fit through the gap in the hedge at a time, but we spill through it like water and walk toward the woods. The children are chasing each other with sticks. Kindred Smith grabs Ruby as she runs past and swings her high in the air. I can hear Linda laughing as she walks close to him. I can't see Papa S.'s face, but I know he must be smiling.

We are quieter when we reach the trees. They make a path for us and we hush to be able to hear the whisper of their leaves. Even the children start to slow down as we walk through the scattered light.

"I wish Elizabeth were here," Jack whispers to me. I squeeze his hand because I know how much he misses her. But she's alone in the house, just her and Nana Willow.

Sylvie didn't die. I can't forget those words. And I can still feel Nana Willow's fingers on my wrist, but they're forced away as we reach the clearing. Papa S.'s Worship Chair sits in the middle. I won't think about what lies underneath, deep in the ground.

Instead I will look at how it gleams, where someone has polished its arms and legs.

Quietly, we form a circle, as Papa S. walks to the middle and sits down on the chair. The sun shines on him and his whole body is covered in light.

We all join hands, making our circle, our family. No beginning, no end. The feeling of happiness spreads through me again, glows among us.

Slowly, Papa S. tips his face toward the sky. We copy him, and above us the color is a striking blue. There is one white cloud. We look up and wait for the sign. At first, there is nothing and then a bird swoops into view, its wings outstretched, its body floating in the curve of the sky.

"We worship you," Papa S. calls out. We copy his words. Ellis, Kate, every one of us.

"We worship you," we say together. "We worship you." Over and over, louder and louder. "We worship you!" Until the words spin in my head and my body seems to float from the ground. The worship soaks through my skin and embeds itself in my bones, turning them to dust. My voice is all that's left.

Gradually we become quieter. Gradually our words fade into the air and we stand in silence under the ceiling of sky.

"We are done," Papa S. says. I look at the circle around me and I know that everyone has been with me to that place. Linda leans her head into Kindred Smith as she whispers words I cannot hear. This is her first time in the worship circle, and her face is layered with happiness.

We watch Papa S. He is rubbing his arms, nodding his head. "Nature has told me," he suddenly says, "that our eyes have become greedy. Our mouths too. We have neglected our hands, the gift of touch." We listen, waiting. "Now we shall go back to our house. Nature has ordered me to take your eyes from you."

There is a sharp breath from Bobby. But Papa S. laughs.

"Your eyes are a gift from her," he says, smiling. "I will not take them forever. I have been told to simply cover them. For one whole day, you will see with your hands."

That is all he says, it is all he needs to say. His words make me uneasy, but when I look at Papa S.'s warm face, I know I must trust him. We follow him from the clearing, through the watching trees, back toward Seed.

I wait outside Papa S.'s room. Jack goes before me and when he comes out, his eyes are covered by a blindfold, his steps timid, his arms stammering.

"Are you there, Pearl?" he asks. I tap him on the shoulder without a word. "Pearl?" I tap his other shoulder. He spins around. "Who is it?" he asks.

"It's me." I laugh.

"Where are you?" He's smiling.

"Here," I say.

"It's your turn now. I'll wait for you," he says.

I don't hesitate. I push open the door and Papa S. is standing there, smiling at me. Across his hands lies a strip of black cloth.

"Come closer, Pearl," he says. And I go to him. "Turn around," he says. And I do. I am looking at his closed door when I hear him step up to me. He is rarely this close to me. His arm brushes my shoulder and then the blindfold is over my eyes and I can see nothing.

At once, I hear more. His gentle breathing. The ticking of a clock. The sound of the material slipping against itself as Papa S. ties it into a knot. Then he places his hands over my eyes, over the blindfold. I can feel his skin, his very being, through the tiny strip of black and I feel a strength I have never known. If it was not forbidden, I think I might cry.

Then Papa S. steps away from me. His hands have left me and I feel suddenly cold.

"You are done," he says, his voice behind me. His hand is on my elbow as he leads me to the door. There is the sound of it opening and as I leave Papa S., the door closes behind me.

"Jack?" I ask.

"I'm here," he says, somewhere beside me. I reach out and he must too, because his hand is there and now he holds mine.

Papa S. is right. I notice so much more. The smallest noises.

The gentleness of my skirt, the rough surface of the dining table. The breeze on my face. I listen more when people speak. I want to hear every word they say.

And everything is more difficult in this bubble of black. Even walking, we knock into each other. We're clumsy as we fill the plates with food. I feel the knife near my fingers as I slice the bread.

Ruby spends much of the day clinging to me, scared that she will be lost on her own. I wish that she could enjoy it as I do. Because somehow, it makes me feel even more alive. But she is too young and so I hold her hand as we walk toward the sweet-corn field, where we will work this afternoon.

"Where is Bobby?" she asks.

"He will be near us somewhere."

"Bobby?" Ruby calls, but no one replies.

Slowly, we make our way. My fingers feel nothing, until they hit the bramble hedge. We follow it until we walk steadily through the hole, my arm pulled forward in the air.

I hear the sound of the corn rustling before I feel them. Touch the height of the plants with my hands, feel their thick leaves, the ears ready for picking. There are rows and rows of them.

"Can I give you the basket now?" Ruby asks. I reach out until I feel the roughness of its weave.

It will be difficult to tell if the corn is ripe with blindfolds on. I won't be able to squeeze the liquid out of the kernels and check for its milky color. I'll just have to guess and hope that I'm not wrong.

"Ruby!" We hear Bobby call. Ruby giggles and I hear her walking away, her body brushing the leaves as she pushes through the stalks toward his voice. Then nothing. I stop, listen, but now it is only the corn knocking in the breeze. I reach up to try to pick one.

My hands hit something. Someone.

"Ruby?" I ask. I go to feel her face, but a hand holds my wrist back gently. I know it's not her. This person is too tall. The breathing too low.

"Ellis?" I whisper. I feel his fingers sliding through my hair. "Is that you?"

The fingers are on my face. On my neck. The hand sweeps over my chest, to my waist. It feels wrong. I want to take off my blindfold, but I daren't.

"Ellis?" I ask again. The hand is on my skirt and I push it away. I hear his breathing. I reach up to feel his face. There is the coarseness of hair, of a beard. He stops my scream by pressing on my mouth. He has hold of my wrist. But I shake my head free from him.

"Ruby," I shout and it makes him drop my arm.

I run blindly away from him. The leaves of the corn hit at me and I can't find my way through.

"Kate!" I call, but she doesn't answer. I'm blind as I reach out into the beating air, as I stumble through the endless plants.

"Pearl." It's Rachel's voice. I follow it with my hands. She is here. I touch her face and the skin is smooth. "Did you get lost?" There is a smile in her voice.

I must not cry. There is nothing to cry about. Rachel is here and I am safe.

At the end of the day, we take off our blindfolds. Everyone else is laughing, blinking in the evening sun. I'm free of the material that bound my eyes. But that touch is still on me, his breathing is in me. I try to push the thoughts away as Jack runs up.

"It's nice to see you again." He laughs. "It made you think, though, didn't it? Not being able to see."

"Yes," I say.

It feels like my blindfold is now pulled tight across my mouth. The truth soaks into the material and stays trapped there.

CHAPTER TWENTY-SIX

•••••••••●•••••••••

I'm collecting eggs when I hear the scream. It's coming from
the work barn. It's Jack, or Ellis.

Before I even reach the barn, they're bringing Ellis out.
There is blood. Everywhere, there is blood. Kindred Smith and
Jack half carry, half drag him onto the driveway. Kindred John
walks behind them. They've tried to wrap a sheet around Ellis,
but I can see. His hand is not there. There is no hand, it is gone
and the white sheet is soaked with red.

"Ellis!" It's Linda. She runs from the house, still clutching a
cloth from the kitchen. She kneels beside him and touches his
face. He's completely still. Ellis's blood is on her fingers. "What
happened?" No one answers. "You need to hurry." But no one
moves. "You have to take him to the hospital!" Linda is shouting
at us.

"We can't do that," Kindred John says. I see his beard and I
drown the thought it brings.

Linda pushes the sheet into Ellis. "But I can't stop the
bleeding."

This can't be Ellis. He is strong. But this person is not moving. His eyes are rolled back in his head.

"Do something," Linda screams at Kindred Smith. For a second he looks stunned, but then he turns to Kindred John.

"He must go to the hospital," he says firmly. Kindred John seems to want to speak. "We don't have time." And Kindred Smith pushes him out of the way. He stumbles as he begins to lift Ellis.

"You are taking him to the hospital?" I ask. I feel numb. Jack is helping Kindred Smith to put Ellis into the front seat of the van.

Linda tries to clamber into the seat next to her son.

"You have to stay here," Kindred Smith tells her. But he has panic in his eyes.

"No!" she screams.

"I will take Ellis," Kindred John says. And before anyone can question him, he runs around to the front seat and he is starting the engine. Kindred Smith pulls Linda away from the door. He holds her close to him, so that she cannot see as the van disappears around the side of the house. It will go down the driveway. It will go to the hospital on the Outside.

Jack is next to me. He's covered in Ellis's blood. There is some smudged down his cheek. I reach up and touch it. It's still wet.

"What happened?" I ask, although my words hardly form.

Jack is looking at the house, where the van disappeared. "Jack?" I ask again. He turns to look at me and he opens his mouth, but he can't seem to speak.

"It was an accident," Kindred Smith says. He is stroking Linda's hair as he leads her toward the house.

"What happened, though?" I ask. I can see Sophie running back through the fields.

"I don't know," Jack finally says. "Kindred John was with him."

Sophie rushes up. She's gasping for breath, but I know what she wants to ask. I bend down to her. There's blood on my skirt as I take her onto my lap.

"Ellis is hurt," I say. But I am scared as I say it. I don't want to tell her that they've taken him to the hospital.

"Can I see him?" she asks. She is staring at the blood on Jack's shirt and her bottom lip begins to tremble.

"They have taken him to make him better," I say. Bobby comes up and he starts to cry. "Hush now," I say. I look toward the house and I can't see Papa S., but Bobby is crying. "Come on. I need help with the eggs in the barn." I take Sophie's and Bobby's hands in mine and we walk away. Away from Ellis's blood on the driveway.

The egg is smooth and still warm. I lift it from where it lies, curled in the straw, and put it carefully in the basket. I look through the barn door, the frame of daytime, but there is no one there. All I can see in my mind is Ellis's blood. Red as berries.

Kindred John has taken him. He'll look after him, won't he? The sound of the corn knocking is loud in my mind.

Sophie stayed by my side for a while, but now she and Bobby run in and out of the straw, hunting for golden gifts from the chickens. If I was a child, I too could cut Ellis from my mind. Forget how his face was so strangely tipped back. His beautiful face. Because I know now that even someone from the Outside can be beautiful. And the thought of him in a hospital makes me feel so sick that I have to breathe and keep looking at the patch of sky.

I need to talk to Kate, but she's still Papa S.'s Companion. Who will tell her about Ellis? I want to be the one, so that I can hold her hand and we can talk and know that the doctors won't hurt him and he will come home soon.

I can't be in here any longer. I have to find Jack. I watch my hands put down the basket on the dry mud floor, and I hear myself walk out of the barn and into the air so that I can breathe again.

I see Jack straight away. He's sitting at the table in the meadow, alone. His head is bent forward, his hands around a glass in front of him. He doesn't hear me as I go up.

"Jack?" I ask quietly. He jumps a little, tries to smile, but his jaw is set rigid. Sitting next to him, I put my head on his arm. Ellis's blood has dried on his shirt. I reach out to touch it. It's hard, cold. But it is part of Ellis. And I want to find him, push it back into him.

"What happened?" I ask.

"I don't know." Jack shakes his head, as though trying to free his thoughts.

"Were you with him?"

"No. He was working with Kindred John. His hand . . . I don't know. I don't know how it happened." He looks up at me and into me and our thoughts are the same. Because Ellis's soul lies in his hands. His hands are his music. I hear his piano notes on the breeze and they twist down into my stomach.

"Can they put it back on?" I ask.

"I don't think so," Jack whispers as he looks down at his own fingers, where they can move with their blood and their skin and their bone.

"Then why did they take him to the hospital?" I ask. "Because we could have helped him here."

"You saw the blood, Pearl."

"But we could have stopped him bleeding. We have everything here to heal him. Now he's there, who knows what they will do to him." I shiver, even though I'm not cold. I think of the doctors with their knives and their experiments.

Jack looks up at me. His eyes are different now. "Not all doctors are bad," he says. "I think hospitals might sometimes be good places."

"How can you say that?" I ask him. "You didn't want to go when you cut your chest."

"That was different. I wasn't that hurt." He stares into his glass, where the water sits waiting. "And since then, I've talked to Ellis. They have medicines that heal." Jack says it so quietly.

My thoughts are messy. Because isn't it against everything?

"Papa S. says we have to follow Nature's path, Jack. It's the only way."

"If Ellis hadn't gone to the hospital, he might have died. Is that the right way?" Jack asks. "Would you have been happy with that?"

I know my answer. I know that I could never have held Ellis's head on my lap and accepted that it was his time.

"He might already be dead, Pearl." The pain in Jack's words show in every part of his gentle face.

"No," I say. Because that can't be true. I can't let it be true.

"They might have been too late."

I can't hear any more. I stand up from the bench, clutch my long skirt into my fist, and hitch it high above my knees so that I can run away. Through the meadow, through the field. Away, but

I don't know where. I just want to keep running until my lungs hurt enough to block out the pain.

Above me, a buzzard circles as I run.

CHAPTER TWENTY-SEVEN

········•••●•••········

I don't want to go back. I sit in an apple tree with the ghost of
Ellis. He holds my hands in both of his. We watch the sun sink
out of the sky and the gray turn to black.

Only when the cold soaks into my veins do I go back to
the house.

Kindred John is sitting with Kindred Smith at the kitchen
table.

"Ellis is well," Kindred Smith says to me, and he stands up
so that he can wrap me in his big, safe arms. I must not cry, not
now. So instead I laugh as I kiss my palm and hold it to the night
sky beyond the window.

But it was not Nature who saved Ellis.

"Where is he?" I ask.

"He is still at the hospital," Kindred Smith says.

"Why?" I ask. I look at Kindred John.

"They're looking after him," he says, but his face looks
strained. I should comfort him, but I don't want to.

"But Papa S. says that hospitals are bad places," I say. "And now you've left Ellis there."

"The doctors will help him," Kindred Smith says. But it's against everything we've ever been taught, everything we've ever known. I don't know what truths to hold on to.

The door opens and Heather comes in. She looks tired. Her hair, which she always wears loose, is pulled back into a knot.

"Pearl, I need you to take a bowl of cold water to Elizabeth," she says. She's reaching for her apron, tying the strings behind her back. They are all being so normal. Do they not remember about the doctors? Are the experiments not true?

"I know it is strange, Pearl. But Ellis is well and he will come back to us," Kindred Smith says.

"You must go now, Pearl," Heather says.

I'm glad to leave the room, to walk away from them all.

Elizabeth is worse than yesterday. Her face is so pale, and her eyes are scrunched with pain. She tries to smile when she sees me. I sit next to her bed and push her hair back from her face, where it is sticky with sweat.

I put the flannel in the fresh water, squeeze it in the cold and put it on Elizabeth's forehead.

"Thank you," she says and her body sinks back slightly into her bed.

"Have you eaten?" I ask, and she nods.

"Jack brought me food." Then she grimaces, breathes quickly.

"What is it?"

"It's nothing. It just hurts."

"Is the baby coming?" I ask.

"No." She laughs lightly. "It's not ready yet. I just have a pain under my ribs."

"How can I make it better?" I ask. It's almost impossible to see her like this.

"Tell me about your day. Let me think of something else." She reaches out to me, to hold my hand. Her arms are swollen. The skin on her fingers stretched.

And so I lie to her. I lie to Elizabeth. I tell her about the barn, about collecting eggs, about sitting in the meadow with Jack, about being in the tree in the orchard. They are all truths. But I don't tell her about Ellis. I won't speak the words that are pushing at my lips. I can't tell her about his blood, his hand. I fill the days with tiny lies that I might have done. Helping Rachel with evening meal, grating carrots and sprinkling them with poppy seeds.

I place my hand on the swell of Elizabeth's belly, rising like a hill under the sheet. "Is it moving?" I ask.

"A bit. It has slowed down, though." Elizabeth is smiling as she reaches out her other hand and strokes it over her belly. "There's not much room left now," she says.

"How long will it be? Until the baby is born?" The flannel is warmed through, so I rinse it and squeeze it in the cold water again.

"Maybe three weeks now." I bend down and kiss the stretched sheet, where underneath our baby sleeps. *Together we will run to the shadows of the trees, and I will tell you who your mother is.* Our baby pushes against my palm in reply.

"Do you think it's a boy or a girl?" I ask.

"Nature will decide," Elizabeth says with a smile. But then she winces again, her neck stretching back.

"Tell me what I can do," I say.

Elizabeth shakes her head as she puts her hand into mine and squeezes some of her pain into me. "My feet hurt," she finally says. Her breathing is more level now, but there is a flicker of fear darkening her eyes.

I move to the end of the bed and lift up the thin sheet. I try to hide my shock. Elizabeth's thin, elegant feet are so swollen that I don't recognize them as her own. They look filled with water, the skin shiny. I'm scared to touch them. But this is Elizabeth, my mother. When she grew me, she must have been in this pain.

I take the flannel and place it over one of her feet. Gently I massage her swollen toes. I try to imagine her running in the grass, her hair tied with flowers, her laughter growing wings and disappearing into the trees. The baby lying in the meadow, watching the birds swooping up to the clouds.

Elizabeth is asleep. Her breathing is settled and, for now, I don't think she can feel the pain.

As I lay my head down onto her bed and close my eyes, I let Ellis back into the room. They have cleaned up his blood and he comes to sit next to me. He is smiling. But where his hand once was, there is only air.

•••••••••••••••••••••◆◆◆◆◆◆◆◆•••••••••••••••••••••

Enough. I won't eat. I won't drink. He has taken everything from me, but he cannot take the final thing away. My choice. To live, or not to live.

He loves me, he loves me not. He loves me, he loves me not. He controls me, he controls me not.

No more.

Papa S. is here. He walks toward me with the food. I clamp my mouth shut tight and padlock it with the years he has locked me away. He slams down the spoon and his fingers rip at my lips. He tries to force my teeth apart, but I bite down hard. Because I won't eat, I won't drink. I won't be his puppet anymore.

I kick out at the bowl and it crashes and spills and my arm thrashes out and knocks his precious water tumbling.

Now his eyes burn with anger. His arms shake with rage and he pushes into my closed mouth, over my nose, blocking my air.

I can't breathe. It's what I want, but I can't breathe and I am not ready. Not yet, not this way. Not him. I fight him and struggle, but I am nothing against him.

Suddenly he lets go and the musty air rushes back to me.

He kicks me hard in the stomach before he leaves the room.

He closes the door quietly behind him.

CHAPTER TWENTY-EIGHT

........●●●●●●............

K ate comes to the table for morning meal, her hands linked
with Papa S. She holds a flower to her lips, but this time
she looks at me. Her eyes are filled with fire. Papa S. does
not smile.

We go through the ritual that we always do, but today it seems
stilted. There are too many empty places, too many thoughts
buzzing around our heads. The four days Ellis has been away
have been too long.

"Begin to eat," Papa S. says. And we do. But the porridge
tastes wrong. Everything feels wrong.

It is our free day, but Kate will have to be with Papa S. and
Ellis isn't here. I can't think of him and what they are doing to
him. Kindred Smith is sitting next to Papa S., but they don't talk.
Normally their heads would be bent together and there would be
smiles and laughter. But Papa S.'s face is rigid as he spoons the
food into his mouth. Kindred John is also silent and their unease
trickles down the table, even settling on the children.

Linda barely moves as she eats. The dry patches on her skin

have appeared again and she has scratched them raw. Thankfully Papa S. has forbidden her to go to the hospital, but since Ellis has been gone, the thin, gray cloud has settled back around her.

We eat the porridge. Bobby taps Jack on his arm.

"We're going to make a den in the forest," he says quietly.

Jack smiles at him. "I'll help you," he says.

No one says another word.

———

The clouds are gathering, but it doesn't look like rain. They are too white, too far away. And the blue of the sky doesn't want to disappear.

I have a basket of food that Bobby helped me prepare and he is clutching an armful of bamboo sticks, his eyes concentrating on the trees ahead. Sophie and Ruby hold a blanket between them, stretched out flat as they run in front of us through the field, their laughter warming the air. I want to have some of their happiness, but nothing is right without Ellis.

I imagine that he is here. Maybe he would be carrying the bamboo. Maybe he'd be chasing Sophie, rolling her in the blanket, throwing her in the air. But then he's wrapped in the soaked red sheet again.

"Are you OK?" Jack asks. He's carrying twists of thick rope.

"Yes," I say, but Jack knows me better than that.

"He'll be fine," he says. "Kindred Smith says he'll be back in a few days."

He won't be fine, though, will he? I want to say. *He'll never be fine again.*

"Has Kindred John told you yet what happened?"

Jack adjusts the rope on his shoulders. "He says the machine slipped."

"Do you believe that?" Am I really questioning Kindred John?

"I have to believe it," Jack says finally. He starts to walk quickly and I know he doesn't want to speak about it anymore.

We go into the trees. The air is green and I breathe in the beauty of it. We let Bobby lead. Follow the little figure of him as he grasps the tricky bamboos. We wind in and out among the tall trees until we get to the place he decides. I don't know why he has chosen here, but he has.

"Shall we collect sticks first?" Jack asks.

"No," Bobby says. "First, we collect leaves." And so we do. We lay the blanket and start to fill it with leaves scooped from the ground. Jack and I pick up handfuls and look at each other in silent conversation.

We're sprinkling the leaves for the bottom of the den when I hear something, not far away. I look up, but no one is near. Then I see a hand, reaching around the trunk. I see his face only for a second, but I know it's him.

Simon.

I shouldn't go to him, but I do. Jack is busy gathering sticks and I walk away, toward the boy from the Outside. I turn behind the tree and he's here. His face is soft, concerned. His body is so close to mine. We are tucked in together so we won't be seen.

"Why are you here?" I force myself to stay next to him.

"Where's Kate?" Hearing him say her name makes my stomach twist, and I don't know what to do.

"She's not here."

"I need to see her." His breath is so close that I take it in mine. Nerves trickle down my arms but I have to keep myself here.

"Why?" I ask. "Why do you need to see her?"

"She said she would meet me here."

"She wouldn't say that. She hardly knows you."

Simon looks me straight in the eye. "I've known her for months."

"Months?" Is he lying?

"Where is she?"

"She's not here," I say again. I know I should walk away.

Simon reaches out and touches my arm. "I'll wait here. Will you get her for me?" His eyes are different from Ellis's. They are a startling blue, his eyelashes pale. "Will you?" he asks me again.

"She can't come here," I say as I move my arm from him.

Simon doesn't seem so calm anymore. "Why? Where is she? Is she with him?"

"With who?" I ask.

"That old man," he says.

I know now he must go. "You are not welcome here," I tell him. And I mean to turn and go, to leave him there. But something makes me stop and look at him. At his Outside skin. At his forehead, his eyes. He's not one of us, but he's like us and there's something about him that makes me know he is not evil.

It's Simon who turns his back on me and starts to walk away. "Tell her I'll come back for her," he says.

Then he is gone.

I stand where he has left me. I'm unsure what to do. Everything used to be so clear, so definite. But now my thoughts are like the roots around me, twisting into each other. I can't find where they start, and however hard I try, they keep ending in darkness.

Jack is knotting the rope on a tree. His movements are sharp and he yanks on the rope so hard that it must almost cut his skin.

"Who was he?" he asks. The children are close by, making a pile with the sticks they have found, so Jack speaks quietly. I thought he hadn't seen us. I don't want to answer, but I won't lie to Jack.

"Simon," I say.

"Simon?" Jack pulls the rope taut and begins to tie it round another tree. The children are here, resting sticks up against the rope to make the walls of their den. Bobby is directing them.

"Yes," I say. Isn't that enough?

We weave ivy in and out, making the walls strong. All the time, I can feel Jack looking at me. Ruby and Sophie drag the blanket inside and Bobby pulls the basket in with them.

Jack and I are alone, outside the den of sticks.

"What did he want?" Jack asks.

"Kate."

"Kate?" When I look at him, he seems hurt, not angry.

"They met at the market," I whisper. I won't tell him any more. "I don't know what to do."

"We must tell the Kindreds," he says.

"No." I know it's wrong, but I don't want them to find out.

"What do you mean?" Jack asks, confused. But how can I explain? It's like the jigsaw of my life has been shaken up and put back together all wrong. I need someone to put the pieces straight, one by one.

"I don't know, Jack. I'm worried Kate will get in trouble."

Jack pulls his suspenders back over his shoulders. He's looking around. For Simon? For the trees to give him answers?

"OK," he says, but he doesn't sound sure. "We won't tell the Kindreds. But if we ever see him again, then I will."

Ruby rushes out of the den. "We're ready!" she says, her smile out of place in my thoughts. She takes our hands in hers and pulls us into the den. They've laid the food out like a feast. Cherry-red tomatoes, chunks of cucumber, the hard-boiled eggs, free of their shells.

———————

Kate is sitting alone at the kitchen table when we get back. The children are cold, huddled together under the blanket and they scuttle upstairs to jump into their beds. My ankles feel like ice. Jack and I spent far too long sitting with our feet dangling into the lake. Trying to make sense of Ellis. Wondering when he will come home.

"Where've you been?" Kate asks. She sounds tired.

"In the woods," I say. "I thought you were with Papa S."

"I was. But I'm not now."

Jack looks awkward. I'm sure he's remembering Simon. He walks out the door and we listen as he crosses the hallway.

"What's going on, Kate?" I ask. I reach out for her hand. "Are you still his Companion?"

Kate doesn't answer, but she shakes her head. Suddenly she's crying. She's trying to keep quiet, trying to stop her life spirit from leaving her, but the tears won't let her. I have never seen her like this. I move my chair and wrap my arms around her.

"What is it?" I ask. "It'll be OK." But Kate's tears don't stop. Her body shakes under my arms.

The door opens. Heather rushes in. "I can hear you from the stairs," she says. "Shh, now. Shh." She brushes Kate's hair back from her eyes. And when they look at each other, I feel like a child again. I am not part of what they know.

Kate breathes deep gulps of air. Heather fills a glass with water and holds it out to her. I think of Simon, hiding among the trees. Did he only run to the edge of the forest? Is he still hiding there now? His body being swallowed by the creeping dark?

I watch Kate. Her eyes are red from tears. *Tell Kate,* he'd asked me. *Tell her I'll come back for her.*

But I don't say a word.

※———‹———※

"Kate," I whisper from my bed. She's probably asleep. I've been lying here for so long, listening to Ruby and Sophie breathing, watching the night sky blear through the cracks in the curtain. Wondering what is the right thing to do.

"Yes," Kate replies. She sounds wide awake.

It's easy to find my way to her bed. I sit on the end of it, clasp my arms round my knees. "He was here again," I whisper. I've said it now. "Simon."

Kate sits up quickly. Her face is close enough for me to see, but I can't work out her expression. "Where?"

"In the woods. He was asking for you."

She smiles and her face lights up.

"He's from the Outside, Kate. He can't come back." I want to tell her that I know. I know their secret.

"Did anyone else see him?"

I look down at my arms, crossed over my legs. "Jack."

"Jack saw Simon?"

"Yes."

"What did he say?"

"He says if he sees him again, he's going to tell the Kindreds." Sophie moves in the bed nearby, but she's still fast asleep. "You have to make him stay away, Kate." But she shakes her head. Panic rushes into me. "You have to. He's from the Outside. He will poison you."

"That's rubbish. Ellis is from the Outside. And Sophie. And Linda."

"That's different."

"Why?" Kate stares at me and I can't answer her. "I like him," she says, so quietly.

"But it's wrong, Kate." And I think of Jack. How hurt he looked when he saw Simon in the trees.

"No. These feelings aren't wrong." She closes her fingers into a fist and brings them close to her heart.

And I understand her. Because ever since I saw Ellis, I have felt it too.

"What are you going to do?"

Kate's eyes are wide as she looks at me. "I don't know," she says.

There is a noise from the corridor. Just the house creaking, as it does when we sleep.

"I don't know," Kate whispers again.

* * *

No. I push him away. My arms are weak, but I can slap at him. And I shake my head so that the spoon can't go between my teeth.

No.

My life, not yours. My choice, not yours.

He kicks me hard on the arm before he goes. The pain seeps into the pain in my stomach, the pain in my head. Little snakes swimming in my blood, squeezing past my bones.

I am with my daughter. Today it is the blonde one and we hold hands and run through the meadow. I pick flowers and weave them into her hair. Her hair is growing now and it is like mine. Maybe she is mine.

I'm too tired to stand up and see through the window. So I lie here and I am with her and I hold her hand.

Hold my hand, my daughter.

I am going.

Hold my hand.

CHAPTER TWENTY-NINE

．．．．．．●．●．●．．．．．．

The light switches on. We are snatched from sleep. Rachel is standing in the doorway and I can see that the sun hasn't risen outside. It's not a deep black, though. Morning is close.

"Papa S. wants us all in the Eagle Room," she says.

"Is it Ellis?" I ask, the words coming before I'm fully awake.

"No, it isn't Ellis," she answers.

Sophie stretches in her bed. She slept head to toe with Ruby again last night. They've done that the last five nights, since Ellis was taken away.

We're quiet as we walk down the stairs, having dressed sleepily. It's cold. Autumn is definitely coming. In the Eagle Room, we gather in a circle. I smile as I see, tucked into the corner, the trunk with the messages sewn into the hems. The room works its magic as it always does, and as we stand and hold hands, I know everyone must feel the same as I do. A happiness lifting from the floor, circling the closed curtains, touching the painted red walls. This is the first time I've felt happy since Ellis left. I hope that Linda can feel it too. Nothing can hurt us here.

When Papa S. comes in, we kiss our palms and face them toward him. He smiles and takes his place in the middle of us all. I won't look at Kate, but squeeze her hand to let her know I know.

"My family," Papa S. says, his voice swimming toward me. He turns, looking at each of us. I smile when his eyes meet mine. "Nature made us. Nature knows us. Every movement, every thought, Nature sees." A prickle of fear sweeps around my neck. I must concentrate on Papa S., his wise, wonderful face helping to guide us.

"We cannot all be perfect," he says, "but we can right our wrongs. Clean the dirt away. Make ourselves pure again . . ." He pauses. Turns slowly. "So. I have made a box. Made from Nature's gift of wood. Big enough to hold those thoughts that weigh you down. It will take your wrong and we will lock it in. And we shall send it in flames so you may be cleansed." His voice is rising as he holds his hand toward the ceiling.

I catch sight of Jack and his face is lifted toward Papa S. He looks like our real Jack again, the Jack who is never unhappy. And seeing him gives me hope. Hope for everything. Simon will go. Kate will be happy. Ellis will come home and my thoughts will be clean.

Papa S. is walking from the room. Bobby looks up at me, his eyes sleepy.

"It's good," I say quietly to him. "We can put all of our bad thoughts into the box." He looks confused. "Watch," I say, and I point to Kindred John as he takes Rachel first. No one says a word. I look over at Kate, but she is staring toward the curtains and I can't tell her thoughts. Heather is here and I have a moment of fear for Elizabeth, alone upstairs. But Heather smiles at me and nods, and my worry disappears.

One by one, we are taken by Kindred John. When it's my turn, he reaches out his hand for me and I take it. His skin on mine makes a memory shrivel deep within me. We have to walk from the room, down the corridor and then knock on Papa S.'s door.

"Enter," says Papa S. Kindred John leaves me and closes the door behind him.

On the floor is a long wooden box. It is like the coffin Kindred John once made to bury the deer we found dead in the meadow. But this coffin is much bigger. I could lie down inside it.

Papa S. must see my surprise. "I know," he says. "But Nature told me it had to be like this. There are so many impure thoughts." He looks at me, right into me. I feel his hands reaching down and dragging out the bones of Simon. "Put those thoughts into the box," he says. "Spit them. Be free of them."

I spit into the coffin. The secret of Simon. The impure thoughts of Ellis. I spit them away and I feel free. Those thoughts are dead.

"Thank you," I say and I run up to Papa S. and reach up to

him and kiss his cheek. I want to hold on to him, onto all that is good. He seems surprised. But pleased. He puts his arms round me and I feel his goodness seep into all the hollows left by my bad thoughts. He kisses my hair.

"You have done well," he says and then he points me to the door. I walk past the coffin and out of his room.

Kindred John tells me to go out and wait with the others on the driveway. I am surprised by the light. It's gray and the sun isn't strong, but the night has nearly gone. Everyone who went before me is standing around a huge pile of sticks and logs. A bonfire waiting to be lit.

Flames. These are the flames. Papa S. will burn the coffin. The flames will take our bad thoughts forever.

Ruby jumps into my arms, beaming. "There's going to be a fire."

In all my life, I only remember one bonfire. Years ago, before Ruby was even born. All I remember is the heat and the strength of the flames.

I beckon Bobby over and he comes to hold my hand. Together we watch Kindred Smith as he flutters like a moth, tucking in bits of stray wood. We wait like this. One by one, our family comes out to the bonfire. I watch each of their faces in turn. Jack looks so happy. His smile is free. Even Kate's eyes come alive at the sight of the logs piled high.

I wish that Elizabeth could see it. I will remember the crackling and tell her of the heat on my skin.

We wait.

Then they come, Papa S. and Kindred John. They carry the coffin between them. It looks heavy with our bad thoughts. It weighs down their shoulders and I want to help, but they brush away Kindred Smith and Jack when they step forward. Carefully the coffin is put on the bonfire. Then they begin to pile more sticks on top of the wooden box. Now we can help.

The bonfire gets higher and higher until the coffin is covered.

Then Papa S. kisses his palm, faces it to the sky. We do the same.

"You are free!" he shouts. And I feel free. The coffin with my badness inside is hidden in the sticks and I want to dance with happiness.

Papa S. scrunches up some paper and pushes it in. He lights a match, presses it to the paper, and it catches, the tiny flame growing quickly. Papa S. walks around, lights another and another. The sticks crackle and hiss as the flames step onto them, growing bigger and bigger.

We have to move back. Ruby jumps from my arm and she and Sophie laugh and clap their hands. Bobby still holds on to me, the flames reflected in his eyes. Yellows, reds, greens, growing taller and hotter, burning the logs. I see flashes of the coffin, the flames beginning to eat at its wood. I watch the boiling hot logs. The wood of the coffin burning away.

There is a hand. In the bonfire, there is a hand. In the coffin, there is hair. It fizzes up and is gone. I see a face. I am screaming and pointing, but the fire is so loud.

"Jack!" I scream, and he looks where I point, but the flames are thick and he cannot see.

And now I can't. But it was there. A face, a hand. I know it. I must still be screaming because Kindred John has his arms around me. I am screaming and pointing, but Kindred John holds my arms down. He pulls my head into him, but I want to see. I need to be sure. I push myself away from him and the heat of the flames scratches my face as I step closer.

"Elizabeth!" I am screaming. Is it her?

They're pushing us inside and I'm running, through the front door, across the hall. The stairs are too many. I am at the top. My feet loud on the corridor and I crash open Elizabeth's door.

She's lying in her bed. She is here. She's not in the flames. I must not wake her. I run over to her, touch her face. She's real. She's alive.

"Pearl?"

I run out of her room and down to Nana Willow. When I rush in, I see the shape of her fragile bones sticking through the blanket. The steady rise and fall of her breathing.

Who was it? I want to scream. *If it wasn't you, Nana Willow, whose face was burning in the coffin?*

In the bathroom, my knees are on the cold floor. A feeling of sickness grinds in my belly, but nothing comes up. I breathe. Slowly, I breathe.

Did I imagine it? It was so quick.

My hair sticks to my neck with sweat, with the memory of the heat of the fire. The hand, its fingers melting.

Someone knocks on the door. "Pearl?" It's Heather. "I need to prepare morning meal. Will you sit with Elizabeth?"

My legs shake as I stand up. I brush my skirt straight with my hands, walk to the basin, turn on the tap, and splash cool water onto my face.

"Pearl?" Heather again.

"I'm coming," I say.

I open the door and walk back toward Elizabeth's room.

She has gotten worse. Her lips are so pale and her forehead is creased with pain.

"Do you need to drink?" I ask her. I'm still shaking as I sit on her bed. My stomach is trying to smooth itself as my mind seeks sense. Elizabeth shakes her head. She's breathing deeply, but the air sounds trapped. Her red and swollen fingers grip the sheet.

She opens her eyes and looks at me. "I'm scared, Pearl," she says.

"Don't be," I say. I take her hand in mine and kiss her palm. There was a hand in the fire. I want to tell Elizabeth, but I can't. "You have had a baby before." I try to smile. "You will be fine."

"It wasn't like this," Elizabeth says, then she breathes in sharply.

"Shall I rub some berry oil onto your stomach?"

"It doesn't help," she says, her words disappearing into wheezes of pain.

I'm frightened too. But I won't show it as I kiss her hand again. "Everything will be fine," I say.

Elizabeth closes her eyes.

CHAPTER THIRTY

●●●●●●●●●●●●●

I'm sitting on my bed, trying to brush my hair, but all I can hear is the bonfire. The crackle as the hair disappeared to the bone. I blink my eyes, but it is still here.

When Heather comes into the room, the fire disappears. "Papa S. has asked for you," she says.

"What do you mean?" I ask, standing up. But already I know. It can only mean one thing, that I am to be his new Companion.

"He wants to see you in his chamber." Heather's words are flat. Does she have a forbidden feeling of jealousy? Or is it more?

"Now?" I ask. Heather nods. I have waited so long for this moment. I should be happy. Yet a feeling of dread is weighing thick in my stomach. "But what shall I wear?"

Heather looks at me, standing in my nightdress. "You can just go like that," she says and then she walks from the room.

I look over at Kate, but she's busy straightening the sheets on her bed. Her back is to me and she doesn't turn around. It's Ruby who runs over to me and starts jumping on my mattress.

"You're going to be a Companion," she says, her voice almost a song.

"We don't know that," I tell her. I want to share her excitement, and I don't know why I can't.

"You will be," she says, her young arms stretching up to the ceiling.

To be Papa S.'s Companion. It's what we all dream of.

I reach for my dressing gown and put it on and slip my feet into my slippers. It seems wrong that I'm going into Papa S.'s chambers, yet I am only in my nightdress. I wish I could wear one of my skirts. My silk one, or the purple one that Rachel gave me.

I look at Kate as she pulls her nightdress over her head.

"Where do I go?" I ask. "Kate?"

"Go through the closed door at the end of the corridor," she answers. But she's avoiding my eyes.

"Really?" I want to reach out to her. Have her tell me that I'll be all right.

"You'll find the way from there." She looks at me for just a second, before she goes to the basin in the corner and picks up her toothbrush. So I walk out of the room without saying another word.

Jack is coming up the top of the stairs, just as I go down the corridor. He must have been working with the horses, as even from here I can smell them on him. He bounds up the last two stairs to get to me.

"Where are you off to?" he asks.

I feel suddenly awkward. "I'm going to see Papa S." I say the words slowly.

"What, now?" Jack looks confused.

"Yes." I look into his face and I see understanding creep into his eyes.

"Oh," he says. I nod at him and then I walk on, because I know how big this moment is, that I am about to become a Companion for the very first time and I don't want Jack to see the confusion in my eyes.

No one is in the corridor. The soft noises from the other rooms get left behind. I reach out to touch the wood-paneled wall. My fingers feel its smoothness and for a few seconds I close my eyes, so there's nothing else, just me and its ancient secrets. I breathe in the air that Papa S. must breathe as he walks down here every day.

Opening my eyes, the door is almost in front of me. The door that I have never been through. It's made of a wood so dark that it's almost black. Its handle is a carving of a lotus flower, painted and varnished so that it shines. I reach out and touch it, turn it, and slowly push it open.

The door makes no sound. No one would even know that I've walked through it as I close it behind me.

I'm in another short corridor. There is a small, round window that must look out over the fields, but all I see is black. I'm cold, so I pull my dressing gown tighter over me as I go to the door at the end.

I stand and wait. What shall I say to him? How shall I be? How will I become his Companion? Suddenly I feel an overwhelming fear and my feet are moving backward, but the door swings open. And Papa S. is standing here.

"Pearl," he says, in that voice I love. And I no longer understand anything, because he is Papa S. and surely he is everything? I go into his arms as he wraps them around me. And I try to feel safe. "Let's look at you," he says, stepping back. His skin looks older in this light, where the sun has touched it and turned it to wrinkles.

He has changed from his day clothes. Now he's wearing a long cloak that reaches to the floor. It is made of shimmering gold and I just stop myself from reaching out to touch it. His long, gray hair flows around his shoulders and it makes me think of a waterfall in the moonlight.

"Come in," he says, and he takes my hand. I am holding the hand of Papa S. Am I now his Companion? Was this really what I had been frightened of? I want to laugh with relief.

I pause just inside the room, because it's like nothing I have ever seen. The walls are covered with tapestries of sunsets and birds and flowers. I remember the long winter hours spent watching the women of the house with their colorful threads. I have sat, cross-legged, with a tapestry of my own, jabbing the needle through the holes, pricking my skin, but never enough to draw blood.

"Here," Papa S. says. He's still holding my hand as he leads me over to the corner. I recognize it instantly. The small tapestry I did of a robin a few years ago. I giggle as I remember my frustration at getting the lines of the beak straight. How worried I'd been that I might run out of the right red for his chest. At the bottom, my name is sewn in black thread.

Papa S. smiles. "It is very good."

There is carpet on the floor in here. It's not like the carpet in the sitting room, which is almost worn through to the wooden boards. Here, it is deep and soft. Papa S. sees me looking.

"It is the color of pearls," he says. "Why don't you take off your slippers, feel it on your feet?"

I look up at him and he nods, so I do as he says. It feels like I'm walking on clouds.

I gaze over at the heavy curtains that reach to the ground, closed tight against the dark outside. And in the middle of the room, there is the biggest bed I have ever seen. It has posts rising up from each of its corners and material sweeping down all around it.

"It's so peaceful in here, isn't it?" Papa S. asks.

"Yes," I say, my voice sounding like a child.

"Let us lie down," he says. And still holding his hand, I follow him to the bed.

We do not go under the covers. We lie, side by side, my hand in his. My heart is beating so loudly that I wonder if Papa S. can hear it. Finally, I am in his chamber. Finally, I see what it looks like. I am alone with Papa S. I might even be his Companion.

I feel Papa S. squeeze my hand. It doesn't feel like Elizabeth's, or Jack's, or Kate's. His hand feels bigger and bony. I hear his breathing next to me. I dare not look at him, so instead I look up at the purple velvet above my head. But why do I not feel happy? Why does this not feel right? The doubts that had been whispering to me are now scratching to be heard.

"Do you like it?" Papa S. eventually asks. His voice helps me remember how I feel about him. Reminds me that I am in the chamber of the most important person in my world.

"Very much," I say, and I look at him and he smiles at me and I feel good that I have said the right thing, that I have pleased him.

"My cloak is made of satin," he says.

"It looks like golden water," I reply.

"Do you want to touch it?" His eyes look into mine. But for some reason, now I don't want to. "Come," Papa S. says and he gently pulls my hand onto the cloak. He moves my fingers to stroke the material. He's right. I have never felt anything so soft. But underneath, I can feel the top of his leg and I don't want to be touching it.

I manage to pull my hand back. He looks at me and I'm scared that I have offended him.

"I've never felt anything so beautiful," I say and smile at him, and he smiles back.

I am in Papa S.'s bed. What would Kate say if she saw me now? She must have been here. Did it unsettle her? Did she want to run away? I breathe in, trying to find her smell under the layers of air, but there is nothing.

"Let me tell you something, Pearl," Papa S. says quietly. "Nature is such a powerful force. Sometimes she does things that we just don't understand. But she controls us all. Our days, our nights, the food we eat, the water we drink." He pauses, licks his lips slightly as if they are dry. "We must listen to Nature. Sometimes we must do things that we are unsure of. But they are always what Nature wants, they are always good." He looks at me and there's something in his eyes that makes me think I have displeased him. "Do you understand, Pearl?"

I nod, although I don't know what he means.

"Good." Then he unlocks his hand from mine, turns away from me and clicks off the light.

We are in darkness. Total darkness.

I lie here, but Papa S. does not say anything else. Am I to sleep like this?

In my memory, I see the coffin cracking open, the flames slipping through. Winding around the face, melting the skin.

I feel the walls closing in on me. The darkness is suffocating. I want to run away, but I cannot move, cannot breathe.

Papa S. touches my arm.

And I hate it.

"Who was in the coffin?" I ask, my voice a stranger in his bedroom. He pulls his arm back. "Who was it in the bonfire?"

I'm sitting up now, searching the dark for his face. But I can't see him. I can only hear him. A low, animal-like growl.

"Pearl," he says, his voice raw. "The poison has reached you. I must cleanse you."

He's moving toward me. The mattress creaks, his cloak rustles.

I jump from the bed, run blindly to where I hope the door is.

"Pearl!" His voice is strong and it tries to pull me back, but I will not go. My arms are outstretched in front of me. I can feel the wall, the rough texture of a tapestry. I move along until it is only wood under my fingers, so it must be the door. My hands go down and I feel the handle. Its lotus shape is jagged in my palm.

I hear Papa S. coming toward me. His hand is on my

shoulder. His fingers digging deep into my skin. "You will be punished," he whispers.

I turn the handle. And I go from him.

I am outside his chamber. I am free. The floor is cold and hard underneath my feet as I run. My slippers are back in his room, next to the bed of Papa S. But I can't go back there. I won't ever go back there.

I'm through the second door, scared of something I don't understand. The corridor is so quiet now. All of the lights have been turned out. There is no noise, so everyone must be sleeping. My bare feet sound sticky on the floor.

There's a figure standing near my room. I walk toward it, and as I get closer I can see that it's Heather.

"Are you all right, Pearl?" she asks.

I nod my head. I don't want her to ask any more. Heather reaches out to hug me. I thought she might be jealous that I've just been with Papa S., but there is something strange about her, something sad.

"Go to sleep now," she says. "It is a new day tomorrow." She turns from me and goes back to her room. I walk the few steps more to mine and gently push open the door. I can hear the sound of sleeping. I feel my way to my bed, lift the blanket up and climb underneath it. There is a shock of cold. I hope it will numb my thoughts.

CHAPTER THIRTY-ONE

......•••••••••••

Ellis is standing in the kitchen. He has been gone for ten days, but now he's back. I should stop myself, but I don't—I run to him and he puts one arm around me. His other, thick with a bandage, stays by his side.

"We missed you," I say. I pull back from him and we smile at each other. Now I can forget everything else. Ellis is here. He has come home.

"I missed you too," he says.

Kate comes in. She stops in the doorway and looks at him. "Hey, you," she says, her smile in her eyes. Envy sits in my stomach, but I won't let it stay. She walks up to him and I watch as she kisses his cheek.

I want to step between them, remind them I am here.

"So the hospital did heal you," Kate says.

"Of course," Ellis replies. And it's true. He is here, alive. Nothing bad seems to have happened to him there.

"Now, I need to get a drink for Elizabeth," Kate says and she turns away, opens the fridge door and gets out a bottle of milk.

"How is she?" Ellis asks.

"Not so good," Kate says quietly.

"Did they hurt you?" I ask.

Ellis half laughs. "No. The food was rubbish, though."

"Your hand?" I ask. Kate stops moving, then I hear the milk as she pours it into a glass. Ellis shrugs his shoulders, but they are stiff and his jaw is hard.

"I'm sorry," I say.

"Yeah," he replies.

"How did it happen?" I ask. "Were you too close to the machine?" He starts to shake his head, but suddenly the door opens and Linda rushes in. She is drying her hands on her apron.

"I wanted to come and see you," she says, almost to herself. And then she hugs him so tight.

"I'm OK, Mom," Ellis says awkwardly. He's not even smiling.

She reaches up and puts her palm softly on his cheek. "You came back," she whispers. Ellis doesn't say anything. "You belong here." And I see Linda smile for the first time in days. Then she's laughing, but as she hugs Ellis again, he keeps his arms by his sides.

When Kindred John walks in, something in the air changes. He goes over to Ellis, puts his hand on his shoulder. "How are you?" he asks.

Ellis moves away. "Never better," he replies. He's staring hard at Kindred John.

"You helped save him," Linda says. She goes toward Kindred John, kisses her palm, and places it on his chest. His cheeks sprinkle red, just a bit, as he puts his arms around her and she tucks her head into him, like a child. She looks safe, like nothing in the world can hurt her.

"I never want him to go near that hospital again," Linda says.

"They saved my life," Ellis says.

"If you hadn't lost all that blood, I never would have allowed it," Linda says.

"He's back now." Kindred John smiles at her. "That's all that matters."

Ellis walks out of the room. When he goes, something pulls me with him and I can't help but follow. Out in the hallway, when I reach out to him, it's his bandaged arm that I touch. A shiver goes through me. I try not to show it.

When he was at the hospital, I kept hoping that everyone had got it wrong. That Ellis would come back and play piano with Ruby on his lap. He'd take my hands in both of his.

The bandage is rough under my fingers.

Ellis pulls his arm away. "What work are you doing today?" he asks.

Looking in his eyes, I can see that he's changed. Maybe they have done something to him after all. "I'm in the orchard. With Kate and the children."

"I'll come with you," Ellis says, just as Kindred John comes out of the kitchen.

"Ready for work, Ellis?" he asks. Has he been listening to us?

"I'm going to help Pearl in the orchard," Ellis replies. I can hear the sound of plates being washed in the kitchen. The clatter of the clean dishes on the draining board.

"I'm not sure you should do that," Kindred John says. He's taller than Ellis and he's standing close to him.

"I can't work the engines with one hand," Ellis says. And then he turns his back on Kindred John and walks away. I hold my breath. In the kitchen, someone splashes water into the sink.

Kindred John looks at me. He doesn't move. He looks lost and I should reach out to him, but I don't.

"Be careful," he says to me. His words make me run out the door.

The children are already waiting by the baskets outside. Sophie and Ruby dance around Ellis, and he reaches out to touch their heads as they duck and weave away from him. Their laughter is all I can hear. Things will get better now. Autumn will bring its shorter days and we'll all curl up and listen to the stories that the Kindreds will tell. There's so much to look forward to.

"Right, who wants this one," I say, holding up the smallest basket. Bobby looks up from the tiny mound of sticks he's piling up.

"Is it an ants' house?" I ask him.

"It's a bonfire," he says.

The skin was melting.

"We had a bonfire," Sophie says to Ellis. She's pulling on his hand, jumping from foot to foot.

The memory of it makes me feel sick. At night, the burning face keeps me awake. It creeps into my bed. The hand holds my mouth so I can't scream.

I breathe in the fresh air. "Here," I say, and I put the basket in Sophie's arm to make her stop talking about the flames.

Kate comes out just as we're walking through the meadow. She runs to catch up with us, hitching her skirt so high that you can see her bare thighs. "How did you manage to avoid the work barn?" she asks when she reaches us.

"I told Kindred John I was coming here," Ellis replies.

Kate looks at him. "Race you, then," she laughs. She's running ahead with her basket in her hand. Ellis chases after her, easily overtaking her. I run too, but all I can see is the bandage on Ellis's arm. He can't hold the basket in that hand. He won't be able to pick the apples with both. I want to scream into the air. I want time to go back. Back to the sunshine days by the lake, where Ellis pushed through the water with both of his hands. Back to happiness.

There's so much fruit in the orchard. I kiss my palm and touch the giving trunk of a tree. I feel its heart within as I close my eyes. I must remember that Seed is good. That Nature protects us. That here, we are safe, we are free.

"This one?" Ellis breaks the spell. He's standing with Kate underneath some branches. She tucks her skirt into her underwear and begins to climb.

"Throw your basket up," she says to him when she's settled on a bough, her own basket hooked over a sturdy branch.

"No, I can do this," he says. And he follows her. He is slow, awkward, his arm pressing against the bark, where his hand should grip. I want to look away. I want to help him. I do neither. When he gets to her branch, Kate laughs at him.

"You took your time," she says. She puts her legs on either side of her branch, lies flat on her front and starts to pull herself along.

"You might have to hold me. I don't want to fall," she says, looking back over her shoulder at Ellis.

He reaches out his hand and puts it on her bare leg. She stops moving, stretches out her arms until her fingers are on an apple.

"Ready, Pearl?" she asks. I run underneath her, just as she unhooks the first apple and drops it from the tree. "Good catch," she laughs as I put it in the basket. There's another and another. And all the time, Ellis has his hand on her leg.

We pick apples until the baskets are full, almost too heavy to carry. The children have already struggled back to the house, so we can walk slowly, just us three.

The sky is white. Maybe it will rain.

"Pearl saw someone in the bonfire," Kate says. I look at her. She had asked why I had been screaming, and I had whispered it to her when we'd been collecting eggs. I hadn't expected her to tell.

"What do you mean?" Ellis asks. He doesn't laugh at me the way Kate did.

"Shapes in the flames," she says. I move my basket from one arm to the other and stare ahead at the house as we get closer.

"What sort of shapes?" Ellis asks.

"A hand, a face," Kate says, her voice whispering like the wind.

"I saw it, Kate," I say, the heat rushing up my neck. "Bobby believes me. He saw it too."

Ellis looks at me, as though he wants to say something, but he stops as Ruby comes running out of the kitchen door.

"Pearl," she's shouting. "Linda needs you to take cold flannels to Elizabeth." I put the basket on the grass and run into the house.

Elizabeth's room smells sickly sweet. She's twisting in her bed as Linda tries to hold a cloth on her swollen arms.

"Is the baby coming?" I ask. Cold water splashes from the bowl I'm carrying and falls onto the wooden floor.

"I don't know," Linda replies. She looks at me and I know she's frightened. Elizabeth's blonde hair is spread in wet strips across the pillow. She's grinding her teeth, rocking her head from side to side. I put the bowl on the table next to the flowers Jack picked this morning, before I squeeze a flannel and press it onto her forehead.

"I'm here, Elizabeth," I whisper close to her.

"Pearl?" she says, but she doesn't open her eyes.

"Yes," I say. "I'm here." The cold flannel on her skin seems to calm her. I hold it there.

"Help me," Elizabeth says, her words slicing through her teeth. She opens her eyes and tries to touch me with her hand.

"What can we do?" I ask Linda as she rinses her cloth.

"This will help keep her temperature down. And we have to try to get her to eat. She needs strength to deliver the baby."

Elizabeth moans. She's twisting her body again, moving onto her side. Her hands grip the pillow.

I feel angry, suddenly. Because this baby is doing this to her.

I want the baby to disappear, to shrivel up to nothing. Leave Elizabeth's skin alone, let her run, cook, and eat with us again.

Elizabeth's swollen fingers clutch at her pillow. Her hair sweeps around her neck like white ivy. She's whispering, over and over.

"Hurry," she says. It's her only word. "Hurry."

CHAPTER THIRTY-TWO

·······•••••••········

In this murky day, where everything seems wrong, Papa S. comes to us. He has gathered us under the afternoon sky, where we sit at the edge of the meadow in the creeping cold. I had wanted to stay with Elizabeth, but he wouldn't allow it. She was asleep when I left her, but still I don't like to think of her alone upstairs.

Papa S. turns and looks at all of us. One at a time. I wait for his eyes to meet mine. He has not spoken to me since my time in his chamber, and I am waiting for his anger. But he is smiling. Has he forgotten that I ran from him? That he wants to punish me? Fear makes me want to run away now, but Papa S. holds me with his invisible thread.

He will go first, as he always does. Even the children do not move. They barely breathe. Maybe they're afraid, as I used to be.

We all watch as Papa S. picks up the knife, presses it to his skin. The blade cuts, and there is the sparkle of red on his palm. He raises his hand to Heather's lips and she takes his blood into her. Her eyes are closed. He has chosen her. This only happens once a year and he has chosen her.

Rachel sits on the other side of Papa S. He passes her the knife and we see her skin as she pushes it into her palm. She does not flinch as the blood oozes out and she holds her hand up to Papa S.'s waiting lips.

Bobby takes the knife. We watch as he leans it into his tiny palm. His skin doesn't break. He presses hard again, his eyes a mixture of panic and fear.

Kindred Smith walks across the circle. He pushes the knife gently into Bobby's palm until his blood eases out. Bobby has a proud little look on his face as he raises his hand to Sophie. She looks bewildered.

"Go on," Linda says encouragingly. Sophie bobs her head in quickly, her lips wrinkling with disgust as she feels Bobby's blood on her mouth.

Then Bobby passes the knife to Sophie.

"I don't want to," I hear her whisper.

"You have to," Linda says. Sophie's lip trembles. She's going to cry in front of Papa S. Someone is moving. It's Ellis. He's trying to stand up, but Kate is holding him back, her hand on his bandaged arm. He stays sitting, but his fist is clenched and he glares straight ahead.

We are all watching Sophie, who still has the knife in her hand. Perhaps Papa S. will tell her that she won't have to do it, that she's too young, too new? But he doesn't say a word. His smile has disappeared and he's staring at her. I want him to comfort her, but he doesn't.

Linda takes the knife and holds her daughter's little wrist. "It won't hurt," Linda tells her softly, but Sophie screams as the blade is pushed into her palm. Then Linda is licking her blood. "See, it is done. All over." And Sophie becomes silent.

When it's Ruby's turn, Kindred John helps her. She winces, but doesn't cry. The knife is passed to Ellis, but he passes it on.

"I shall help you," Kindred Smith says, coming toward him.

"No. I won't be doing it," Ellis says, staring hard at Kindred Smith. No one else moves. Then Kate, too, passes the knife to Jack. What is she doing? We've done this many times. It's something we love. Isn't it? It binds our family, holds us to each other. I cannot look at Papa S. But I can hear the angered breathing of Kindred John beside me.

Jack hesitates. Surely Kate will change her mind? But she doesn't. So he cuts himself. He holds his palm up to Kate, but she looks at him and gently shakes her head. Jack blushes as he looks down at the blood waiting in his palm, but then he passes the knife to me.

My left hand is on my lap, palm facing toward the sun. Slowly I press the blade into my skin. It won't cut through, so I push down harder. There is a pain, but I force it away. I feel my skin pop as the knife cuts it and my blood breaks free. Just a bubble at first, so

I slice a tiny bit more until there is a little pool of red.

Jack is next to me. I raise my palm to his lips. His eyes don't leave mine as he takes my blood in his mouth. We are one and nothing will ever break us.

I turn to Kindred John sitting next to me. He cuts his hand and holds my head as I bend my lips to his palm. The taste of his blood shocks me, but I won't show it. The rusty metal hidden in its liquid red. It feels wrong. For the first time ever, it feels wrong.

We usually now hold hands, this circle of us. Our family. But instead, Papa S. makes a low, growl-like noise and stands up suddenly.

"So this is what going back to the Outside has done to you!" His words storm toward Ellis. "The doctors, they have dripped poison into your blood."

Ellis does not look away from him. Papa S. drops his head back violently. "Punish them," he screams to the sky. His face is contorted by anger, his eyes wide and cold. He's not the Papa S. I know. "Punish them!" he shouts again, his words like steel in my stomach.

Please, no, I say in my mind. *Please, Nature, I beg you, no.*

⤜⟶⟵⤛

Bobby takes my hand as we walk back toward the house. When he looks at me, I see a strangeness in his eyes.

"The woman has gone," he whispers to me.

"What woman?" I ask.

"The woman behind the window," he tells me.

"Who?"

"She lived in the room. Now she has gone."

"Which room?" I ask. Bobby watches the backs of everyone as they scatter toward Seed. With no one looking, he points toward the tiny window sunk into the roof of the house. Then he looks at me as if I should understand.

"There's no one there," I tell him.

"There was. She lived there," Bobby says quickly.

I smile at him. "You must have seen the sun planting shadows."

"No," he says angrily. "She was there. Now she's gone."

"Well, if she's no longer there, then you don't need to worry." I smile at him again, but I look up at the window.

"But where has she gone?" Bobby asks.

"Come on," I say. "They're already starting work in the fields." I point to Kate as she comes out of the back door, a basket in each hand.

I start to walk and Bobby follows me. He's by my side, staring intently at the window in the roof. I glance up again, but there's no one there. There is no trick of the light, no shadow.

But I look down quickly. Somewhere, I feel that Papa S. is watching and I don't want him to see.

CHAPTER THIRTY-THREE

·········●●●·········

I stay with Elizabeth through the night. The pain ebbed away enough for her to eat, just a bit. But her whole body seems on fire. Even through the sheet, the skin on her belly burns. But still she says that the baby is not coming yet. Linda dripped hemlock juice into Elizabeth's mouth and Heather wrapped her feet in damp dock leaves, but nothing helps the swelling. Nothing is working.

The music sweeps up through the cracks in the floor. The notes crash against each other. Elizabeth wakes and she smiles. I haven't seen her eyes alive for days, but the sound of the piano brings magic. Surely it is Ellis. It is only with one hand, but he can still play.

"Go to him," Elizabeth says. She reaches out and touches my face. I don't want to leave her, but she's calm and Ellis is playing music again.

"I'll send Heather to you," I say as I kiss her on her cheek.

I follow the notes. They come to greet me on the stairs and hold my hand as I go down. The music takes me across the hall and pushes open the day room's door.

Ellis is sitting at the piano. His back is to me. Quietly, I walk through the furious sound. He doesn't stop. His hair has fallen into his eyes, his lips are slightly parted, as if he is about to speak. The music isn't as full, but it still peaks and swells and fills the room as it stamps to every corner and throws its strength into the air. I sit down next to him and put my arm across his waist.

He has come home to us.

"It's amazing to hear you play."

Suddenly he smashes his fist onto the notes. His body is shaking. He reaches for the piano lid and slams it down. I try to keep my arm round him, but he is frightening me. I have seen anger, but this is coming from somewhere else.

"He won't get away with it," he says, turning to me with furious eyes.

"Who?" I ask. "Did they do something to you at the hospital?"

Ellis moves away. He's shaking his head at me. "Can you really not see it, Pearl? Or do you just not want to look?" he says quietly.

"See what? Ellis, you're scaring me. What have they done to you?"

He grips my arm and is staring into my eyes. He's so close that I can feel his breath on my cheeks. I don't scream. I want him to let go. But I want him to kiss me.

He raises his bandaged arm. "This wasn't an accident, Pearl," he says. He doesn't look away from me.

"What do you mean?" I ask. But somewhere, deep inside me, I hear a flicker of truth that I must already know.

"Your precious Kindred John," Ellis says.

"He wouldn't have," I say.

"Wouldn't he?"

"But why?"

"To warn me. Because I know the truth," he says quietly. "I know what he's like. I know that everything here is based on lies. And power. And fear." Ellis reaches out for me and I let him take my hand. The feeling of his skin on mine spreads through me. "Kindred John threatened me, Pearl. He said that if I told the doctors that we lived here and about what he'd done, then he'd hurt my mom. And Sophie." I try to pull my hand away, but he won't let me. "And now I know what he's really capable of."

"You're lying."

"It's Papa S. who's the liar. He hasn't been chosen by Nature. He's just a normal man, in stupid clothes, who gets his kicks out of controlling you all."

I try to put my hands over my ears, but Ellis moves his arm and pushes them back. His bandage rubs against my skin.

"Listen to me, Pearl. The world outside isn't such a bad place. Papa S. is making it up to force you to stay here."

"No one is forcing me," I say, moving my head roughly from his hand.

Ellis stares at me. There is fury in his eyes, but something else too. Then he stands up from me. He kicks the wall hard and storms out of the room.

Your precious Kindred John. Those were Ellis's words.

It wasn't an accident.

CHAPTER THIRTY-FOUR

············●●●············

"Let's go and watch the sunset at the dip," Kate says. We've finished the washing and Jack is helping us put away the plates.

"Can I come too?" Sophie asks. She's sitting on Ellis's lap at the table. They're making a toy for Elizabeth's baby, weaving thread in and out of sticks.

"Not this time," Ellis says. "It's late. You should be thinking about sleep."

"I need to give this to Elizabeth first," she says. She's up and out of the door before Ellis can argue.

"The dip," Ellis says. "I haven't been there since I came back." He stands up, stretches his arms above his head. The sight of his bandage makes my thoughts spin. Ellis's words about Kindred John, about Papa S., are in me now and I can't get rid of them.

"Let's go now then, before anyone can stop us," Kate says. I finish wiping the side and put down the cloth. Jack looks hesitant.

"Come on then," I say and I reach for his hand. I need things to be normal again. I want to forget.

So together we all go quietly out of the kitchen door. We don't look back as we walk across the fields.

Jack is taller again. I notice it when we are side by side. His hand feels strong in mine and he seems to steady me. So much is different now, but just looking at him pulls me back to a place where I am happy.

I breathe in the dampening air. Watch a buzzard as it lazily circles above us.

"This way," Kate says. We follow her down the side of the field to the raspberry bushes. They're spotted with ready fruit and Kate reaches out to pick one. She closes her eyes as she puts it in her mouth.

"Kate," I whisper. "It's not picking time now."

"They won't know." She smiles. She takes another and passes it to me. I look behind us. We are hidden from the house. The raspberry is soft in my fingers.

Everything here is based on lies. On power.

Ellis and Jack watch as I put the raspberry between my teeth. It's like velvet on my tongue.

Kate takes the scarf from her head and we start to fill it with the pink berries. When it's full, she gathers its corners and we walk together toward the dip.

We go around the edge of the forest, to the field at the back. You can never see it from here, but as you get closer, the colors seem to change. Kate runs ahead and I know when she reaches it, because she suddenly disappears over the edge.

We get to the rim of the dip, peer in, and Kate is already at the bottom, lying on her back and looking up at us. We run, almost falling, to join her. The sky is striking. The brightest blue melting into flames of orange and red.

"It's amazing," Ellis says. Nature is covering us with colors of fire.

I push away the burning hair, the melting flesh. Papa S.'s anger when I asked him.

"It's cold," Kate says. She sits up and opens the corners of her scarf. The pile of raspberries seems so small here. Kate picks one up, and without a word she reaches over and puts it into Jack's mouth.

Ellis interrupts the silence. "How are the engines?"

It's getting darker, but I can still see the red in Jack's teeth. "Same as always." He laughs.

"Still making the magic ones?" Ellis asks.

Jack nods. "Trying to," he says. I look for doubt in him, but I don't see any.

Ellis shakes his head and looks at me. Is that all lies too? The hours that Jack has spent rubbing the oil into the engines, the oil that Kindred John says cures pollution? My head aches with the thought of it. I feel unsteady, as if the earth beneath me is rocking and swaying. And I want it all to stop.

I want the doubt to go away. I want only to know the beauty of Seed. I want to believe in magic engines. And to hear Ellis playing piano with both of his hands.

I will close my eyes and when I open them I'll be in the kitchen, looking out the window, and it will be daylight outside and Linda, Ellis, and Sophie will be in their car, coming up the driveway for the very first time.

But I am still in the dip.

The sun falls lower still. It's dragging the blue with it, sucking it down.

"Don't you ever want to leave, Jack?" Ellis asks. Jack doesn't answer.

"I've thought about it," Kate says. Somewhere a fox cries.

"Don't, Kate," I say. "Don't think like that."

"But nothing's right anymore," she says quietly.

"That's not true."

"Tell me then, Pearl," Ellis says sharply. He sits up and even in the gloom I can see anger trickling over him. "What's right about this place?" He tries to take my hand, but I pull it roughly away. "You see, you can't think of anything."

"That's not true."

Suddenly Ellis stands up. I think he's going to say something else, but he just starts to climb up the side of the dip and within seconds he is gone. I want to reach up, pull him back to me. What is it that stops me?

"Thanks, Pearl," Kate says. As she picks up her scarf, the raspberries spill out of it. It's easy for her to run up the grass and disappear.

Jack and I are silent. We watch as the black sky overtakes everything. As the moon silently spreads her wings.

"*Do* you ever want to leave, Jack?" My words are so quiet that I hardly know them myself.

He won't look at me. "Sometimes," he replies.

"Why?" I ask.

"I don't know. Just sometimes . . ."

I don't want to speak anymore, but I do. "Ellis says that it wasn't an accident. His hand."

I feel Jack nod beside me. "I know," he says. "But it's not true. The shock is making him remember it wrong."

"Do you really believe that?"

"I don't know," Jack says quietly. Then he's standing up. "Come on."

We get up and he keeps hold of my hand as we clamber up the edges of the dip. At the top, the field is almost silver.

"We can never escape its beauty," I say.

"I don't want to," Jack answers as we carefully walk back to the house.

It feels like I have a ball of wool inside my head, wound tightly with all my thoughts mixed in. I want to find the end, pull it to unravel them all. But I search and it's not there. And Papa S. and Kindred John and all of Ellis's words stay locked together.

Jack steadies me as we walk. Keeps hold of my hand as we push open the kitchen door. He doesn't let go when we see Linda crying by the sink.

CHAPTER THIRTY-FIVE

......•••••●•••••••...

"What's wrong?" I ask. Linda turns to look at me. She doesn't even try to stop the tears.

I run before she can answer.

Elizabeth is in her bed. The skin on her face is stretched and swollen and her eyes are white with fear. I hardly recognize her as my own. Heather is holding dried petals to her forehead.

"What's wrong?" I ask.

"She's fine," says Heather, but she won't look at me.

"No," Elizabeth says through her blackening breath. "No."

I step forward to her and Heather moves away. A petal falls from her fingers and becomes caught in Elizabeth's sweat-drenched hair.

"Is it worse?" I ask.

Elizabeth grabs my hand. "Yes," she says.

"I'll get some fresh water," Heather says. She gathers the flannels into the bowl and she leaves Elizabeth and me alone.

"You must help us," Elizabeth says. As she breathes, her belly heaves under the sheet.

"Heather is bringing cold water. It will make you feel better," I say.

"No," Elizabeth says. She grips my hand. "Listen to me, Pearl. It wasn't like this before." She twists her head away from me, her teeth tight, her neck red.

"Shh," I say. "The baby will come soon." But there is fear in the room, tapping at me, waiting to be let in.

"Pearl. I will die. My baby will die."

No. She can't mean it. She is having a baby. Soon, she will hold our baby in her arms. But she is crying. Elizabeth is crying.

"You must get me help, Pearl. Please. I don't want this to be my time."

"How? Where is help?"

Elizabeth's chest seems to crackle with her breath. "Please, help me." She closes her eyes tight with pain.

I know that I have to get her a doctor. The doctors helped Ellis. They were not bad, they saved his life. Papa S. is wrong, Nature cannot do everything.

The doctors dripped poison into his blood.

No. No, Ellis is good.

"Please," Elizabeth whispers.

I lean to kiss her on her forehead, just as Heather comes back into the room, carrying a bowl of clear water.

I walk from the room and hurry down the stairs. I go out of

the front door and slip into the night.

No one follows me. No one calls after me, so I run. I don't know what I have to do, but I won't let Elizabeth die. I won't let her baby die. I run across the gravel toward the trees at the edge of the driveway, expecting to feel a hand on my shoulder. Waiting for Papa S. to step out from the darkness. But he doesn't come.

I reach the trees. I won't stop. I run in the blackness, toward the gate at the start of the driveway and the beginning of the Outside.

And I'm on the road. It's dark. Which way will I go? They are both the same. They are both empty, black holes. I choose, because I have to and I cannot stop, I must not stop.

The road is hard and loud under my feet. There is no breathing behind me, no hand around my waist.

The lights of a car. They are getting brighter, coming closer and I shield my eyes. It drives past me. But it stops. It is coming backward, toward me. I want to keep running, but the car is quicker than me and it catches up.

There is a man and a woman inside. The window moves down.

"Are you all right?" the woman asks. The man peers around her, looks up at me.

"Elizabeth is dying," I say, trying to calm my breath.

She looks over at the man. "Where is she?" he asks.

"In our home," I say. "She needs help. She's dying." The truth of the words whip around me.

The man takes one of those small telephones from his pocket. "I'll phone an ambulance," he says.

The woman reaches out to me, but I step back. I want to be swallowed by the darkness behind me. "It'll be OK," she tells me.

The man is talking into the phone. "What's wrong with her?" he asks me.

"She's having a baby," I say.

The woman smiles, lets out a relieved breath. "She'll be fine," she says.

"No. She's dying," I say.

The man smiles as he talks into the phone. "What's your address?" he asks me.

"What do you mean?" I ask.

"Your house, where is it?" he asks.

I point down the road. You can just see our gate in the darkness. "Seed. Our home is Seed."

The man talks into the phone again and the woman watches him. Then he puts it back into his pocket. "The ambulance won't be long," he says. I stare at him. "The doctors will come and help with the baby."

The doctors will come to Seed. Is that really what Elizabeth wanted?

"She'll be fine now," the woman tells me gently. "We can drive you back."

"How long will it be?" I ask. I can feel the walls of the Forgiveness Room crushing my bones. Already I can't breathe.

"Five, ten minutes?" the woman says.

I run from them. Back along the road, their car lights framing the way.

I'm sorry, I silently scream to Papa S.

I should run away. Run away now.

I turn into our driveway. I hear the car hesitate behind me and I know they watch me. But the strangers drive away as I race back toward our home.

Linda and Heather are arguing in the kitchen. "She needs a doctor," I hear Linda say, before I run up the stairs.

Elizabeth is alone. She's not moving, but she is breathing. Thin, rattling breaths. I go to her and she looks at me.

"Someone is coming to help," I tell her. She tries to move, so I reach for her hand. Her breathing is slow.

"Is the baby coming?" I ask.

She looks at me and she is crying. "Pearl," she whispers. It's so quiet that I have to move close to her. She smells of summer flowers. "I love you, Pearl."

"Help is coming," I say.

"I am not your mother," Elizabeth says.

My mind stops. My world stops.

"What do you mean?" I ask.

Her breathing is a whisper from her body. "Sylvie was your mother."

"Sylvie?" I am crying now. I feel her fingers loosen in mine. "Elizabeth, I'm scared. Don't leave us. It isn't your time."

She is closing her eyes. She's drifting away. "Sylvie was my sister," she says.

But I'm screaming. Screaming for Heather. Screaming for Linda. Screaming for help to come as Elizabeth's breaths fade away.

I hear the sound coming up the driveway. The wailing van, with blue lights flashing up through the window.

"They're here, Elizabeth," I say to her. But I know her hand can no longer feel mine.

I hear them come up the stairs. A man and a woman from the Outside are in Elizabeth's bedroom. Their clothes are green. They move me away. They are touching Elizabeth's neck. Her swollen hands. The man has a bag and he's opening it.

Linda is here. Her arms are around me. Something is in the man's hands. He holds it onto Elizabeth's chest. I watch as her body jolts upward. They will hurt the baby. I try to step forward, but Linda holds me and she tries to cover my face, just as I see him pushing onto Elizabeth's chest again.

The sound of people running up the stairs. Jack, Kate, Ellis are in the room. They stare at Elizabeth, but I can't look at her. Instead I see Kate put her hand up to her mouth.

I hear the thud of those things on Elizabeth's chest. The sound of her body breaking free from the bed again and again. Until nothing.

Nothing.

Now that they've stopped hurting her, I will look. Her head is bent back. The pillow has fallen on the floor. Her hair is across her face, but no one brushes it away. They're talking about the baby. They will take Elizabeth's body, try to save the baby.

But I know the baby has gone too.

I am screaming so loudly that I can't hear anymore.

CHAPTER THIRTY-SIX

·············•●•·············

They are taking Elizabeth. The man and the woman from the Outside are taking Elizabeth and we are letting them. We are all standing and watching and letting them take her away.

She's gone. *You're too late,* I want to scream at them. *Leave her with us. Give us back our baby.*

Linda holds me as we watch them take her down the stairs. Papa S. is at the bottom, standing by the open front door. His eyes are wide, his mouth is silent.

Linda lets go of me and she runs after Elizabeth. But Papa S. puts out his arm. Papa S. *Is it your fault? All your ideas about doctors and the Outside.*

I breathe. Try to swallow a hideous anger that is beginning to curdle my blood. But my love for Elizabeth is too strong. I am walking up to Papa S. I am so close that his beard brushes against me.

"This is your fault," I shout at him. I cannot stop. "You let Elizabeth die."

I notice nothing but his hand, holding back my arms. Then he pushes me hard and I stumble as he walks away. He doesn't see what we do. That Kindred John is talking to the man and the woman and letting them put Elizabeth into their white van.

The flashes of blue start again. They are going. They are taking Elizabeth and her baby and we just stand and watch as they go down the driveway and disappear.

Bobby has woken. He's standing at the top of the stairs and he walks down to me, his bare little feet hardly making a sound. Wordlessly, I sit, and Bobby curls onto my lap.

"Why have they taken Elizabeth?" he whispers to me. I cannot answer him. "What about the baby?"

"I think Nature has taken the baby," I say.

Nature? We could have stopped it.

"Why?" he asks.

I thought I'd know, but I don't. How can it have been the baby's time, when it had not yet stepped a foot on the Earth?

"Because that is Nature's plan," I say. But my words feel hollow.

"When will she give them back?" Bobby asks.

Never. They are never coming back.

It is a physical pain I feel. My heart is cut. It hurts to breathe. We cannot be happy without Elizabeth.

I am not your mother, Pearl.

Kate comes from the kitchen. She puts her arms around Bobby and me. Her tears are wet against my cheek.

—————————⟶——⟵—————————

Kate and I have watched the dark outside the window change into a morning of gray light. Bobby is still sleeping on my lap. He is not my brother.

Kindred Smith walks in. His boots seem too heavy and his face no longer looks the same. He shakes his head and I know now, for definite, that the baby is with Elizabeth, will always be with Elizabeth.

"It was a boy," Kindred Smith says, his voice low, and he looks like he wants to say more but he walks past us. We listen to him going wearily up the stairs.

A boy. I want to count his fingers, count his toes. I want to see him kick his feet. I want to hear him laugh, I want to hear him cry.

I want to see Elizabeth. To hold her hand, to hear her voice, to stand with her in the meadow, weave flowers into her hair. Anger takes root in my bones.

Kate reaches up and silently brushes away the tears on my cheek. But I don't care who sees them.

"We have to make morning meal," Heather says. She's standing in front of us, her arms by her side, her hair falling uselessly over her shoulder. Bobby opens his eyes. He looks confused, as he finds his mouth with his thumb and nestles into me again.

I realize that I am aching. I've not moved for hours. My bones and my muscles hurt. My neck is stiff. My arm numb from holding Bobby.

"I need some help for morning meal," Heather says again.

"We heard you," Kate snaps at her. Elizabeth would hate this.

"Come on, Bobby," I say quietly to him. And I move, so that he has to sit up and peel himself away from me. "Go and wake the others. You can tidy your room before we eat." Slowly, he stands and walks up the stairs. Already I miss his warmth.

Elizabeth's room. Her sweat on the sheets.

I let her die.

Papa S. let her die.

The pain reaches into me and squeezes me and I have to blink and breathe, blink and breathe.

Kate gets up and reaches out her hand for me. When she hugs me, she's crying again. "I don't think I can do this," she says.

"You can," I say. But I don't know how. "We have to."

Then we follow where Heather went, into the kitchen, because there is nothing else we can do.

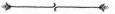

We've finished preparing morning meal and are sitting at the table, silent. Jack's head is bent forward, as though it is too heavy to hold. Ellis's eyes are filled with fury.

Papa S. walks into the dining room, with Rachel by his side. I should be terrified that I shouted at him, but I'm not.

I look at his face, at his eyes. The mole on his cheek and the dry hair of his beard. *Is Ellis right? Are you just a normal man?*

Rachel is holding a flower to her lips, but I don't like it there. Elizabeth is gone, yet Rachel is walking in as though nothing has changed. Anger fuses in me, but it's so mixed with grief that I find it hard to know it.

Papa S. kisses his palm and faces it to the sky outside the window. I do the same, but I can't look there, because I want to reach up into Nature's endless blue and rip it into little shreds. And then burn it.

Ruby sits by my side. Her thin arms rest in her lap. She's looking at Papa S. and I know that she doesn't understand why Elizabeth has gone.

I'm struggling to eat the porridge. It is sticking in my throat and I can't swallow.

"It is my fault," Linda starts as a whisper. "I knew she was ill. She died because of me."

"Shh, now," Kindred Smith says. "You did the right thing." He reaches over to take her hand.

She looks up at him. "I should have got her help."

Suddenly Papa S. slams his fist onto the table. "It is Nature's way," he shouts, and he stares at Linda with a look I never want to see again.

There is silence.

———————

The air in the Eagle Room is thick with grief. We have been told that this was the way it was meant to be. But how can we live without Elizabeth, without the baby we were promised?

Jack holds my hand, but he hasn't said a word, not one word. Papa S. comes in. He is carrying a stick wound with leaves. He steps into the middle of our circle and when he looks at us, his face is gentle, his eyes warm. But I feel cold.

"We must feel hope," he says. "We must feel happiness. Because Elizabeth can now travel on the wind, fly to the sun. She will grow in the flowers, in the fruits, in the fields." He smiles. "We may no longer be able to see the shape she had on earth, but you can still feel her warmth, her voice, her laughter in the trees."

I look over at Ellis. His face holds hard as a stone. He stares at the wall, won't look at Papa S.

"The pain we all feel is rooted in love," says Papa S. "And we must thank Elizabeth. Thank her for all that she gave us." Papa S. kisses his palm and raises it up. "Thank you, Elizabeth," he says. "Thank you."

We kiss our palms. "Thank you, Elizabeth," we say. But it hurts. It doesn't feel right, because I just want her here with me. "Thank you." Louder, over and over. "Thank you," we call. Papa S. stands in the middle of us all, both hands raised, his arms striking the air. "Thank you."

I see a figure move. It's Ellis standing up, walking from the circle, leaving the room.

Kate follows him.

CHAPTER THIRTY-SEVEN

•••••••••●•••••••••

We stand around the hole dug in the forest. The soil is dark. They lower the coffin, with Elizabeth and her baby, into the ground. The Kindreds and Jack hold the rope, letting it slip slowly through their fingers. Bit by bit, the coffin goes down. I don't want to think what is in it. I cannot think of the baby curled with Elizabeth.

They throw the rope down into the hole and it thuds onto the wood. The memory of the coffin in the fire grasps at me, but I have to move it into blackness or I won't be able to breathe.

Papa S. stands in front of us. He's smiling as he kisses his palm and points it toward the deep, black hole. I cannot do the same, when all I want is for Elizabeth to climb out and stand with me and hold my hand.

They're pushing the soil over the coffin. It is trickling down and locking her in.

I look toward the sky.

They fill the hole.

"Thank you," I whisper under my breath.

I love you, I hear her reply.

Kate and I stay, standing at the mound of earth. One by one the others have left us, but I can't leave, not yet.

Kate touches my arm and I turn to her. Grief sits in her eyes, in her mouth. "We have to go," she says to me.

"You can," I reply. "I want to stay here, just a bit longer."

"No," she says. "We must leave Seed."

Leave Seed?

"It's bad here," Kate says. She's looking at the mound of earth that holds Elizabeth and our baby to the ground. "I want to go."

"We'll be all right." I'm trying to convince myself.

Kate looks at me. "This place isn't what you think," she says.

Then she's running away through the trees, back toward the house.

I look once more at the dark earth.

Everything here is based on lies. And fear.

I try to straighten my thoughts as I look at the leaves twisted into the mud. But nothing is right. We let Elizabeth die. And Kate doesn't want to live here anymore. Is there a part of me, somewhere, that wants to run away too? Looking around me, the trees whisper their reply.

Slowly I walk away, and leave Elizabeth and her baby there.

CHAPTER THIRTY-EIGHT

........●..........

"Elizabeth wasn't my mother," I say. The days she has been gone are hollow circles, and I can't get her back.

"How do you know?" Kate asks. She stands up, a fresh egg in her hand.

"Elizabeth told me."

"Are you sure?" Kate looks at me and I nod my head. "Then it must be true." She bends down again, sweeps her hand over the straw.

I wait. She has more she wants to say. She finds a new egg, brushes it clean, and puts it in the basket.

"Was I her real daughter?" Kate asks. The question shocks me. I have never, ever thought that Kate might be Elizabeth's daughter. It had always been me. "Pearl?"

"I don't know," I say quietly. "She didn't say." I push my hand into the straw and it scratches me.

"I always hoped I was," Kate says, sitting down. "But I always thought it was you." I sit next to her and she takes my hand. "I really miss her, Pearl," she whispers. "Papa S. says she is everywhere, but I can't see her anywhere."

When she looks at me, her eyes are wide, like a child. "I feel like I've lost her, but I don't know where to look." She roughly wipes away her tears. "And I don't care about my stupid life spirit. I don't believe in it anyway."

"Shh," I say, looking quickly around the barn. "He'll make you go into the Forgiveness Room again."

"I'm not scared of that." But she's crying so much now that her body is shaking, her face is red and wet. The noise of her tears echoes up to the ceiling and out the open door. I put my arms around her, but she doesn't stop. Maybe she doesn't need to.

There's the noise of someone coming in, walking closer, standing in front of us. I won't look up. *Is it you, Papa S.? How will you punish Kate now, if your Forgiveness Room doesn't work? Are you going to punish me?*

There is a hand on my shoulder.

"It's shit, isn't it?" It's Ellis.

I'm so relieved that I throw my arms around him as he sits down. My kiss is on his neck and the feel of his skin makes me pull away. Kate has curled her head into her knees and Ellis reaches for her. He lets her cry and there's no fear in his eyes.

Slowly, Kate is quiet.

"I'll get you out of here," Ellis whispers.

Kate looks at me. I can tell by her eyes that she has talked about this with Ellis before. "You'll come too," she whispers, looking at me. "And Jack."

"But this is our home, Kate."

"I won't go without you," Kate says to me. "I'm not leaving you here."

"We've got it planned," Ellis says. He comes closer to me, as if the air will take his secrets. "We'll be fine, I promise."

"I want to be free, Pearl," Kate says, looking up at me.

"You are free," I say. "You have everything here."

But nothing I'm saying feels right. We don't have everything, because Elizabeth has gone. Papa S. let her die.

"I need to show you something," Ellis says.

"What?"

"Come with me," he says and he stands up, tall against me.

"I don't want to," I say.

"Please," he says. I see the bandage on his arm and I know I must follow him. He turns to Kate. "We need you to cover for us," he tells her, and quietly she gets up too.

We walk into the house, through the coldness of the hall, until we're standing outside the Forgiveness Room.

"Why are we here?" I ask, looking around. Ellis ignores me and he's pushing open the door.

"No," I say.

"You've got to see," Kate tells me. Her hand is gentle on my back, but she's pushing me into the room. She stays on the outside, closing the door behind us. It is just me and Ellis with the red door in front of us.

"This is where he put my mom because she helped Elizabeth," he says. "And I know you've been in here too." Ellis starts to walk around the edge of the wall.

"I don't want to be in here," I whisper to him.

He looks back over his shoulder. "I have to show you," he says.

My breath is short and I need to run away. Will Papa S. be waiting, standing quietly? But still I follow Ellis.

Around the corner, there's a tape recorder on the floor. Ellis steps toward it, but then stops and looks at me. Then he pushes against the wall and it starts to move. He's pushing it forward, making the Forgiveness Room inside it smaller and smaller.

"It was Papa S.," he says. "Nature wasn't crushing you, it was Papa S."

No. No. He's got it wrong.

But Ellis is pushing the walls and they're going in.

"Nature could still have moved them," I say. But I know I don't believe it.

"Look," Ellis says and he steps back toward the tape recorder. He kneels down and presses one of the buttons. Instantly the woman's screams crush into my head. I cover my ears, until Ellis presses another button and they stop.

"Did Papa S. tell you that these screams came from your bones?" Ellis asks me. I don't reply. He knows the answer. "It's just a tape. He just pressed Play."

"But why?" I ask.

"Because he wants to control you. And if you're frightened, you'll do whatever he tells you. And he was using terror to control her too. Whoever she was, Pearl, she was terrified."

I stare at Ellis. I don't want to ask, but I know I have to. Because her screams were real. She was begging them to stop.

"Who is she?"

"I don't know." Ellis shakes his head. The coffin in the fire crackles in my mind. "But there's more." He presses the Forward button and there's a whirring sound. Then it's Papa S.'s voice I hear, coming from the tape recorder.

". . . unconscious. I'll take her upstairs." His voice sounds strained. There's someone else talking, a man, in the background. Papa S. shouts. "No! Leave us."

Kate is knocking at the door. We have to get out of here. Ellis stops the tape and we run to the door. Kate has opened it. We walk through, just as Kindred John appears around the corner. He comes up close to us.

"What are you doing here?" he asks. There's no warmth in his voice and he's staring hard at Ellis.

"I was looking for you," Ellis says. "I thought that I could help you with that table you're working on. You could teach me." Ellis smiles at him, doesn't flinch for a second.

Kindred John looks around, at the Forgiveness Room door shut tight behind us. "Of course," he says, his words squeezing through his teeth.

Kate takes my hand. My arm brushes Kindred John as I walk past.

CHAPTER THIRTY-NINE

........•••••●•••••........

The only sound I can hear is the thread pulling through the material. I am sitting with Kate. She concentrates on the skirt she's sewing, her forehead folded into a frown.

"Sylvie was my mother. Elizabeth told me." My words stop Kate and she puts the needle onto her lap. "And now I will never see her."

She reaches out to hold my hand. "She would have looked just like you."

"But I will never know her. I will never hear her voice."

The door opens and Rachel is here. "There you are." She smiles at me. "Papa S. wants to see you."

Kate doesn't let go of my hand.

"He's in the kitchen," Rachel says.

Kate looks at me. "I'll have to go," I say. And I move Kate's fingers from mine, feeling the sharp sting of the needle as it scrapes my fingertips.

Papa S. is alone in the kitchen. Is he going to punish me for shouting at him? For blaming him for Elizabeth's dying? I won't say sorry, because I do blame him. He puts his arms out to me, but I don't go to him. Confusion clouds his face.

"Come to me, Pearl," he says.

Do I have a choice? I hesitate, but I walk toward him. He puts his hand on my head and holds me to his chest. I can hear his heart beating, but it doesn't comfort me and I want to pull away. His hair brushes my cheek and instantly I see the hair crackling in the fire.

"Come now," he says. His hand feels large in mine. He leads me from the kitchen, across the hallway.

The Forgiveness Room. Are we going to the Forgiveness Room? Does he know? I need to break away, to run from him.

"Do not be afraid," Papa S. says. He smiles at me. His teeth look gray.

I walk with him, his hand tight on mine. We get closer. I can see the door. But he takes me past. Papa S. leads me toward his study. He smiles at me.

He pushes open his heavy door. And when I step through, he closes it behind me.

"Come," he says. And he takes me to the sofa pushed against his window.

Outside, I can just make out the figure of Jack, standing alone in the field. I want him to come and take me away from here.

"You are hurting, Pearl," Papa S. says as he sits me down.

"Yes," I answer.

"Then I am disappointed in you." His eyes stare into me.

"But Elizabeth . . ." My throat burns.

"It was her time," Papa S. says. "This was the right way, the only way."

"But the baby," I whisper. Doesn't he feel any sadness?

"The baby grew, so that it could take Elizabeth back to Nature."

Nature didn't take Elizabeth. You let her die.

"We should have taken her to the hospital," I say quietly. Courage is building in me.

"You know that it's your fault?" Papa S. smiles at me. "You left my chamber and Nature waited to punish you. And she chose to take the most precious thing from you."

"No," I whisper. *Please don't let this be true.*

"Yes. Nature punishes all things bad," he says.

But Elizabeth wasn't bad. She was everything pure.

"Did you not see the swarm of flies that came in from Outside?" Papa S. asks me, his voice strong with rage. "They came like a black cloud and Elizabeth opened her mouth and let them in."

No, there was no swarm of flies. I think of the bees in Ellis's stomach, the bees that never hatched.

Papa S. reaches out and touches my cheek. "Soon it will be

your time, Pearl."

"For Nature to take me?" I ask. Papa S. laughs.

And now I am afraid. I imagine my body in the bonfire.

"To be my Companion," he says.

To be his Companion. To be with him in his bed. His breath on my face. My hand on his robe.

Please look at me, Jack. Come and save me.

I must smile.

"Thank you," I say, but my stomach hurts.

"Without each other, we are nothing, Pearl. Without our family, there is no point in anything." Papa S. slips his fingers into my hair. "Like liquid sun," he breathes.

"Who is Sylvie?" I ask. He freezes and my breath stops. I didn't mean to ask.

"Who is Sylvie?" His voice is low, his words slow. "Is that what you asked?" He puts both hands on my shoulders and won't let me look away. "Why do you mention that name?"

"It is something Nana Willow said."

Papa S. drops his hands from me. "Her mind is rotten with age, Pearl," Papa S. says.

Elizabeth told me too.

"Soon," he says. "You will walk with me. We will be as one." He smiles as he leans forward, and he's kissing me on my lips. I jump back. There is a flash of fury in his eyes, but then he kisses his palm and holds it over my heart. His fingers press at my skin through my shirt.

"Soon," he says. Then he takes his hand from me. "Now go."

I get up. He sees me walk out of his room. He sees me doing as he asks. *But Papa S., you cannot see my thoughts. You cannot see where they are leading me.*

CHAPTER FORTY

•••••••••●•••••••••

I can't sleep. It's no good. Shadows from the moon are filtering through cracks in the curtains, and I'm willing sleep to come, but it won't. Words and thoughts are fighting for space in my head. Somewhere, I can hear Elizabeth whispering my name. Somewhere, I can hear the crying of her baby.

I am hot in these sheets, the blanket heavy on me and I can't bear it any longer. I think I know where I am going as I leave my bed and creep silently across our bedroom floor.

The darkness is my friend, I tell myself as I go down the corridor. It is just Nature sleeping.

I hold my breath as I walk, quiet as air, down the stairs. There's no one here. No one to see me. Is there? I won't look behind me.

In the kitchen, the drawer makes too much noise as I pull it open. But the flashlight is there and I hold it in my hand as I tiptoe to Nana Willow's door.

I turn the handle. The door opens and I'm inside, in total blackness. I click the flashlight on and it glares at Nana Willow as she lies sleeping in her bed. She doesn't move.

Gently, I walk toward her. I want to say her name, but I don't say a word. Her face is thinner than before. Her body is fading away. Soon she will sink into her sheets and disappear.

She opens her eyes, blinks wildly in the light, twists her head away. I move the beam quickly, so that it shines on her empty table instead.

"I'm sorry," she says, her eyes shut tight. "Please don't hurt me again." She moves her hand up to her eyes. There is a deep bruise on her arm, rotten and green.

"I won't hurt you, Nana Willow," I say, stepping toward her.

She flinches. "I'll be good. I promise, I'll be good," she whimpers.

"I am Pearl," I say. But she won't look at me. Her fingers stay covering her eyes, her face on the edge of the flashlight's beam.

"Who hurt you?" I ask her. She's crying. I can see the tears on her cheeks.

"Please don't hurt me again," she says. "I won't tell a soul."

"Nana Willow, where is Sylvie?" I ask.

She opens her eyes, cracks her head toward me. And she's staring right at me, through to my bones. "Pearl?" she asks.

"Yes. Where is my mother?"

"They took her away from me," she whispers. "They said they would keep her safe. But if I told, then Nature would punish her."

"Where is she now? I want to see her."

"They hid her away. They said if I was quiet I would see her again."

"Who hid her away?" I don't want to ask. My world is crumbling around me and I think her words will crush me. But I have to know.

"They hurt her."

"Who hurt her? Where is she?"

"She is gone," Nana Willow says. It's difficult to hear her, as she struggles with her tears. "He locked her away. For years, he locked her away. But now he says she is gone."

Gone.

"What did he do to her?" I ask, but she curls onto her side and brings her knees up tight. "Nana Willow?" Suddenly in my memory I see the fire, and sickness sweeps through me. Have I seen my mother, her face covered by the flames? "Nana Willow." I start to shake her shoulder.

But someone is walking upstairs. I can hear the floorboards creak above us. I try to work out whose room it is, but my mind can't make sense of anything. I turn the flashlight off and run to the door, closing it quietly behind me. I don't have time to go to the kitchen, so I leave the flashlight on the table in the hall as I pass. I run up the stairs, lifted by fear, because I know I will get caught.

There are two shapes coming out of our bedroom. One is Kate, the other is Kindred John. His hand is on her shoulder. He is leading her from our room. They stop when they see me.

I keep walking. I have to be calm. "What's wrong?" I ask. "Kate, where are you going?"

Her eyes may still be sleepy, but I know that she doesn't want to be here.

They hurt her. She is gone.

I stare at Kindred John. *Was it my mother in the coffin? Did you watch my mother burn?*

"I will look after her now," I say. And I take Kate's hand. But he still holds her shoulder. "We're fine," I say. There is challenge in my eyes.

Before he can reply, I pull Kate with me, back into the room. His hand falls from her and I close the door on him.

Kate stares at me. She's shivering in her nightdress. She puts her head on my shoulder. Her tears are in my hair.

As I tuck the blanket around her bed, I imagine us running from here. But every time we get through the gate, there's another one we cannot see. It's made of the hands of Papa S. The skin twitches as we get close, and his whispers cover my breath and drag me back to Seed.

CHAPTER FORTY-ONE

••••••••••●••••••••••

H eather is Papa S.'s Companion as we walk up to Dawn Rocks. Normally her smile would light her face, but there is a sadness that holds her down.

The darkness shifts around us. It is trying to disappear. Birds are calling for the sun to rise.

Maybe Elizabeth didn't die, and she is walking behind me. If I listen, I'll be able to hear the murmurs of our baby clutched tight in Rachel's arms. But there's nothing except the sound of our feet, crunching on the fallen leaves.

At the rocks, I sit between Ellis and Kate. We look straight ahead, but our thoughts loop in and out of each other's. Jack holds Ruby on his lap. Her head is tucked into him. She can't see the sorrow in his eyes.

Papa S. turns to us. My skin prickles at the sight of his beard. *Did you kill my mother?*

He opens his mouth to speak. His eyes are wide and he's staring at the muddy sky. No words come. No sound.

He sinks to the ground and falls forward until his face is on the wet grass. Papa S.'s hands claw at the green shoots. Earth blackens his fingers.

Jack holds Ruby's head, so she can't see.

Do I imagine the shape that walks quietly forward on the grass? A woman. She has hair like mine, like Elizabeth's. Even in this scratchy light, it shines bright, floating like white water down her back. It's my mother. I know it's my mother. I want to go to her, but I can barely breathe. I think she will comfort him. I think she will put her arms around Papa S. and make everything better.

But she places her bare feet on his sprawled back. She walks up his spine.

And then Papa S. howls. A sound of the deepest, darkest night, just as the sun shows herself above the horizon. I look at the sky, so quickly. But when I look back, my mother has gone.

And Papa S. is standing up. Smears of mud are on his skin. He is smiling at us, but it feels so wrong.

"I am dying," he says.

I know I have heard the words right. He's nodding at us and I won't look away from him. Heather gasps, reaches her hand out and clasps his cloak in her fingers. Gently, he touches her hair.

"Yes, I am dying." His voice is soft, like honey. "I do not have much time."

I feel Kate squeeze my hand. I glance at Ellis and he's looking at me. In his eyes, I see Kindred John. In his eyes, I see Elizabeth lifeless on her bed. And through the trees, my mother walks and slowly burns to ash.

Papa S. is hugging everyone. Kindred Smith. Linda. Bobby. Ellis stays as still as the rock when Papa S. holds his arms round him. When it is my turn, I have to put my arms round his back. His cloak feels soft. I ache at the memories of happiness.

Kate flinches back. She won't let Papa S. touch her. Disbelief sparks in his eyes, but his strange smile never disappears as he steps away from her.

Then everyone is walking back down to the house and the sun is rising in the sky. I watch as, one by one, they follow Papa S. Jack, with Ruby still in his arms, looks back at me. I want to call out to him, to ask him to stay with us. But my words don't come and slowly he walks away.

The rock is cold under me. Kate, Ellis, and I sit in silence, watching our family as they are swallowed by the trees.

Who are you, Papa S.?

"Don't believe him," Ellis says. "He isn't dying. He just wants to freak you out. It's another way he can control you."

Soon it will be your time, Pearl. To be my Companion.

"If we leave, where will we go?" I ask quietly. Kate looks at me quickly. We are both surprised by my words.

"Simon is helping us," Ellis says. Simon, with his Outside

skin. "I know you saw him in the woods. We've been arranging things and he's getting in touch with a friend of my mom. Friends of mine." Friends of Ellis? I reach out to touch the rock, to steady me.

"He's finding us somewhere to stay on the Outside, Pearl," Kate says softly.

"I tried to find Mom's car keys, but they're nowhere."

Car keys? Does Ellis think we can just drive out of Seed?

"And they've hidden my phone."

"Kate," I say. "What are we doing?"

"We'll be all right. We'll be together," she says.

Maybe together we can break through the gate of Papa S.'s flesh and bones.

"I won't go anywhere without Jack," I say. Does he know? Does he know that we really have to leave?

"We'll persuade him," she says, and she looks to the ground.

Jack on the Outside.

"We'll take my mom too. And Sophie," Ellis says. My thoughts buckle and knot and it is difficult to breathe.

I stand up, pulling my hand free from Ellis. And I'm running away from them, across the hard ground. My mother is calling to me.

But there is nowhere to go.

CHAPTER FORTY-TWO

······●············

"Jack," I say. "Do you trust me?"

We're sitting in the almost-dark at the edge of the forest, on a curve of a fallen branch.

Jack turns to me. "Of course I do."

"But really trust me. More than you trust the Kindreds." I hesitate. "More than you trust Papa S."

Jack stares back toward the house, where the evening has turned its red bricks black. Some of the windows glow orange, others are empty squares. Papa S. is somewhere there.

"I don't know what I think anymore," he says. "Kate is saying things I don't want to hear. I don't know what's going on." He breathes out heavily. "How can everything have turned so bad?"

"Maybe it always was," I whisper.

Jack shakes his head. "No. We had everything here. We were happy."

The forest is silent behind us. It's strange. Not an animal moving, not a tree creaking.

"Do you believe that Papa S. is dying?" I ask.

Jack doesn't reply.

"Have you ever been to the Forgiveness Room?" My voice is so quiet.

Jack looks at me. Memories flicker somewhere in him. He closes his eyes briefly and nods his head.

"It was just Papa S., Jack. He was pushing those walls."

"But they were moving in on me. They were going to crush me."

"It was him. He was just pushing them forward with his hands."

A feeling of strength is growing in me, and it's bigger than my fear of the now, my fear of the future. I can change what happens to me. I know we can break free.

Jack shakes his head. "When I was there, a woman was screaming."

"It was a tape recorder. That was all. Papa S. pressed Start and Stop."

Jack looks down at the ground. He rests his elbows on his knees. "But who was she? She wasn't pretending, Pearl. Someone was hurting her."

A breathless pain squeezes my chest. "I think she was my mother," I whisper. I want to cry, but the tears are shut inside me. The hand of Papa S. is pushing them down.

"What are you talking about?" Jack says sharply.

I forget how much he doesn't know, how much he doesn't want to hear. How he still loves Seed, as I once did. I must be careful. I can't lose Jack.

"She was Nana Willow's daughter."

"And Nana Willow told you this?"

"She told me she had a daughter called Sylvie, and that they took her away."

"But she doesn't think straight, Pearl. You know that."

"Elizabeth told me as well," I tell him. Jack can't question that. His love and trust in Elizabeth is unbreakable. "And she said that Sylvie was my mother and she thought she died giving birth. But she didn't die. They locked her away."

Jack looks at me and I know that he wants me to stop. I know he wants it all to go away. But to save us, he has to believe me. I won't run without him.

"I think the screams were her. Papa S. was hurting her." Tears burn my throat. I will keep strong for Sylvie. For my mother.

But I won't tell Jack my darkest thoughts. That I think I have seen my mother in the fire, her hair scorched black. Her hand being burned to dust.

The thoughts stick in my blood.

"I don't want to stay," I say.

Jack bends his head forward and rests it in his palms. For a while, he doesn't move.

"Jack?" I whisper. I put my hand on his back.

He turns, buries his tears in my shoulder, and I hold him as the evening grows darker.

CHAPTER FORTY-THREE

....•••••●•••••....

"Ready?" I whisper.

The dark has sunk half of Kate's face into shadow, but I can still tell that she's scared. "I don't think we should do it," she says.

"We have to. We have to get someone to help us."

"Simon is helping us. He's going to get people."

"But what if he can't? What if he doesn't and we're waiting here and no one comes?" I say.

I've never seen Kate look so agitated. She pulls at her hair, which has fallen over the shoulder of her nightdress. She glances down at her feet, bare on the floor. "What if Papa S. catches us, Pearl? What will he do to us?"

They hid her away. Nana Willow's words creep into me. *She is gone.*

"I won't let him hurt you, Kate." Her hand is ice-cold as I reach for it. "And he won't catch us. No one will. It's the middle of the night and everyone is asleep."

I pull her with me from the bedroom, walking so quietly that we are almost not here.

How many hours have we spent running along this corridor, laughing? Jack chasing us with a pillow, Bobby bounding like a fox. The memories almost stop me.

But how many secrets do these walls know? If I scraped away their top layer, how many lies would I find? If I stopped and pressed my ear against it, would I hear my mother's voice?

Keep going, she would say to me.

Be free, she says.

The tiles on the hall floor are freezing under my feet. We run across them quickly, hand in hand.

The Eagle Room door is large in front of us. I've never noticed if it makes a noise, if its hinges groan, but now we must open it.

The handle squeaks slightly as I turn it, but the door itself is silent. Kate closes it, shuts us in. The curtains are open and the light in here is gray enough to see.

"You get the skirts," I whisper, and Kate goes to the trunk and lifts the lid. I walk toward the desk. The drawer scrapes as I open it, and lift out a pen. The noise slices around us as I rip the paper into small pieces. But no one can hear this from upstairs.

I pick up the pen, hold it steady in my fingers.

Help us, I write. *We are at Seed.*

Help us, I write on another. *We are at Seed.*

Again and again.

"Quickly," Kate whispers.

So I go to her and she unpicks a tiny part of a hem. I fold a piece of the paper with my writing and I push it in. I watch as Kate sews it up, the needle rushing through the material.

I fold another piece. Watch my words disappear.

Someone is outside the room. It is more than the nighttime noises of the house. It's the sound of boots on the floorboards.

Kate and I stare at each other. Why can't I move? Kate grabs me and we crawl behind the sofa, pulling the skirts with us.

The handle creaks. The door opens. Someone is here. Someone is standing in the Eagle Room. And by the trunk, in a little pile of white, I can see the shreds of paper filled with my words, on the floor where I left them. I can't reach out for them. They sit there, looking at me, waiting to be found.

Help us. Help me.

My breath is tiny and silent. I must not move. Someone is in this room, looking around. Surely he can hear the blood beating in my body?

Help us. We are at Seed.

If he steps in farther, he will find my words. He will find us.

The door closes with a gentle thud.

Has he gone? Still I don't move. Because what if he's tricking us? What if he's still here, waiting as we crawl from behind the sofa? Waiting to punish us.

I listen for the sound of boots in the corridor. I can't hear them. Somewhere in the house, another door shuts. Was it him?

Slowly, I turn to Kate. Silently, she sews closed the hem of a skirt, my message inside.

I move along the length of the sofa, twist myself until I can see. It's just a door. Nothing else. He has gone.

"No more," Kate whispers, her face the color of ash. She folds the skirts, lifts the lid of the trunk, and silently slips them back inside.

I reach for the pieces of paper on the floor, scrunch them into my palm. Feel my words sticking into my skin as slowly we tiptoe out of the room.

CHAPTER FORTY-FOUR

........•••••●•••••••...

Ruby gasps when Papa S. comes in for morning meal. And for a tiny second I don't know who he is, because his beard has gone. It's hacked short to rough, gray stubble clinging to his chin. He looks strange and naked and my heart clenches in sorrow.

But when I look at his eyes, they are wild with anger. And behind them, I see my mother burning. And Elizabeth's baby locked in the earth.

Heather stands by Papa S. as his Companion, but she does not hold a flower to her lips. Her head is bent, her hair falling over her face.

"Bad thoughts did this to me," Papa S. suddenly yells. It is so loud, so terrifying, that Sophie ducks her head into Linda's arms.

Papa S. grabs at his hair, starts slapping at his chin. I hear Ellis laugh slightly beside me.

"The poison has entered Seed. It came into my chamber and ripped at my beard." Papa S. is shaking, his cheeks boiling red. "I fought it, but it was too strong."

He slumps onto the table, his bowl crashing to the ground.

I have never heard it before, never even imagined it, but Papa S. is crying. Great, heaving sobs have taken over his body. His fingers curl in and out, grasping at the empty air.

The shock among us is so strong that you can almost touch it. Even Ellis is silent now.

"Poisoned!" Papa S. raises his head and screams.

Kindred Smith gets up and goes to him. He puts his arms on him, tries to lift him. But Papa S. roars and smashes out with his fists.

Suddenly he is still. He glares at Kindred Smith with a look that should melt his skin. "This is all your fault," he hisses. "You persuaded me to let them in. That woman, that boy, brought poison with them."

Ruby curls into me. I tuck her head so she can't see. Her little body is shaking. Linda's face is white. She loves Papa S. She loves Seed.

"Nature will punish us. Punish us all," Papa S. screams. He pushes Kindred Smith out of the way as he stumbles out of the room.

Bobby's eyes are wide. I turn to Jack, but he is staring at the empty doorway. When he looks, slowly, toward me, I know the words he doesn't say.

I believe you, his eyes tell me. *I believe you.*

❦ ———— ❦

"He will be all right," Kindred Smith says.

He has come up to me as I stare through the sitting room window, at Jack pulling potatoes from the cold ground. He doesn't mention Papa S. Has he spoken to him since this morning?

I move away from him, just slightly, but enough to make him look at me and frown. Guilt weaves into me. Because I have loved Kindred Smith all my life and now I want to run from him.

"It's hard without Elizabeth," I say.

"I know." He turns to me and touches my arm. "She would be so proud of you."

Did you hurt Sylvie? I want to ask. *Did you hurt my mother?*

We watch as a car appears on the driveway. It comes closer. I can hear it through the glass of the window, as it slows down and stops.

A man and a woman get out. They are in smart, dark clothes. The woman wears a white shirt under her black jacket. Her hair is short, cropped even to her ears.

"Who are they?" I ask. But Kindred Smith doesn't answer. He walks to the door.

Seconds later I see him on the driveway, walking to them, shaking their hands. Their voices are too quiet to hear, but I can tell that Kindred Smith doesn't know them.

Ruby runs toward them from across the grass, but something makes her stop as she gets close. The woman waves and smiles to her, but Ruby must sense the danger floating around them. When they see me watching, I cannot look away. I stare at them. They smile, but I don't smile back.

They start to walk toward the house. Kindred Smith is bringing them into our home. I hear the noise of the front door open, their feet in our hallway, their voices in our air.

As quiet as I can, I push up the window and climb out onto the gravel. I close it silently behind me and run across the driveway toward Jack in the fields.

"Did you see them?" I ask.

He straightens up and looks at the car before he looks at me. "Who are they?" he asks.

"I don't know. They're in our house."

He's crumbling the mud off a potato. "What are they saying?"

"I don't know." I take the potato from him and put it into the almost full bag. I want to feel excitement. Are they Ellis's friends? Have they come to save us?

"Let's find out then." Jack reaches out for my hand as we walk.

I trust him to lead me through the empty kitchen and into the hall. They are not here. But I can hear them, in the sitting room, the room I just slipped away from.

"Come on," Jack says and he squeezes my hand.

"Are we just going to walk in?" I ask.

"Yes," he says. And so we do. We push open the wooden door and watch as Kindred Smith and the strangers look up at us. The woman's nose is like the beak of a hawk. I don't like her empty smile.

"Hello," she says, standing up from our sofa. "My name is Jean. I was sorry to hear about your friend Elizabeth. It must have been a shock to you all."

Jack and I don't say anything.

"We didn't know that children were living here."

Still we don't say anything. Kindred Smith is watching us.

"I'm Stuart," the man says. He doesn't stand up. He reminds me of a few of the people I see at the market, with rolling skin on his chin and fat hands. "Do you want to come in for a quick chat?"

"No." I'm startled by Jack's rudeness.

"We have work to do," I say.

Is this really who has come to save us? I don't know what I was expecting, but it wasn't this. I thought I would want to go with them, that I would trust them, but I don't.

"It won't take long," the woman says, moving toward us. "How long have you lived here?"

"All our lives," I say, glancing briefly at Kindred Smith.

"Are you happy here?" she asks.

My cheeks redden. I feel Jack's fingers in mine.

Behind them, outside the window, Papa S. has crept up and he is looking in. The stubble on his chin presses against the glass.

"What work are you doing?" Stuart asks, from where he still sits.

"We're digging the potatoes," I say.

"Not school work, then?" he asks. School. Where Ellis has been.

"We alternate," Kindred Smith interrupts. "All the children here have a balance of education. As well as their school work, they learn to work the land." But we don't do school work, only the reading and writing in winter. Kindred Smith is lying. "And Jack is a budding mechanic." He smiles encouragingly at us. "Aren't you, Jack?"

"Yes," Jack answers.

"Would you like to see?" Kindred Smith asks.

"We'd prefer to see their school books," Jean answers. She turns to me. "What are you learning?"

"Everything," I answer. Stuart snorts, his jelly cheeks shaking. I glare at him and he tries to smile. Doubt begins to find me. Can we really give up Seed for people like this?

"Would you like to show us your books?" the woman asks.

I feel Papa S.'s eyes on me.

"Not now," Kindred Smith says and he claps his hands together. "Plenty of time for that. But that sun won't wait for us, and they need to bring more potatoes in before it gets dark." He walks toward us, puts his hand on Jack's shoulder. "We'll come and get you if we need to talk to you more."

So we turn our backs on the strangers, walk through the door, and away from them.

Jack and I pretend not to look as we bend over the spades, but I can see the black shape walking toward us. It's the crow-like woman, coming closer. She reaches me first.

"That looks like hard work," she says.

"I enjoy it," I reply. I stop digging and look at her.

Tell her now, Pearl, tell her.

But I know that Papa S. is watching me.

"Do you see a lot of Steve?" she asks.

"Who is Steve?"

"Steve Elmack. The man who runs it here."

I don't understand.

"Your leader," she says.

"Papa S. is our leader," I say. Steve?

"How often do you see him?" she asks. Jack is still.

"All the time," I say.

"What's he like?"

I don't answer.

"Does he make you do anything you don't want to?" she asks.

Still I don't reply. I want to talk to her, to tell her everything. But I'm scared that Papa S. is hiding, watching.

"There's help away from here, if you need it," the woman says.

I look at Jack, but his face shows nothing.

"We've told Steve that we're coming back in two days, so that we can see your school work. You might want to tell me more then?"

Two days. In two days I'll find a place to hide, where Papa S. cannot see and I will tell this woman everything.

It's strange when she touches my arm, as though she wants to say something more. I glance toward the house. Then she turns from me and walks back toward the driveway. As I dig my spade into the earth, their car starts. I listen as it takes them away.

Jack is staring into the distance.

"I don't think we have long," he says. As I brush my hair away, mud smudges near my eyes. "For this," he says, sweeping his arm from our home to our forest. I wrap my cardigan closer to me.

"We'll stay together, Jack," I whisper. "I promise I won't go without you."

Jack tightens his hand around the spade. His knuckles go white. I touch them, try to soothe blood back into them.

"I don't want to live here without Elizabeth," I say. But there is more, so much more. *One day, Jack, I will tell it all to you.*

Suddenly Jack picks up his spade. He swings it high and slams it into the ground. He tips his head and he yells toward the sky. I want to touch him, but I'm scared. I have never, ever seen Jack like this, and when he doesn't stop, I run from him. I lift my skirt so I can run over the muddy field, back into Seed.

CHAPTER FORTY-FIVE

......•••●●●●●●●......

The sun is barely up when we turn the corner to the field. Immediately, I know that they are dead. Two of our cows lie side by side, their bodies slumped into the grass, their eyes wide open, their mouths gaping.

Kate drops her bucket and it clangs on the ground as she runs to them. She kneels next to the body of the first, thumps hard onto its skin.

"It's dead, Kate," I say.

She looks up at me, her hair wild. "What's going on?" she shouts.

Someone is running up behind us. I turn to see Kindred John getting closer. "I saw from the window," he calls to us. "We'll have to get the tractor with the wagon up here."

"What's happened to them?" Kate asks. She stands up, her feet wide, her hands on her hips.

"They were old," Kindred John says. He puts his hand gently on Kate's arm, but she shakes it off roughly.

"Oh, Kate," he says as he smiles. For an instant, I think she might hit him.

I grab her arm and pull her away, hurry her from the field, my empty basket knocking against my leg.

I lead her without speaking, all the way to the forest. We stop only when we're covered by trees. She stares at me.

"Cows don't just die like that," I say. "Two of them at the same time."

"What's happening?" Kate asks. She's looking around us, but there are no answers in the air.

I can't hold my words in anymore. "Sylvie didn't die when I was born." I meant to whisper, but my voice is too strong. I can't see behind the trunks of the trees. I can't see if anyone is near enough to hear me.

I take Kate's hand and she lets me lead her again. In and out of the trees in silence, until we start to walk across the West field.

Run, Pearl, run. My mother's voice fills my bones.

We're standing in the middle, with nothing around us but the green grass stretching to the house and the white sky reaching down to touch the trees that line the fence to the Outside.

"They locked her away." I say it without hesitating.

"Who?"

"They locked Sylvie away."

"What do you mean?"

"She didn't die when I was born, Kate. They hid her away."

The words catch in my breath.

Kate looks toward the red bricks that make up our home. "Where?"

"I don't know. But they did something to her. They hurt her. And now she's gone."

Kate turns back to me. There's a sadness in her eyes I have never seen before. I need to ask her whether we put sticks on top of my mother's coffin. Did the children laugh as we watched her body burn? But sickness grips me and it hurts too much to say it.

"We can't stay," Kate says. She puts her hands on my shoulders. "Do you want to stay?" Her face is so close to mine that I can feel her anger.

"I don't want to be his Companion," I whisper.

She takes her hands from me and starts to walk away. Her blonde hair hangs, lifeless, down her back. She is going toward the fence that keeps us from the Outside.

"Kate?"

"Quickly," she says.

I have to run to catch up with her. Side by side we are hurrying to the edge.

Run, Pearl, run.

The air pushes into me, as the shadows of the trees creep over us. The wooden fence is here for me to touch.

"This is where I meet Simon. If we go now, we can find him

and he will help us." But Kate sounds hesitant and she no longer looks strong.

I touch the damp wood. It's green on this side, where the sun never reaches. If I stand on my toes, I can see the road. It's blank, until it turns a corner and disappears. There are no swarms of flies. Kate is looking back toward the house. She doesn't move. She doesn't climb over the fence.

I know we won't go yet, because Jack is at Seed. And Ellis. I won't go without them. And Elizabeth is calling to me. I cannot leave her and our baby without saying good-bye.

"Tomorrow," I say. "Tomorrow, when that woman comes back, I'll find a place to hide where Papa S. can't see and I'll tell her everything. And we'll leave here. We will," I promise Kate.

Raindrops begin to knock quietly on the leaves above us.

CHAPTER FORTY-SIX

A hand jolts me awake. I'm in bed and it's still dark, but some-one is shaking me.

"Papa S. says we must all go to the work barn." It's Heather's voice. She moves away. I see the figure of her going to Kate's bed, waking her too.

"Why?" Kate asks wearily. Something is not right. I know that I don't want to go.

"It's not for us to question him," Heather says gently. Then she's waking Ruby and Sophie.

Kate flicks on a bedside lamp. She looks sleepy, confused.

"Your shoes, not your slippers," Heather says to Sophie. "We will be walking outside."

Ruby sits in her bed, but doesn't move. Her eyes are mostly closed. I take a sweater to her.

"Come on," I say. She lets me put the sweater over her head, helps me by stretching her arms through.

Kate puts her coat on and does her buttons all the way up to her chin. "Do you know why, Pearl?"

"No," I reply. "He must want to tell us something."

"In the middle of the night?" Kate says.

This feels so wrong. I need to wake up properly. I need to think.

Jack is coming out of his bedroom when we walk into the corridor. His face looks strange, as though he's been pulled from a bad dream. He has his coat over his pajamas, his shoes on his feet. Ruby reaches out to hold his hand. We walk down the stairs with the silence of the night whittling around us.

The starlit air clears away the last dregs of sleep. It's cold on my lips as we walk. We catch up with Ellis and he takes Sophie's hand.

"What shall we do?" I ask.

The door of the work barn is open, spilling out a little light. I don't want to go inside.

"I don't know," Ellis says. But it's too late. There's no time to talk before we are all going through the doors.

Papa S. is standing on an upturned box, near two of the cars. His arms are spread wide. His deep-brown cloak makes him look like an eagle. I expect to see claws at the ends of his fingers.

Steve. Steve Elmack. Papa S., you have a name.

I hear the sound of Kindred John closing the work barn door behind us. The heavy wood shutting us in.

"My family," Papa S. says, smiling. I kiss my palm and face it to him. I must do everything as he expects. I cannot make him suspicious that I am going to leave him. When I lower my palm, Kate takes my hand. I know she's afraid.

Don't be, I want to tell her. *Soon we'll be free.*

"You may sit," Papa S. says, his voice soft but clear.

It's uncomfortable on the floor. Bobby crawls into Heather's lap and she strokes his hair. His eyes are already closing back to sleep.

"Nature has asked me to bring you here," Papa S. says. "To tell you bad news." I look over at the others. Rachel's eyes are wide as she looks up at him. Kindred Smith has Linda's hand in his. Together they look up at Papa S. At Steve Elmack.

"Outside has been taken over," he says. Heather gasps slightly, but quickly covers her mouth with her hand. Jack doesn't move. "Dreadful things are happening. There have been fires, floods, storms that have swallowed houses. And now, only bad people are roaming the land."

"That's bullshit," I hear Ellis whisper.

Kate looks at me and I shake my head so slightly that only she can see.

"They are swarming across the streets and the hills, and will destroy everything in their path."

Like the flies that he said swarmed into Elizabeth? There weren't any flies and Elizabeth was pure.

"They are coming closer," Papa S. says. "Listen, you can hear them."

He is silent as we all listen. I hear nothing but the sound of our breathing. Linda is nodding her head and Kindred Smith too. But there is nothing. There is no sound of people swarming over the hills.

"But no one will break up this family. We will never leave Seed," Papa S. says, his voice getting louder. "We must all call on Nature to help us, to save us." He is pointing to each of us. "We can only be saved together," he shouts. "Close your eyes. All of you, close your eyes."

I look at Jack. Just briefly he sees me, but then his eyes are closed too. Kate holds my hand tight. I close my eyes.

"Nature, save us," I hear Papa S. call. Kindred John's voice joins him, then Linda and Kindred Smith.

"Save us," I whisper. *Save me from him. From Papa S.* All around me, the voices get louder. "Save us," I say. Because I want to be saved. "Please, save us." I am shouting now too. Our cries fly up above our heads, crash around the walls. "Nature, save us."

Through it, I can still hear Papa S. And something else. It is an engine. "Save us," I shout. The words fill my skin, my bones. Everything will be all right. We will be saved. On and on we call, until I feel as if I'm no longer here, as if my body is drifting away. The voices turn into a musical note that hums through me and lifts me and rolls me on the air.

Someone puts something in my hand. I open my eyes. I'm back here, in the work barn.

"Drink it," Papa S. whispers in my ear. In my hand is a mug with white liquid. "It will save you," he says.

His forehead is shiny with sweat. Instantly, I remember Elizabeth's hair stuck tight to her lifeless skin. I don't move and Papa S. leans toward me. His fingers are cold on mine as he pushes the mug up toward my lips. My mother is calling to me, but I can't hear her words.

Suddenly Jack pushes the mug from my hands. It falls to the floor, the liquid spilling. For a few seconds, we do not move. Papa S. stares at Jack with fury in his eyes. Jack doesn't say anything. He just stares back.

Kate has opened her eyes. Ellis too. He looks over at Linda. Her head is tipped back as she calls to Nature. There's an empty mug in front of her.

"Mom," Ellis whispers. He's moving his arm out to Linda, but he can't reach her. There are empty mugs in front of Heather and Rachel. Bobby holds his mug in his hand. I can see that there is no liquid in it. But there is white on his lips. He looks at me.

A strange noise comes from Heather's mouth and suddenly she folds in on herself in pain, her eyes white. Kindred John holds a mug to Ruby's lips and she's drinking.

"Ruby!" I scream. She glances at me in confusion as she swallows the liquid. I crawl over to her and hit her hard on the back. Her bones under her skin feel like sticks that will crack.

"No, Pearl," she whimpers as she tries to get away from me. She curls into Kindred John's lap and pushes me away.

"Spit it out," I shout. But I'm too late.

"We have to get out of here," Jack says as he grabs my arm. "Now."

"We can't leave them," I say. But already I can see the paleness sliding into Bobby. My Bobby.

Kate gets up, pulling Sophie with her. Ellis doesn't take his eyes from Linda.

"Sit down," Papa S. says, smiling at Sophie. He reaches out his arms to her, but Kate grabs her away. "Sit down!" he yells.

Papa S. begins to shake and I try to stand up, but he turns and grabs my cheeks. He is forcing my lips open with his fingers, pushing through another cup with white liquid. I bite him. My hard teeth sink into his flesh and he shouts and pulls back, just enough for me to escape him.

"Nature will punish you," Papa S. screams.

I run with Kate and Sophie, but Kindred John is bigger than us, faster than us and he gets to the door first.

"Sit down," he orders. His spit catches in his beard. Suddenly Kate puts Sophie down and she lashes out at him, her fingers scratching at his skin. He raises his hand and strikes her hard across the face. I catch her as she falls, just as a heavy wrench flashes in the air beside me. It's Jack who swings it, who crashes it into Kindred John.

His heavy body crumples to the floor. I drag Sophie to the door. It is bolted. I pull at the handle. Ellis is behind us, but I can't get the bolt open. It won't move. I yank at it until it slips loose in my hand.

Jack and Ellis push us all through the door.

"Go," shouts Ellis. "Look after Sophie." He's holding the door closed, because someone is pushing it from the other side. "I'll follow."

We are running toward the woods. Jack picks up Sophie and I take Kate's hand in mine. We run through the meadow in the cold darkness, the grass whipping at our legs. The trees' shadows are clear in the moonlight, coming closer. Jack's breathing is heavy in front of us. Sophie's eyes are wide, her arms outstretched toward the barn.

I only look back for a second, but it's enough to see two figures in the distance, coming toward us. Sophie starts to scream, but Kate runs to her and puts a hand over her mouth. It slows us down, but we get to the forest.

"This way," Kate breathes in the dark, and I know where she's leading.

The trees hide us until we are in the clearing. Kate pulls the Worship Chair aside and yanks the trapdoor up. With no light, it is just a black, empty hole.

"There are steps," I whisper to Jack. I go down first, feel my way to the bottom. Jack stumbles with Sophie, and then Kate is inside and she pulls the door flat to the ground above us. I hear her feet on the steps and I reach out blindly in the dark until I have her hand.

Sophie is crying. Our breathing fills the tiny space.

"What is this place?" Jack whispers.

"It's where they put us when we become women," Kate says, in the total blackness. Jack doesn't reply.

Sophie is weeping and I reach out to try to stroke her hair. Ruby was drinking the liquid. Little Bobby's cup was empty. My heart feels like it's on fire.

"Where's my mommy?" Sophie asks, her words difficult against her tears. Linda. There was an empty cup in front of her. She drank the poison. "Where's Ellis?" Sophie whispers.

Ellis had been one of the figures running from the barn. He was coming toward us. We had turned our backs on him. We closed the door in the ground before he even knew where we were. And someone had been following him.

"He'll be hiding safely," I say. "Won't he?"

No one replies. There is just the sound of our breathing.

"What if he's not?" Jack sounds terrified. "We've got to go to him." I can hear him moving toward the steps.

"No," Kate says sharply. "We can't."

"We have to," Jack tells her.

"Ellis asked us to look after Sophie. If we go up now, Papa S. will be waiting for us."

"But Ellis." I can't say anymore. My mind is finding only blackness when I think of him. He is alone, out there. And I do not go to him.

The dark keeps us silent.

CHAPTER FORTY-SEVEN

........●●●●●●●●●......

I don't know how long it's been. Hours, I think. Sophie has fallen asleep.

"We can't stay here," I say. Yet what choice do we have? The alternative could be darker than down here.

"We're safe here," Kate says. "He doesn't know where we are." But I can tell by her voice that she thinks it's useless. Because soon Papa S. will notice that the Worship Chair has been moved. And if he doesn't, we'll die if we stay in this hole.

"I'll go first," Jack says. I feel him passing Sophie into my arms. Her sleeping body is heavy.

"Can't we stay?" Kate asks. "Maybe Ellis will find us."

Ellis. Where are you?

Will you kiss me, Pearl?

There is the sound of Jack going up the steps. He must push the door open, as there's a gust of faint light. The deep black of night has passed and dawn must be close.

I follow him, carrying Sophie awkwardly, up the steps. I hear Kate behind us. Jack is crouching at the top, in the middle of the worship circle. He puts his fingers to his lips, telling me not to say a word. It's light enough to see his face, as he points to himself and then toward the trees.

Jack starts to crawl. He gets to the edge of the circle and then he beckons us over. Sophie is still asleep in my arms. I put a hand behind her head as I run toward him.

We huddle together. The leaves whisper to us, but I can't hear what they tell us to do. Jack looks around, his breathing quick. Kate takes his hand. She points silently to the driveway, but to get there we must go close to the house, and maybe Papa S. is waiting for us.

Papa S. I loved you. Grief crashes into me.

Kate is shaking my arm. Sophie is awake, her wide eyes looking into mine. Kate takes her from me and points toward the wall of the vegetable garden. We have to cross the open space of the meadow. Step over the empty plants in the strawberry field.

I begin to walk, crouching low, the morning dew painting my calves wet. A pigeon calls out.

And then suddenly we see him. But I can't know. I won't. Because his legs are twisted under him and his blood on his body has turned black.

Sophie is screaming as Jack runs to him. *"Ellis!"*

But Ellis cannot hear her. His life has gone. Jack grabs Ellis's shirt in his fist. He's hitting Ellis's chest.

I want him to stop.

Push the blood back inside him.

I want everything to stop. I want my heart to stop too.

Ellis, wake up.

Don't go. Please. Please don't leave me.

Breathe again. Breathe, Ellis.

Stand up, Ellis.

Come with me.

"Pearl!" Kate's voice whips at us. She's running with Sophie toward the safety of the wall. Because Papa S. is here. He has crept up and he is so close and he's holding something and I know it is a gun.

The sky is so white. So cold.

Run, Pearl, run.

But I can't move. I stare at Papa S. At Steve Elmack. And it is only hatred I feel now.

I stare at the metal in his hand that has taken Ellis from me. Ellis has gone.

Jack stares at Papa S. Then he stands up, his arms spread wide. "Do it to me," he shouts. "If you can do it to Ellis, then do it to me."

Papa S. raises his gun. We are close enough to see the hole at its end. Somewhere, Kate screams at us, as Jack closes his eyes.

But Papa S. moves it toward his own head. The shot cracks

through the air.

I grab Jack's hand and we run. The grass lashes my ankles. The echo of the gun is in the air. We run without looking back. Our feet are on the hard of the driveway. Our house is behind us. Ahead of us, Kate has Sophie in her arms as my mother calls me toward freedom. A freedom she never had.

The gate is coming closer. Jack's breath is with mine.

We are so close.

There is nothing but us.

Us and the Outside.

ACKNOWLEDGMENTS

The biggest thank you goes to my mother—for letting me spend hours with my mind in books. And for telling me I could reach my dreams.

To Veronique Baxter, the best agent in the world. Thank you for taking me on and for your unwavering faith. And to Laura West, for your early input that helped shape *Seed*.

To Ali Dougal—I can never thank you enough for making all this a reality. And for your perfect edits, enthusiasm, and warmth. I hope *Seed* does you proud. Thank you also to the whole team at Egmont, especially Lucy Pearse—you spotted my book in the inbox and made enough of a fuss to get it noticed. And to my brilliant copy editor, Marisa Pintado—I'm in awe of your eye for detail!

For my husband, Miles, thank you for always believing I could do it. And for giving me Frank, Arthur, and Albert—sunshine I can hold. I love you all to the stars and back again.

To my siblings, Philip, Lara, Emma, and Anna. You all proudly called me a writer before I trusted I was one. Thank you for stumbling through life with me and making me laugh until I cry.

Thank you to the wonderful Whinneys, for all your love, support, and endless food.

To Lucy and Martin—thank you for the strength of your friendship. And your undiluted excitement when we knew I would be published!

To Stephen M. Nash. You may not be able to say "consumerism" but you write like a diamond. Start your book today. Ditto Toots. *Tynna dy feiro allan o dy drwyn. Rwyt ti'n ardderchog.* Nick M. M., for your love. And Shanaz, for keeping small, yet still managing to run Chaat, the best restaurant in London.

Thank you to Carlene, Cathy, Fabia, Francoise, Rosie, and Sam for everything and more.

Thank you, Mari, for listening to me witter on about books and for reigning in my imagination when it creates yet another ailment. *Rwyt ti'n ardderchog hefyd!* Andrew—thank you for sharing my amazement that this is actually happening. And Ian, for your "500 words a day" rule that got me started. To Lou Channon and all at Brighton Goes Gospel—for joy and sanity. And to Laura Treneer, for being an angel on earth.

To Jo, Barbara, Jackie, and Catherine—thank you for making me read books I would have missed. And thank you to Allie, Debs, Lucy, Sandi, and Suzanna for your wisdom, kindness, and talent. And especially to Nikki—it's been great to share this journey with you.

A big thank you to Sophie Gordon—you believed in me at the beginning of this road and I'm forever indebted to you.

A big thank you to Carlsen, Running Press, and Albatros Publishers, for taking a chance on a debut author from across the sea.

And finally, to my writing spirit. Thank you for choosing me.

LISA HEATHFIELD is a former secondary school English teacher, specializing in working with hearing-impaired children. *Seed* is her debut novel. She lives in Brighton, England, with her husband and three children.